D-Da

C000070839

TIME PATROL

BOB MAYER

"The world will not be destroyed by those who do evil, but by those who watch them without doing anything." — Albert Einstein

Dedication

For all those young soldiers who parachuted, glided, or landed into Normandy on the Day of Days, and the members of the Resistance who put their lives on the line for freedom!

The Time Patrol

There once was a place called Atlantis. Ten thousand years ago, it was attacked by a force known only as the Shadow, on the same day over the course of six years. The last attack led to Atlantis being obliterated to the point where it is just a legend.

There are many Earth timelines. The Shadow comes from one of those alternate timelines (or perhaps more than one). It is attacking our timeline by punching bubbles into our past that can last no more than twenty-four hours. In each bubble, the Shadow is trying to change our history and cause a time ripple.

By itself, a single time ripple can be dealt with, corrected, and absorbed. But a significant time ripple that is unchecked can become a Cascade. And six Cascades combine to become a Time Tsunami.

That would be the end of our timeline, and our existence .

To achieve its goal, the Shadow attacks six points in time simultaneously; the same date, in different years.

The Time Patrol's job is to keep our timeline intact.

The Time Patrol sends an agent back to each of those six dates to keep history the same. This is one of those dates: **6 June** *.*

Where The Time Patrol Ended Up This Particular Day: 6 June

"The eyes of the world are upon you. The hopes and prayers of liberty-loving people everywhere march with you." — General Dwight D Eisenhower

Normandy France, 6 June 1944 A.D.

"STAND IN THE DOOR!"

Mac barely had a chance to grip the metal frame around the opening in the side of the plane before he was slapped on the rump and the jumpmaster screamed, "Go!"

Mac went on pure instinct, throwing himself out of a perfectly good airplane, chin tucked, hands around the reserve across his belly. The airplane's prop blast immediately ripped away the leg bag containing the Thompson submachine gun and the blasting caps. Mac was automatically counting, "One thousand, two thousand, three thous—" then the opening shock of the parachute jerked him upright.

He checked above, and the twenty-eight-foot diameter hemisphere above his head appeared intact. He looked down. He was 700 feet above ground, just the dark mass of Earth below. There was a little time, so he glanced about. Quiet, other than the fading sound of a plane's engines. Lights here and there in the countryside. But no flak, no artillery, nothing martial to foreshadow the greatest invasion the world would ever know. The Day of Days was yet to kick off with fireworks.

Mac was going to be one of the first with boots on the ground, but he would be gone before the day came to a close.

Hopefully.

Where was the drop zone? The Resistance should be showing a light. Why else had he, whoever he was before he left the plane, jumped? Fortunately, there was an opening among the trees almost directly below.

This was a T-7 chute, the download reminded him—no toggles to steer with, so he reached up and grabbed the risers, pulling, trying to gain some control. He felt like a target. The green chute was silhouetted against the dark sky, and he felt a moment of empathy for Roland, who'd been the first to jump in on so many Nightstalker missions.

If a bullet came, he knew he wouldn't hear it; it would just be one moment here and then not here, sort of like traveling in time, except with no consciousness in the not-here. He took a deep breath then exhaled, hearing the air rush around his canopy.

Feet and knees together, knees slightly bent; the training from the Black Hats at Fort Benning during Airborne School was deeply ingrained. He glanced down once more, and then he saw the deeper black opening of the well directly below him.

It is 1944 A.D. The world's population is 2.2 billion. World War II is well on its way to taking fifty to eighty million, depending on who is doing the math, out of that number. National Velvet, *starring Elizabeth Taylor, is released; Auschwitz is photographed by a British surveillance aircraft; Anne Frank and family are arrested; IBM dedicates the first program-controlled calculator; Hitler survives another assassination attempt; George Lucas is born; the 1944 Summer Olympics, scheduled for London, are postponed; The siege of Leningrad is lifted; Jimmy Page is born; Kurt Gerron films a Nazi propaganda film in a concentration camp, then is sent with his entire crew to die in Auschwitz; the Great Escape;* No Exit *is published by Sartre.*

And Mac saw no exit if he went down that well.

Some things change; some don't.

Mac pulled on the risers, trying to 'slip' the canopy, but the ground was rushing up now, the way it always did in the last fifty feet of the jump. There was movement to one side, and he saw the woman with the gun.

Sjaelland Island, Denmark, 6 June 452 A.D.

"Then perhaps you should be dead," Beowulf said. "Perhaps you *are* already dead, which would explain how you got in here, and why you do the bidding of the Goddess Hel."

The hair on the back of Roland's neck tingled, a warning he'd learned never to ignore. He looked at the barred double doors across the entrance to the great hall of Heorot. "Is there another way in here?"

Beowulf shook his head. "Only the front can be opened from the inside. We sealed every other door."

Roland realized his, and Beowulf's, mistake as the monster dropped from the smoke hole in the roof and landed on the stone floor with a solid thud, right next to the fire pit, its massive weight cracking the flagstone beneath.

Nobody ever looks up.

Roland could hear Nada's voice echoing inside his head just as the sound of Grendel's arrival echoed outside of it.

Roland spun to face the monster as it shredded two of Beowulf's thanes before they were awake, blood, viscera and flesh splattering about.

It is 452 A.D. The world's population is 190 million. Fifty-two percent of those humans live in India and China, seventeen percent in the rest of Asia, seventeen percent in Europe, ten percent in Africa, and the rest of the world has only four percent; Attila leads the Huns in an invasion of Italy; King Vortigen marries Rowena and becomes King of the Britons; Saint John the Silent is born and will become known for living alone for seventy-six years; Emperor Valentinian III flees from Ravenna to Rome trying to escape Attila's invasion.

With his first glimpse of Grendel, Roland realized this was a lot worse than he had imagined it could be.

Some things change; some don't.

Kala Chitta Range, Pakistan, 6 June 1998 A.D

"Into the valley of death we go."

Doc blinked, trying to get oriented. The man who'd spoken was definitely inside his personal space, less than a foot in front of him, holding a piece of paper in front of Doc's face. "Message decoded, sir."

Doc took the piece of paper. He was in a small cave, hole, whatever; he couldn't quite make out his surroundings in the dark. Doc read it in the very dim glow from a single chem light that the man cupped in his other hand.

The words were scrawled in block letters:

TASK FORCE KALI A GO
VIA PRESIDENTIAL AUTHORIZATION
CODE FOUR KILO NINE NINE ECHO TERMINUS
REPEAT GO
VERIFY
CODE FOUR KILO NINE NINE ECHO TERMINUS
KALI WHEELS UP IN THREE ZERO MIKES
TIME ON TARGET FOUR HOURS ONE FIVE MIKES
INITIATE CLOCK AT MESSAGE TRANSMISSION DATE TIME STAMP
MAY GOD BE WITH YOU XXX

Doc had to read it twice to process what it meant.

It is 1998 A.D. The world's population is 5.943 billion. The Lunar Prospector finds water on the moon, and NASA predicts it is enough to support human colonies; Frank Sinatra dies; Nineteen European nations agree to forbid human cloning; Matthew Shepard is beaten and left to die in a field in Laramie, Wyoming; Pol Pot dies (no one will miss him); the High-Z Supernova team is the first to publish evidence that the universe is expanding at an accelerating rate; the Unabomber pleads guilty; the story of President Clinton's 'did not have sex' with Monica Lewinsky breaks; Google is founded; a Soviet sailor kills five others, barricades himself in the torpedo room of a nuclear submarine, and threatens to explode it, causing a nuclear meltdown; Saddam Hussein brokers a deal with the U.N. to allow weapons inspectors back in, preventing war (for the time being).

Doc very much wished at the moment that Pakistan was at the same developmental stage in weapons of mass destruction as Iraq, but it was in vain, since Pakistan had had the capability for nuclear weapons since 1984.

Some things change; some don't.

Doc looked about, noted it was dark outside through the narrow observation slit, then realized exactly where he was: The TF Kali surveillance position in Pakistan, overlooking the nuclear storage facility. Accessing the download, he found the duty roster and learned the identity of the other man in the hole with him: Staff Sergeant Duane Lockhart.

But this was not where he'd expected to be. Not at all.

It was surprisingly cold for June, but they were at altitude. Lockhart reached inside his field jacket then retrieved a red envelope. He ripped it open and leaned next to Doc, checking the authentication code against the one in the message.

"Crap," he muttered when the codes matched. "Yours, sir?" he prompted.

Doc fumbled around inside his camouflage Gore-tex jacket and felt an envelope. He retrieved it, then opened and checked it.

Identical.

"Ours is but to do and die," Lockhart said. "And I'd put my money on the dying part."

Delphi, Greece, 6 June 478 B.C.

"You're too late."

The first thing Scout saw was the body lying in a pool of blood on the floor of the cave. Then a small fire. And on the other side of the fire, an old woman dressed in a white robe, with a heavy red cape over her shoulders. She was clutching the cape tight around her neck and had a purple veil over the lower part of her face.

"I'm too late?" Scout asked, trying to understand where she was, who was dead, and who the old woman was, although that answer popped up instantly: *the Oracle of Delphi.*

"Can't you see?" the Oracle asked bitterly, pointing at the body.

It is 478 B.C. The world's population is roughly 100 million humans, minus 300 Spartans and a lot of Persian troops from a battle two years previously at the Gates of Fire in Thermopylae, and tens of thousands more from the battles the next year which finally pushed the Persians out of Greece, allowing them to once more celebrate these games, the Pythian, in honor of Apollo and the Oracle of Delphi; Fifty-one percent of those humans alive are in India and China, twenty-one percent in the rest of Asia, eighteen percent in Europe, seven percent in Africa, and the rest of the world has only three percent; despite objections from the Spartans, Athens is rebuilt after the Persians destroyed it; there are no plans to rebuild a structure called the Parthenon, which was utterly destroyed by the Persians, although about a century and a half later, a guy named Alexander would sow revenge on the Persians for that act and many others by destroying their empire.

Scout looked more closely at the dead man lying facedown, his white robe stained with blood. "Who is this? What happened?"

"That's Pythagoras," the Oracle said. "The man you were supposed to save."

Some things change; some don't.

United States Military Academy, West Point, New York, 6 June 1843 A.D.

"A man does not beat an animal," Cadet Ulysses S. Grant snapped, holding tight to the bridle of the Hell-Beast. "Never!"

"An honorable man does not intrude between another man and his lady." George Pickett's face was flushed with anger. He stepped up to Grant, barely two feet between them, the horse on one side. He slapped Grant across the face. "On your honor, sir!"

Grant nodded. "Accepted!"

"One half-hour," Pickett said. "The river field with pistols. We will see who has honor. And courage."

It is 1843 A.D. The world's population is 1.2 billion. Roughly twenty million live in the United States. Former West Point cadet Edgar Allan Poe's short story, The Tell-Tale Heart, *is published; the world's first bored tunnel opens underneath the River Thames in London; the Indian Slavery Act removes legal support for slavery within the territories controlled by the East India Company; the first major wagon train departs for the western United States; Charles Dickens' Christmas Carol is published and sells out by Christmas Eve; the world's first Christmas cards are sent in London; James Joule finds the mechanical equivalent of heat; Saint Louis University becomes the first law school west of the Mississippi; Henry James is born.*

Ivar sighed. He'd barely been here ten minutes, and Grant was in a duel for his life with the man who would lead the most important charges in both the Mexican War and Civil War.

Some things change; some don't.

Chauvet Cave, Southern France, 6 June 32,415 Years B.P. (Before Present)

The point man raised a fist as he came abreast of Moms's position. The other four warriors and the woman froze. The point man looked left, then right. Moms was hidden under the bush to the right of the trail, and had also gone still at the signal. She stopped breathing, her hands on the Naga staff, knowing that even with the weapon, these were very bad odds.

Seconds passed, an eternity, then the point man signaled for them to continue.

The female hesitated for a moment, and Moms felt the woman's gaze rake over the area where she was hidden. It was tangible, and it took everything Moms had not to stand up.

Then the woman moved on.

They disappeared up the valley, following those whom Moms was here to protect.

Moms took a deep breath and got to her knees, then stood. She estimated there was about an hour of daylight left.

They'd attack once the tribe was settled in for the night inside the cave.

Moms giggled uncontrollably for a moment, her mind a swirl of images she couldn't process and her body coursing with emotions she couldn't control. She closed her eyes, took several deep breaths, and managed to regain control.

Moms stepped onto the trail then followed.

It is 32,415 Years B.P., which stands for either Before Present, or can be interpreted as Before Physics, based on radiocarbon dating becoming commonly used in the 1950s; it is dated back from 1 January 1950 A.D., because after that, the proportion of carbon isotopes in the atmosphere from nuclear testing makes carbon dating unreliable.

There was killing to be done.

Some things change; some don't.

But *Before* D-Day, and *As* They Came Back From The Ides Of March

New York City: The Present

"THE NEEDLE'S FINE," Edith Frobish said, referring to Cleopatra's Needle, located in Central Park behind the Metropolitan Museum of Art in New York City.

The hieroglyphics that had been missing (at least to Edith and the other members of the Time Patrol) were back. Edith, not trusting her eyes or Ivar's, had asked three different passersby. All confirmed they saw what she and Ivar saw, then hurried away from the crazy couple standing next to the obelisk. New Yorkers were tolerant, but asking them if they saw what was clearly there made even a cynical "New Yawker" a bit nervous.

"The team did it," Edith said.

"They did," Ivar agreed. "I hope everyone is all right."

Edith had her satchel, and Ivar had a large backpack full of notes over one shoulder. They'd come back to the *here* and *now* to do some research. They'd just met back up at the Needle before heading to the Possibility Palace.

"We'll know shortly," Edith said. "Let's get out of here before we run into another policeman wondering why we're wondering."

She had an extra bounce in her step now that all was in place in her world. She pushed open the metal door on the side of the Metropolitan Museum of Art labeled' *Authorized Personnel Only*'.

There was no security guard on duty.

"That's odd," Edith said.

Ivar shifted the heavy load he was carrying. "Let's go. I want to look at this data for—"

"No," Edith said. "This isn't right." She remembered the last time something wasn't right and how it had involved death and mayhem.

Edith led them down a corridor, but turned left toward the Museum proper instead of right toward the elevator down to the Gate leading to the Possibility Palace.

"Edith," Ivar complained, but then she pushed open a door and stepped through. Having no choice, Ivar followed. They were on a balcony overlooking one of the exhibit halls. The usual throng of people were milling and moving below them, taking in the paintings and sculptures.

"Everything's fine," Ivar said. "Can we—"

Edith gasped. She lifted a hand, fingers trembling. "Look!"

Ivar stared where she was pointing. A row of paintings. "I don't—" he faltered as one of the paintings faded from sight, leaving a blank canvas.

No one in the crowd seemed to notice.

"I don't—" Ivar began, but then another painting faded out.

"Oh, dear!" Edith exclaimed. "Not the art."

"It's just some paintings," Ivar said.

Edith turned to him and grabbed him by the shirt. "Don't you understand? The art is the beginning of everything. If it all disappears, it's the end of everything."

Still *Before* D-Day and *After* They Came Back From The Ides Of March

Hunter Army Airfield, Georgia

Scout stood alone in the dark, watching the house's windows, trying to decide on a course of action in the face of the red rage she could feel pulsing forth from the dwelling.

Time travel, Fireflies from another timeline, assassins sent by the Shadow; those, she could handle. This was different. The shades were drawn on every window, and all she could make out were the silhouettes of those inside occasionally moving about. A man. A woman. Just by the way they held themselves, she could discern the relationship.

The woman was Nada's ex-wife. The man, her current husband. After arriving back from the Ides mission and getting debriefed, Scout had checked her cell phone and there had been a message from Nada's daughter Isabella to meet. Scout had played phone tag and left a message for Isabella that she would be here, as requested, this evening.

Beyond the demeanor of the silhouettes, Scout could sense the vibe roiling off the house: anger, confusion, despair, hopelessness; an enmeshment from which Isabella wanted to extract her mother.

Headlights pierced the darkness to the left, a car rolling down the street. It came to a halt short of the house, on this side of the street. A young woman got out. Scout emerged from the shadows of a large oak tree and flashed her penlight.

"Are they in there?" Isabella asked.

"Yes."

"Let's go." Isabella took a step into the street and toward the house.

"Hold on," Scout said.

Isabella paused, but didn't come back. "What?"

"He's angry," Scout said.

"I know he's angry," Isabella said. "That's why I left you the message. He beat the crap out of my mother last week. You told me to call you if I needed anything. I need something. I called. You agreed to meet here. Now we have to help her."

"Getting her killed, or us killed, isn't going to help anyone," Scout said. "I can feel him. He won't allow us to just walk in and take your mother out. It's dangerous. More than you think."

"You can 'feel him?'" Isabella turned back to Scout then stepped up, face-to-face. "More than I have? I felt him many times. I felt his fist. His slap. He broke my arm once, and my mother made me tell everyone I'd fallen off my bike. My teachers knew. I could see it in their eyes, but everyone played the game. Because if we weren't going to do anything about it, how could they?

"I got out of there when I was sixteen. You think my mother would have learned from my dad." She stepped closer to Scout. "My father might have been a great soldier, but at home, he was a drunk and abusive. Why my mother had to hook up with another one like him—" She left the rest unsaid.

"We repeat patterns."

Scout and Isabella turned at the low voice coming out of the dark. A tall woman, almost six feet, slender with wide shoulders, was shadowed by a dim streetlight.

"Moms," Scout said, relieved but not overly surprised at the apparition of her team-leader. "What are you doing here?"

"We take care of our own," Moms said. Scout's team leader came up and put her hand out to Isabella. "I'm Moms. You must be Isabella. I served with your dad for years. I know what you remember about him, but trust me, he ultimately did what was best for you. And he helped a lot of people," she added with a glance at Scout.

Isabella shook Moms's hand. "What do you mean, we repeat patterns?"

"We go for the known," Moms said, nodding toward the house. "We all do. We prefer the horrible known over the paralyzing fear of the unknown and different. It's not surprising your mother would marry a man just like Nada was."

"'Nada'?" Isabella was confused.

Moms smiled sadly. "That's what we called your dad on our team. It's hard for me to think of him by any other name. As hard as it is for you to think outside of what he was in your early childhood. But he finally recognized what he was, and he left. Sometimes that's the best a person can do. Remove themselves. And he did change after he left, but it was too late for him to come back. You need to know that. And remember it. Your mother didn't leave, and she didn't kick him out. *He* made the decision to remove himself from your life. Wasn't his absence better than his presence?"

"His absence was an absence," Isabella said bitterly. "A father is supposed to be a father." She looked at the house. "And a mother a mother."

"If only it were that easy," Moms said. "My own mother wasn't much different, even though she ended up alone. She was broken young. It killed her, but she took a long time dying. At least *you're* not broken."

"You don't know me," Isabella said.

"Scout does," Moms said. "She's here. If she's here, it's because she believes in you." She shifted her attention to the house. "He's in the Ranger Battalion, Scout."

"I know," Scout said. "I've been trying to figure the best way to approach this. I can feel his rage. He's on a hair trigger. We should wait until he deploys to get Isabella's mother out. The Rangers are always deploying, right?"

Isabella disagreed. "She could be dead by then. And if she isn't, he'll go after her when he gets back. We tried leaving once while he was gone. When I was little. He found us. His buddies helped him. Tracked us down and brought us back as if he owned us. Like we were dogs that had strayed."

"His buddies won't help him anymore," Moms said.

"You said it yourself," Isabella said. "He's in the Rangers. Those guys cover for each other. What are the three of us going to be able to do against him?"

"Follow my lead," Moms said as she led the way toward the house, Scout on her right, Isabella to her left.

When they reached the front door, Moms rapped on it with her knuckles.

Nothing.

Moms knocked again, louder.

The door creaked open an inch, and someone peered out. "Yes?" The woman's voice was barely a whisper. Just below the eye, a chain was visible.

"Time to leave," Moms said.

The eye blinked. "What?"

In the background, a man yelled, "Who the hell is it?"

The eye disappeared. "Nobody." The door began to close, but Moms jammed the toe of her boot into the gap. The door opened as far as the chain would allow, two inches. Isabella's mother was shaking her head, looking past Moms at her daughter. "Please leave, Izzy. I'm fine. Really."

Moms withdrew her boot.

"Damn it!" A large figure was behind the woman. "Who the hell are you?" He partly shut the door to unhook the chain, then swung it wide open. "Brought some of your dyke friends this time?" he demanded of Isabella. He was a large man, Isabella's mother a slight presence in front of him. The odor of alcohol wafted out of the house. He wore camouflage pants and a brown T-shirt that had seen better days.

"You need to listen very carefully," Moms said.

"Screw you, bitch. Get off my porch, or I'll wipe it up with your blood and brains." He lifted a large pistol and pointed it at Moms's head.

"Listen carefully," Moms repeated. "If you shoot me, you die. The Cellar doesn't usually give warnings. You're getting one right now. Back up. Let us take her. Then you never try to see her again."

The man blinked. "What?"

"The Cellar," Moms said. "You've heard whispers of it. It exists."

Scout focused, looking into his bloodshot eyes, seeing through them, into him. His thoughts were confused, jumbled. Too many breaching charges going off near his head in training and on missions, each one causing a mini-concussion, over and over again. Too many nighttime raids into villages, where innocents were killed as well as the bad guys. Too much alcohol when not deployed. Too many meds prescribed by Army doctors trying to put a Band-Aid on a wound that was far too big and deep, and started long ago, before all those other things. People were attracted to elite units for many different reasons, and some of them were dark ones.

He owned a legacy of pain from generations of pain.

"We can get you help," Scout said, putting all the calmness she could muster into her voice.

It was a lot.

The muzzle dropped only slightly. "The Cellar?" He shook his head. "I've done nothing for the Cellar to get involved in."

"I'm here," Moms said, "to give you a message from the Cellar."

"The Cellar don't send messages." He looked from Moms, to his wife, to his stepdaughter, and then he focused on Scout. "What the hell are you doing? Why are you in my head?"

But Scout was confused, shifting her focus from the man to the mother.

"Get out of my head!" the man screamed as he lifted the gun.

Scout and Moms moved at the same time, but with different targets. Moms knocked the gun aside, gripping the hand, twisting, causing him to drop it. She pressed the attack, surprising the Ranger, hitting him with several short punches before landing a solid snap kick to the groin. He was a Ranger, but he was still a man. He went down.

As Moms launched her attack, the mother was reaching into a deep pocket on the front of her dress. Scout was ready, snatching the small pistol out of her hand as the woman brought it to bear on Moms. Scout shoved her back, next to her husband, twirling the gun around and pointing it at the two of them.

Moms glanced at Scout, at the pistol, then at the woman, processing it. "How'd you know?" she asked Scout.

"I felt it," Scout said. "There are two people here. No prisoner. Partners."

Moms was silent for a few seconds, then she nodded. "You're right."

Isabella tried to move forward, to get her mother, but Moms put an arm out, blocking her.

The woman was kneeling next to her husband, trying to comfort him. "Are you all right? Do you want me to call the cops on them?" She had an arm around his shoulder. "You'll be okay, baby. You'll be okay."

"Mom?" Isabella said.

Her mother looked at her, eyes filled with anger. "Get out! Get out, and never come back. How dare you bring these strangers into my house? Bring them to attack my husband?"

"But Mom..." Isabella looked at Scout in confusion.

"Come on." Moms gently put a hand on Isabella's arm, leading her toward the door. Scout followed, keeping the gun on the couple, closing the door behind as they exited.

"I don't understand," Isabella said. "I don't understand."

They crossed the street. Moms turned to Isabella. "It's the way it is, Isabella. You can't make someone do what they don't want to do. You have your life. It's time for you to move on completely. Leave this behind."

"But we can't leave her with him. He'll kill her someday."

"He might," Moms agreed. "But it's her choice. We all have to make our own choices. It's also possible *she* might kill *him*. I'd make the odds pretty even."

"It's fate," Scout said, and both women turned to her. "There are things we can't change, Isabella. You father knew that. He accepted his fate. And in doing so, he did a very, very good thing. There's another young girl out there who has an older brother who is alive and taking care of her because of your father's sacrifice." Scout pointed at the small house. "That's your mother's fate. But you control *your* future."

Then Moms's and Scout's satphones rang: *Send Lawyers, Guns and Money.*

St. Petersburg, Russia

"We live in a Kafka world," the Curator said.

"Excuse me?" Doc was startled out of his reverie in front of the tomb of Tsar Nicholas II, the Tsarina and their five children (and the remains of sundry help who were killed with them). It was a marble crypt, roughly four feet high by four wide and two deep, inside Peter and Paul Cathedral, located within Peter and Paul Fortress, an island made by the Neva River.

"All of this. This show." The Curator waved his hand. He tapped the crypt. "I tell you a secret, since you paid to see it alone. This is not marble. It is fake. They could not afford marble when they decided to put on a show and finally inter the remains after DNA confirmed it was the Royals. So funny that the last Tsar of the Russian Empire, murdered in the name of the Soviet Union, is now buried so poorly in the name of the new Russia, is it not?"

Doc wanted to tell the Curator that paying to be left alone meant being left alone, but the Curator had warned him that there were security cameras, and his boss would wonder if someone were completely alone in here at night. He could explain away the visit as a request from an American academic, but only if he accompanied Doc into the chapel.

What Doc really wanted to say to the Curator was that he was being Kafkaesque by saying it was a Kafka world, but that was a wormhole he wanted to go down as much as he wanted to time travel again, which meant, not at all.

"The Cathedral was plundered during the Revolution," the Curator said. "The Germans bombed it in World War II. We have restored maybe half, but it will never be the original, even if we manage to make it appear original. There just isn't the money that a monarch like Peter the Great could spend to build such a thing."

"You mean that an empire could spend," Doc said.

"That is the Kafka thing," the Curator said. "Was Tsar Nicholas a monarch we should venerate, or a tyrant whom our country rebelled against? Those in power in the Soviet Union, the insiders, knew where the bodies were for a long time. But it was best to let it be, since responsibility for the murders had always been denied by the regime. But then the new Russia rose out of the Soviet Union, and what was to be done with the knowledge of where the bodies of the last leaders of the Old Russia were buried? The word would get out sooner or later. It is better to act instead of react."

Doc didn't really want to discuss this.

"I wonder what the Tsar would think of all this," the Curator said.

Nicholas II was a weak man with a wife who'd turned to a shaman in her time of need, Doc thought. He remembered his first and last sight of Nicholas II, asking God to look over Russia, just before Doc was taken out and paraded in front of a firing squad.

Doc shivered although it was warm in the Cathedral.

"But in death, there is equality." The Curator tapped the crypt. "The servants who died with them, valet, cook, lady-in-waiting, along with the family physician, their remains are in here, too. But on the bottom." He laughed. "So, even in death, the Tsar is on top."

I could have saved the Tsarina and the Duchesses, Doc thought. Could have? No. He couldn't have. He'd accepted that since he'd returned. Not completely, but enough. The Tsar had been doomed along with his family. Doc wondered what a timeline where the Tsar hadn't died was like. He assumed there had to be one. After all, there were an infinite number of possible timelines. And in one of them at least, Anastasia found her dream. Doc held onto that hope.

"May I have a moment alone?" Doc finally asked. "I've paid enough for that."

The Curator frowned. "I will be right outside the door. Three minutes is all I can allow." He left in a huff, and silence finally reigned.

Doc reached into his pocket then retrieved the pages he'd carefully ripped out of Anastasia's diary before tossing it into the furnace in the bowels of Alexander Palace. He unfolded them then read the young girl's thin script:

I know that I'm a princess, but I don't want a prince. How funny that I'm the only girl who doesn't want a prince, but rather desires an ordinary boy who loves me, and not the shoe which I leave behind. I want no pumpkins which turn into carriages, and certainly no wicked stepsisters, as my sisters are enough for any lifetime. I want a true friend in a boy who will always care for me like Papa cares for Mama, and combs my hair and laughs at my little stories and tells me over and over that I'm the prettiest when I know I'm not.

I don't want a prince at all, and I'm so lucky because I'm the youngest and will be able to have a real marriage for love, and not for country or position or treaty. I know those are needed, but Mama said no to the first who was presented to her by her grandmother. To defy the Great-Grandma Victoria! Even her own son would not do so. But Mama did, and Great-Grandma granted her wish to be with Papa.

And if she had not? I would not be here. I would not be writing this. So strange.

But once Mama met Papa, he was all she had room for in her heart.

Still, Papa was a prince. If only he'd been a farmer. I'd still be here, Mama would still have a full heart, and all these troubles would not lie on our heads.

If only.

If only.

If only HE had not come into 'Mama's life because of my little brother. HE is not real. HE is not of us. I know it, but I cannot tell anyone. They would think me crazy, even though they should see that HE is the crazy one. All the country can see it, but not Mama. Even Papa knows it, but he gives way.

The first time he read it, Doc had had no doubt about the identity of the HE Anastasia was referring to: Rasputin.

During debrief after the mission, Dane, the Time Patrol Administrator, had dismissed Rasputin when Doc claimed he'd been influenced by a Valkyrie from the Shadow to give the Tsarina his visions and to help heal young Alexei.

It raised a troubling question: Rasputin was recorded in history. His prophecies, his effect on the Tsarina and thus the Tsar, were all there, laid out as fact in the many tomes written about that time.

That was a paradox. It meant that if a Valkyrie had influenced Rasputin, and history had recorded what he did as a result of that, then the Shadow had *already* changed our history. And that change was part of the present. Did that mean that the Russian Revolution had been inevitable with or without Rasputin? Or that Rasputin would essentially have been the same without the Shadow's influence? Or that—

"It is late to be visiting a tomb."

Doc slowly turned to face the man who'd spoken.

"I am Lieutenant General Serge of the Russian Federation." He was in dress uniform; the epaulets on his greatcoat had two stars, and the bill of his military cap was decorated with the "scrambled eggs" indicating a senior officer. He waited for Doc to respond, and when he didn't, asked, "And you are...?"

"I am Professor—"

"No, no, no." General Serge smiled and shook his head. "It is a good cover story. The passport you use is even real. But you and I know, you are not the man you pretend to be." He pointed at the pages in Doc's hand. "May I?"

Doc hesitated.

The General seemed disappointed. "I have soldiers outside. I prefer to be civil."

"I'm an American citizen who—"

"You are a secret agent," Serge said. "I could say you were here to spy. Our President is not fond of American spies. Perhaps you've read that in the papers."

"I'm not here—"

"To spy." General Serge nodded. "I know. You are here to pay your respects. The papers, please."

Doc handed them over. He waited while the Russian read them.

"Ah," Serge said when he was done. "So sad. Anastasia, of course?"

"Yes."

"Should I ask how you have these? And why the pages seem fresh, not a century old?"

Doc had no answer that would make sense to the General.

In that, he was mistaken.

"I did not expect an immediate answer to that. How about this: Did you meet my brother in your journeys?"

Doc blinked. "Excuse me?"

"Did you meet Major Alexie Serge? From the Vympel Group of Duga."

Doc took a step back in surprise.

"I take that as an affirmative. Is he well?"

Doc knew it was pointless to lie any further. "No."

"I suspected as much," Serge said. "They were all badly irradiated by Chernobyl. Then they disappeared. In time. No?" He did not wait for an answer to his negative inquiry. "Where did you meet him?"

"I can't tell you that," Doc said. "I was treating him when he died. He wasn't in pain."

"That is good," General Serge said. "But did you kill him?"

"No. He died of the radiation."

"It took a long time," Serge said. "Or did it? That is an interesting question which I'm sure you will not answer. I know, and you know, that he was from our Russian Time Patrol. They were irradiated when Chernobyl went critical, and then disappeared. That is a long while ago as we measure time. We have not reconstituted the Patrol since we no longer have the technology, as it disappeared with them. I assume your American Time Patrol still has the technology. That is how you have this." He waved the papers from Anastasia's diary.

Doc knew he'd made a big mistake coming here. Too late, of course. He could hear Nada listing all the mistakes he'd made.

It was a long list.

General Serge indicated the papers again. "This is the property of the Russian Federation. Of the Russian people. You will agree?"

It really wasn't a question, but Doc nodded anyway.

Serge read the last page aloud: "'*When she died, she was only sixteen. There was a boy somewhere who loved her, without ever having met her. But he knew her very well. He would never be able to tell her that he loved her, because now she was dead. But he thought, and she thought, that in another life, whenever that will be, that they might meet and fill each other's heart. Goodbye. Do not forget us*'.'" He shook his head. "So sad. And so prescient." General Serge slid the pages from Anastasia's diary into his coat. "Did you see them die?"

"No."

"But you saw them?"

Rule one of Time Patrol seemed rather thin right now, given that the Russian had brought it up first. "I saw them."

"I am curious. What was your mission?"

"To make sure history remained the same. That is always our mission."

"And what was this Shadow, which my brother spoke of, trying to change in history?"

"Save the Tsar."

General Serge snorted. "An impossible task. Nicholas was doomed from the start. He had not the strength to rule Russia, and Alexei would never have made it to adulthood. The monarchy was doomed. A stupid plan."

If that was actually the plan, Doc thought, going back to his wonderings about Rasputin and the Shadow's possible influence.

Serge reached out then tapped Doc on the chest with a powerful finger. "I want you to take a message to Mister Dane. Tell him the Russian Federation is ready to take our place once more in the defense of humanity. In the defense of our timeline."

Doc remembered his teammates tracking down Colonel Serge and his men in the Space Between. They'd been reaping people for the necessary body parts to stay alive, one step ahead of the radiation they'd absorbed when the Shadow opened a Gate into Chernobyl. But in doing so, they were affecting the timeline, causing ripples. They had to be stopped. And were. Serge continued. "We know you have managed to finally shut the Rifts."

Doc nodded. "The Nightstalkers did that."

"And now you Nightstalkers are Time Patrol. Ever wonder what happened to the Time Patrol team before you? The American team?"

"I don't know," Doc said.

Serge shrugged. "We know you've recruited a graduate student from the University of North Carolina. And a young girl. What is special about this young girl that you allow her on your most secret team?"

"She was just there in North Carolina," Doc lied. There was also the fact that he couldn't explain what was special about Scout. He didn't quite buy into the whole "'Sight'" thing, but on the other hand, there *was* something very different about her.

"I don't believe you," Serge said. "We have learned here that certain people have special talents. You tell Dane we have found some people he would be interested in. Most curiously, one of them is--" he paused—"let us say special also." Then he abruptly shifted directions. "One of your people was just running some computer simulations in New York City. Very complex. We couldn't get access to all of what he was doing, but it appears the threat from the Shadow is greater than ever. Dane will need our help." General Serge stepped up beside Doc then slipped an arm around his shoulder. "I miss my brother. He was a hero of Russia. A hero of the world. As are you, my friend. You will take my message, no?"

"I will."

"Good. Good." Serge was gently escorting Doc to the door. "My men will take you to the airport and—"

Doc's satphone picked this awkward moment: *Send Lawyers, Guns and Money.*

Austin, Texas

"Beloved son," Mac read, coming up behind the old man sitting in a folding chair in front of a tombstone.

The man was half-asleep, more half-drunk, with an empty bottle of scotch on the perfectly manicured grass next to the chair.

Mac held up a six-pack of Pearl beer. "Why you drinking the hard stuff, Dad? Not our bread and butter?"

Mac's father shook his head, swirling the alcohol around inside his brain, trying to get a glimpse of reality.

"Beloved son," Mac repeated, pointing to the inscription at the top of the tombstone. Then he pulled a beer off the plastic holder and tossed it to his dad, who fumbled it, dropping the beer.

"Scotty wouldn't have approved of that, Dad. Dropping a pass, dropping a beer." Mac picked it up. He popped the top, spraying both of them as it exploded. He handed what remained to his father, then opened one for himself. He squatted next to the chair.

"Miss me, Dad?"

"What do you want?"

"Ah, hell, Dad, I ain't wanted a dang thing in a long, long time. I left, remember? Never asked you for nothing." He took a deep drink out of the can, grimaced, and then put it down on the grass. "Not as good as I remember. I'm kind of tired of drinking, anyway. You can have the rest."

"Get the hell out of here."

"I will," Mac said. "Don't worry. I will. Mom said you were out here. Said you come every day. She didn't want to talk to me, either. Didn't even open the door. Like I had some sort of disease." Mac laughed. "Now that's funny, considering where I just was. I stopped a disease from killing a whole bunch of people. Millions. Hell, Dad, you wouldn't even be here if I hadn't done what I done. Strange how things work. Course if you weren't here, I wouldn't have ever been born and then, well, that does get a person's head spinning, don't it, Dad?"

His father was sobering up, his bloodshot eyes narrowing. "You weren't at the funeral. You have no right to be here now."

"You didn't want me at the funeral." Mac stood. "You told me that in no uncertain terms. Don't you remember?"

By the befuddled look on the old man's face, Mac knew his father couldn't remember. But it didn't matter. It had happened when it happened. There were some things you just 'couldn't take back.

"That's good you don't remember, Dad. Because that means you won't remember what I'm telling you now." Mac leaned over, close to his father. "I know you won't believe me, but it's true. Not long ago, I was given a choice. A true choice. Whether I would go back in time and prevent Scotty's accident, or help a lot of other people. Strangers." He pointed at the tombstone. "You can see the choice I made. You might think that was wrong, but I know it was right. You want to know why? Because Scotty was going to grow up and be just like you. A no good sonofabitch. He had a black heart, just like you."

"Why, you—" Mac's father struggled to his feet, knocking the chair over in the process. He was too inebriated to see the dark light dancing in Mac's eyes, the lust of anticipation for the confrontation.

Mac's satphone rang: *Send Lawyers, Guns and Money*.

Mac laughed. "Damn, Dad. You're not only no-good, you're damn lucky." He turned then walked away.

The Possibility Palace, Headquarters Time Patrol
Where? Can't Tell You. When? Can't Tell You.

"'I will conclude my narrative by simply recording my gratitude, heartfelt and inexpressible, to God, and to many of my fellow-men, for the vast improvement in my condition, both physical and mental; for the great degree of comfort with which I am surrounded; for the good I have been enabled to effect; for the light which has risen upon me; for the religious privileges I enjoy, and the religious hopes I am permitted to cherish; for the prospects opening to my children, so *different from what they might have been; and, finally, for the cheering expectation of benefiting not only the present, but many future generations of my race.'"*

"An unbelievable story," Edith Frobish commented when Eagle finished reading.

She was sitting in a plastic chair at the side of Eagle's hospital bed. His left shoulder was heavily bandaged, and he held the Kindle in his right hand. A trip to the Space Between, and surgery by one of Amelia Earhart's people using a Valkyrie suit and Atlantean technology, gave a prognosis of a full and speedy recovery. While the rest of the team had dispersed back to their present for a little off time after the Ides mission, somehow it had fallen upon Edith to be the one to take care of Eagle. She'd even escorted him, along with Sin Fen as guide, into the Space Between, her first journey there.

The room they were in was on the outer rim of the Possibility Palace, with a view to the world outside through a large bay window. It was early morning and raining, water pelting down onto the grasslands that stretched into the distance. There were mountains on the horizon, but the low clouds precluded seeing them at the moment.

Eagle didn't know when or where the Possibility Palace was located, but the suspicion was very far in the past, since time traveling into the future wasn't possible.

"Josiah Henson was a slave for forty-one years," Eagle said, "and a free man for fifty-three." And Eagle had insured Henson would be born and write the book he'd just quoted, a book published in 1849, and on which *Uncle Tom's Cabin* would be based in 1852. But the price had been high: convincing Henson's mother to return to slavery in order to conceive and bear a child into slavery.

Eagle could tell that he didn't have Edith's complete attention; she was worried about what she'd witnessed in the Met. "Dane will take action when he knows what to do. They haven't pinpointed the date being attacked yet."

"Oh!" Edith's face flushed red. "I'm so sorry. Really, I am. I know you almost gave your life to make that book a reality."

"It *was* a reality," Eagle said. "I made sure the reality didn't change."

Edith was even more flustered. "You're right, of course. I'm sorry. I'm just having a hard time waiting."

"'Hurry up and wait' was pretty much a motto in the regular Army," Eagle said.

"But the art is disappearing!"

"Only to you," Eagle said.

"And Ivar."

"Okay. And Ivar. In fact, only to Time Patrol agents. I've been thinking about that. How we all noticed Cleopatra's Needle was different, but no one else could see it. I think it has to do with the fact that traveling through the Gates, traveling in time, makes us different. Skews our perception of reality. We can see possibilities in time that are caused by ripples before they become permanent."

"What if it is lost forever?"

"We lost Kirk when we first went into the cavern containing the HUB below the Met," Eagle reminded her. "But he's alive now. With his family, back in Arkansas. The timeline can be reset. Ripples can be smoothed out. Once Dane and the Analysts figure out what's causing the art to fade out, what date and which years are being attacked, we'll fix it."

"It's so strange, though." Edith got up and began pacing back and forth. "The fading isn't era-specific. It's across the spectrum. Paintings, sculptures, artifacts. All disappearing. Some faster, some slower. But there's no way to pinpoint a break point in the timeline. The start of the ripple. We've always been able to do that before."

"Then think differently," Eagle said.

She continued back and forth.

"Edith."

She stopped pacing.

"Come here," Eagle said, beckoning from the hospital bed.

She came over and stood next to him.

Eagle tapped the side of his head. "We have to think differently if this is something you've never seen before. How would you end *all* art?"

Edith was shocked at him evening mentioning that possibility. "To end something so big, you'd have to stop it at the beginning."

"And when was the beginning of art?" Eagle asked.

Edith spread her hands. "No one knows that. Art is, well, it's the way humans express our creativity. Our imagination. It's usually visual, but it can also be sensual in terms of touching a sculpture, or auditory, in terms of music. The key is that we are expressing something inside of ourselves to others in a way that touches us emotionally. Dance is art. Film."

"But how did it start?" Eagle pressed.

"No one knows," Edith repeated. "We just assume art evolved. As mankind evolved. Diffusionist theory."

"Which means what?"

"It spread from multiple sources."

"All at once?"

"Over time," Edith said.

"But what if art started in one place, at one time, with one person?" Eagle asked. "A single point in evolution."

Edith was so startled by the idea, she sat down on the edge of Eagle's bed. "But even if one person was the first, others would eventually have come up with the concept. The desire to put something inside their minds out there in a way to get others to feel what they felt."

"True," Eagle agreed. "But there is always a first. And if the first is delayed, perhaps, that could cause a big enough shift that everything afterward is affected. That could explain what's happening. Remember, the Shadow tried to stop the first Internet message. That didn't mean there wouldn't have been another Internet message, maybe even the next day, but perhaps the true first is important."

Edith reached out to his good hand then took it. "It's scary, isn't it? I'm not sure I ever really appreciated what we do here until I went with you to the Space Between. Met Amelia Earhart, even if she's not from our timeline. And now, the thing I was most afraid of, the art disappearing, is happening. And I realize how small my fear was. Is."

"Most of us have small fears," Eagle said. "The ability to see—"

Edith's satphone played: *Moon River.*

Eagle looked at Edith. *"Breakfast at Tiffany's?* Is that your version of a Zevon?"

Edith stood. "I'm afraid so."

Then Eagle's phone Zevoned *Lawyers, Guns and Money* .

"This is the spot," Roland said.

Neeley didn't ask if he were sure, despite a millennia and a half passing since Roland had buried the two men. He wouldn't have said it if he weren't sure. Men like Roland didn't deal in guesses; nor did women like Neeley.

They were in the middle of a field on the outskirts of Ravenna, on the northeast coast of Italy. The dirt had recently been plowed, and they stood on top of a furrow.

Roland shrugged off a backpack then opened it. He removed a six-pack of bottled beer, a leather pouch that jingled, and then a hand trowel. He dug a hole, deep enough to avoid being plowed up during the next crop cycle. He opened the leather pouch and emptied the ancient coins into the hole.

"What you would have won, Eric," Roland said. He pushed the dirt back into place.

Then he grabbed two beers, handing one to Neeley. He opened another then poured it on top of the fresh dirt. When it was empty, he put it back into the cardboard carrier. He opened a fourth beer .

"To fallen comrades," Roland said.

"To fallen comrades," Neeley repeated.

They both drained the beers in one long chug. Roland opened two more beers, handing one to Neeley.

"To Gant," Roland said. "A righteous dude."

"To Gant," Neeley said.

They each took a sip.

"To Nada," Neeley said.

"To Nada," Roland repeated.

And then they began the list of names, fallen comrades from various units.

They ran out of beer long before they ran out of names.

Then Roland got Zevoned.

Assembling For The Missions

The Possibility Palace, Headquarters, Time Patrol
Where? Can't tell you. When? Can't tell you.

"YOU LIED DURING DEBRIEF," Dane said to Ivar.

They were seated on opposite sides of a wooden table, inside one of the nondescript rooms off the spiral ramp at the top of the Possibility Palace. Perched to one side, like a referee between Dane and Ivar, was Frasier, the psychiatrist for the Time Patrol, although his job had nothing to do with mental health.

Ivar was tall and thin, with long, dark hair. He'd been drafted into this whole mess indirectly by being in the wrong place, a lab at the University of North Carolina, at the wrong time, when his professor opened a Rift, a rudimentary form of Gate.

At the moment, he was surprisingly calm, considering the Administrator of the Time Patrol was confronting him. He glanced at Frasier, who made everyone uncomfortable with his solid black, artificial left eye.

"Don't look at him," Dane said. "I decide what happens. We both picked up on the lie. I told you the number one rule of the Time Patrol is to never tell anyone about the Time Patrol. Yet you told someone. Not just someone. You told Meyer Lansky, a notorious gangster."

"You told him," Frasier added, "for the smallest of reasons. To save your life."

"I think that's a pretty good reason," Ivar said. "I succeeded in my mission. Kept the Kennedys alive. Nothing changed. It wasn't like I told him when and where he was going to be whacked and he avoided it. His history before I went back and after I came back remained the same."

"Doesn't matter," Frasier said. "You broke the number one rule."

"Why don't *you* go back some time?" Ivar challenged Frasier.

The psychiatrist turned to Dane. "Curious. Not the reaction I expected."

"I'm in the room," Ivar said.

Dane leaned back in the old wooden chair. Dane was old beyond his years, which, given it was the Time Patrol, might mean anything. Short gray hair, face a little too lean for the bone structure, deep bags under his eyes.

"You've changed," Dane said. "You're not the same person who was recruited into the Nightstalkers."

"I wasn't recruited," Ivar noted.

"They asked you," Dane said.

"Right. As if it were a real question. What if I'd said no? After seeing the fun in North Carolina, you think they were going to just let me go back and finish out my PhD? I've heard about the Cellar. I like Roland, and I think Neeley's neat, but she'd cut my heart out if given the order."

A slight smile cracked Dane's usually grim face. "You have a point."

Ivar leaned forward and put his hands on the table. "Almost dying does change a person. It changed me, at least. When I was going down into Long Island Sound with my cement shoes, a few things occurred to me."

"Such as...?" Dane asked.

"That nothing really matters except the next breath you take," Ivar said. "Moms always makes her speech about how we're standing on some imaginary wall, protecting all the ordinary people from the things they can't conceive of, while they worry about their normal day-to-day crap. But now, I don't care too much even about this stuff we're doing here. Saving our timeline. Because it does occur to me that I told Lansky his future, and it *didn't* change anything. I broke the number one rule, and it didn't make a difference. So what does matter, except the next breath I take?"

Dane and Frasier exchanged glances.

"The 1929 Desk has been looking into what you did," Dane finally said. "So far, they haven't turned up any ripples emanating forward, but the possibilities are so vast, a change could be in our future, so we won't know until it happens."

"The vagaries of the variables," Ivar said.

"Don't get cocky," Frasier warned.

"The team is assembling," Dane said. "You're going on the next op."

"So you're not going to whack me?"

Dane grimaced. "Please stop using that word. Technically, the term is Sanction. Bluntly, we kill people when we have to. We don't whack them."

"And when we do kill them," Frasier added, "they never see it coming."

"Just like Lansky and the mob," Ivar said. "What's the date?"

"You'll find out in the mission briefing," Dane said. He changed the subject, indicating the backpack. "What did you learn when you went back to New York and ran your computer simulations?"

"It would be easier if you have a mainframe here," Ivar said. He held up a hand before Dane could reply. "I know, I know. No computers. One day I'd like to know why."

"Not today," Dane said.

"Doc is on to something," Ivar said. "Now that it's been proven that gravity waves exist, we're looking at a revolution in physics. The technology you're using, we're using, the HUBs that make the Gates, might be within our grasp of understanding."

"How soon?" Frasier asked.

"It would go a lot faster if we took a HUB apart," Ivar said.

"We might not be able to put it back together," Dane said. "We can't take that chance."

Ivar spread his hands. "Then I got no clue. Einstein's theory is a century old. But it was just a theory. Now we know it's true. That makes a difference, but it took a hundred years to prove. Space and time are dynamic, interwoven." He pointed down. "We know time is a variable here, and this process is somehow part of that physics. Now, in our timeline, in our present, physicists have opened up a new door of reality where some pretty crazy stuff is possible. The implications are staggering. In fact, reality as we know, isn't reality."

"It's real enough to save it," Dane said.

"The Shadow probably figured this out a while ago," Ivar said.

"Why do you think that?" Dane asked.

"Because you told us the Shadow is the one creating the time bubbles that we go into on our missions," Ivar said. "The furthest we've gotten in this field, in *our* timeline, our present, is opening Rifts, and that never turned out well. There's a big jump from opening a Rift to opening a Gate. The Shadow can not only open a Gate, but when it does, it affects the entire timeline for that bubble. If we stop it from changing history, then it seems that the bubble snaps out as if it never existed."

"Not quite," Dane said. "We've had ripples from missions even though the mission succeeded. One of the men killed on Eagle's mission on Black Tuesday would have had a son who was thus never born. We felt the effect. It was minor, and the 1980 Desk dealt with it, but it happened. So, the bubble isn't one hundred percent contained. That's the reason for our number one rule."

"I get that," Ivar said. "But that also applies to Doc's Turing Time Computer concept; inventing a way to figure out what combination of events the Shadow is trying to accomplish. It actually makes it worse. Because even if we stop the direct attempt by the Shadow, there are side effects. You told us if the Shadow causes six Cascades, that would lead to a Time Tsunami and wipe our timeline out. But how many ripples lead to a Cascade?"

"We don't know," Dane said.

"Do you see how that adds possible branches to the missions?" Ivar asked. "I think it's possible that the Shadow doesn't even know the consequences of what it's doing. Maybe we're both fighting in the dark here."

"Maybe," Dane agreed, "But they're attacking us. We're not attacking them. We can't afford to lose."

"There's something else," Ivar said. "I took all six missions for each date. Analyzed them via as many variables as I could think of. And then asked Edith for her thoughts. We found possible thematic trends."

Dane frowned. "Meaning...?"

"Black Tuesday was their first six-day attack," Ivar said. "Some of the attempts to change our history were obvious. Saving Walter Raleigh from the executioner's axe, for example. Another was wiping out Joe Kennedy, along with his sons and John and Bobby Kennedy, a by-product being Teddy not being conceived. Some weren't as obviously significant, but had potential: if that plane on Eagle's mission hadn't crashed, and the second Iranian rescue mission had gone forward, that could really have changed things, kept Carter in the White House and Reagan out.

"Roland's mission prevented something that never happened in the first place. It didn't change anything. He stopped a child being born that was obviously something which the Shadow wanted to exist. So a null. Scout's was an outlier. Yes, the Shadow was trying to stop the first Internet message from UCLA, but the technology and theory was also up at Stanford. The message would have gotten sent eventually, and the Internet would still have been invented. It just would have been delayed."

Frasier interrupted. "The real goal was Scout."

Ivar nodded. "Yes. I think the secondary goal was the Internet. Almost a lure. They tried to kill Scout. Because she, herself, is an outlier with her Sight. Pandora showing up on her Ides mission indicated that. But the one that's the oddest is Moms's mission. None of those people who survived that crash in the Andes went on to really do anything significant in terms of what your analysts out there"—He jerked his thumb toward the one of four doors that led to the pit of the Possibility Palace—"would consider historically important. But Moms said it was about hope. That the story those survivors carried with them is an inspiration."

"I don't see how hope applies to the other five missions," Frasier said.

"JFK symbolized hope in his time," Ivar said. "What if he'd been killed by Lansky's cronies as a kid?"

Frasier wasn't buying into it. "That's a stretch. And the other four?"

"I think Scout's our hope," Ivar said.

That led to a moment of silence as Dane and Frasier contemplated that.

"All right," Dane allowed. "And the other three?"

"That's the thing," Ivar said. "I think the Shadow is learning, too. Because when we ran the data from the Ides missions, a theme got a little clearer."

"And that was...?" There was irritation in Dane's voice at having to pull for answers.

"God."

Dane glanced at Frasier, then back at Ivar. "Explain."

"Okay," Ivar said. "Think broader than just God. Thematically. God, theology, mythology, fate. A higher power. Scout, Moms, and Roland all ran into women from mythology: Pandora, Pyrrha, and Diana. In Pyrrha's case, she told Moms that Fate was more powerful than even a God. Roland came back almost born-again, staring at stars, saying they were God. And Mac also had what might be considered a conversion. He's not the same guy who left to go back to 1493."

Dane rubbed the stubble of his beard. "Interesting. But you could also say great leaders was the theme of Ides: Washington, Caesar, Tsar Nicholas, Leonidas, Odoacer. Even Columbus was a leader of a different sort."

Ivar nodded. "I know. But Turing had to search for a commonality when he invented his machine to decode Enigma. Remember what Doc said: maybe the missions are lateral, but also linear. We only have two dates to work with so the data is scant. We need to be open to possibilities. Also, I think that the Shadow isn't exactly sure what it's doing yet. Or, worse, on the opposite end, it could have a very long, strategic plan, and we've only seen the beginning of it."

A short silence followed as they all processed that.

A door opened. A woman in a drab gray jumpsuit walked in, handed six folders and a single piece of paper to Dane, a piece of paper to Frasier, and then left.

"These people speak?" Ivar asked.

"When they need to," Dane said. He put the folders, paper on top, on the desk. "The others will be here shortly. I'll brief you all in the team room," he said, dismissing Ivar.

New York City, The Present

The Time Patrol, minus Eagle and Ivar, stood on the balcony and looked at the hall of the Metropolitan Museum of Art. About a quarter of the paintings were blank canvases. There were several empty pedestals where sculptures had once stood. Others were partly gone, as if melting away.

Yet the crowds on the floor were acting as if nothing were different.

"I don't get it," Roland said.

Everyone glanced at Mac, waiting for his usual repartee, but there was none forthcoming. Even Roland was taken aback, so he blundered on.

"Why can we see what they can't see? Or," Roland reconsidered, "Why can't we see what they can see?"

Roland's reconsideration was as surprising as Mac's lack of comment.

"We've traveled in time," Scout said. "It's affected us."

As simple an answer as any.

"Let's get going," Moms said. "This one is shaping up to be bad."

They trooped back to the elevator that took them six hundred feet below the Met. Moms passed the eye and DNA tests until they were in the large cavern holding the HUB, the device which projected a Gate for them to travel through. As always, Moms led the way.

They exited a Gate into a bland room with four doors. Moms went to the one directly ahead and opened it, revealing the massive open space in the interior of the Possibility Palace. Despite having been here several times, none of the five team members was quite used to standing on the balcony on the outside of the massive pit that descended over a mile down into all of recorded history.

Ivar was waiting for them. He greeted them with the truth. "I lied during my debrief after Black Tuesday. Dane and Frasier know."

"You're not dead," Moms said, "so they must be okay with it." She nodded toward the door where their team room was, indicating they were moving on and his indiscretion was already in the past.

She led the way along the spiral track that rotated down into that pit and was crowded with desks manned by Time Patrol Analysts responsible for every era of history. They didn't go below the top spiral, since it seemed all the admin offices of the Time Patrol were up here.

"Whoa," Scout said, stopping everyone as Moms got ready to open the door to their team room. She was looking up.

Normally the 'roof' of the Palace was a dark, gray cloud, the unknown future that was yet to be made into history. It was still there, but there were streaks of red in it.

"That's probably not good," Roland observed. The big man was on a roll with his observations.

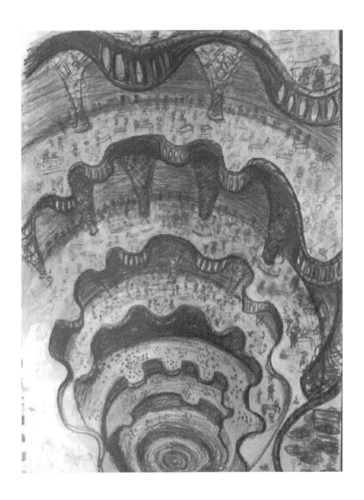

The Possibility Palace
Where? Can't tell you. When? Can't tell you.

"I don't like Ivar's attitude," Frasier said, but he was reading the paper which listed the six dates for the missions, his mind already processing the team members and the likely requirements of the missions.

"Ms. Jones used to recruit members of the Nightstalkers for various attributes," Dane said. "You were part of that process. Did you like everyone's attitude?"

"No."

"All right, then. He answered honestly as soon as we confronted him. We have to remember he was pretty traumatized coming back from Black Tuesday."

"Since when do you cut operatives slack?" Frasier asked.

"Since we need him, with Eagle out of commission," Dane said.

"We need to work on getting replacements in the pipeline," Frasier said.

Dane had the six folders, one for each mission, in front of him. "There's been a development in that area. Doc called while he was on the flight back to New York. He was approached in Russia. The Russians intercepted Ivar's computer work in New York and then tracked Doc down." He quickly updated Frasier on General Serge's offer to Doc. He finished with, "I've contacted the General. We're getting three of their people as candidates for the Time Patrol. They'll be met by Colonel Orlando at Area 51. He'll start Selection and Assessment."

"Why use the Russians?" Frasier asked. "Their Time Patrol team went rogue."

"Their Time Patrol team got fried when the Shadow attacked Chernobyl," Dane noted. "They went rogue to stay alive. As Ivar noted, that's a powerful motivation. Besides, the Russians have agreed to help fund the Patrol. We do need to be practical. We have overhead in the real world. Also—" He paused.

Frasier waited.

"The Russians," Dane said, "have always been on the cutting edge of exploring the boundaries of the human mind. They were far ahead of the CIA in parapsychology. They might bring something interesting to the table."

"You let them catch Ivar's computer work," Frasier conjectured. "You invited them without inviting them."

"Perhaps," Dane allowed. He tapped the paper on top of the folders, ending that discussion. "The first year is"—He paused, searching for words, a rarity—"unique. Outside the parameters."

"Scout," Frasier said, recognizing that mission right away because it was so different. "She's the one with the Sight."

Dane shook his head. "No. Scout's mission is dictated. Back to Greece, just two years after her last trip. That can't be coincidence." He scribbled her name on one folder and pushed it to the side.

"The first year is too vague," Frasier said. "We have no clue what that mission entails. There's no precedent, no data."

"Who is the most adaptable?" Dane asked.

"Moms."

"Then she gets it." Dane wrote on another folder then put it on top of Scout's.

"Pakistan is obvious."

Frasier shook his head. "Doc's Indian. Wrong side."

"He'll understand the stakes," Dane said. "It'll be personal for him."

"That's the other problem," Frasier said. "Let me show you." He held out his hand, and Dane handed over the file. Frasier opened it then began flipping through until he found what he was looking for. "Here." He turned the file around, his finger marking a spot on the page. "He's got family ties there. He might not even be aware of them."

Dane read it, then shrugged. "Not a factor." He wrote Doc's name on the folder and evened the two piles.

"Roland or Mac for D-Day," Frasier said. "Got to be military."

"How is Mac?" Dane asked. "You were concerned about him after Black Tuesday."

"He seems much more stable since he came back from Ides," Frasier said. "Calmer."

"Is that a good thing?" Dane asked. "Where did he go on his leave?"

"To visit his family," Frasier said. "Surveillance indicates he confronted his father at his brother's grave."

"Any violence?"

"No."

Dane drummed his fingers on the three remaining files. "The other two missions require military also. A warrior on one." He wrote Roland's name on a file. "He gets Denmark. Which means Mac gets D-Day. And that leaves Ivar to West Point."

"That's not going to go well for Ivar," Frasier said.

"He'll adapt," Dane said. He had all six folders in one stack. "Tell support to get them geared up."

The Mission Briefing

EAGLE HAD REFUSED PAIN MEDS, leery of anything that might muddle his thinking since his brain was his anchor to the world. He'd been chosen for the Nightstalkers, what the team had been before being recruited into the Time Patrol, because of his tremendous memory—a font of useless information, Nada had often called it, until it suddenly became useful.

Eagle sat in the empty team room, and he realized he'd already let the team down, because it was just a room. The off-white, drab walls, the chalkboard, and the long, white table, combined for zero personality. It could be any room off any of the many doors lining the top spiral of the Possibility Palace.

A team needed personality.

Speaking of which, Roland entered, dressed pretty much the way he'd been for the Black Tuesday mission with the Vikings. He wore a leather tunic, pants, and boots, but instead of a sword, he was carrying a Naga staff, a weapon that could cut through just about any material, especially the armor the Valkyries wore. As far as they knew, the Naga's dated from the time of Atlantis. It was a spear with a pointed, broad blade on one end, and a seven-headed snake on the hilt.

"Back in the game," Eagle said, trying to discern any differences in the attire from the 999 A.D. mission. "I think you're traveling to an earlier time period than Black Tuesday. But taking the staff—that means they expect you might run into a Valkyrie."

Roland didn't really care. He was playing with the staff, getting the feel of the weapon. He was a man easily pleased. "How's the shoulder?"

"Healing," Eagle said. "The prognosis is good as new, which is optimistic for a shoulder injury. It's the most complex joint in the body, while the knee is the largest and—" He paused in his dissertation on joints as one of the four doors opened, and Scout came in.

"Looks like we're both going back to a time we've been in before," Roland said, noting that Scout was dressed just as she had been for her Ides mission. She had on a long, white robe with a red cloak. Leather sandals. Since she hadn't changed the color of her hair after Ides, it was still bright red and short.

"But you get the Naga staff this time," Scout said. She nodded at Eagle. "Looks like you're sitting this one out, unless you're going back as a patient."

"That means Ivar will be operational," Eagle said.

Scout shook her head. "He had a rough time on his last one. I felt bad for him."

All three turned as Doc entered, dressed for combat, wearing desert camouflage and carrying a G-3 carbine.

"Post-Vietnam, but pre-Nine-Eleven." Eagle placed Doc's mission, noting the dated Alice web gear that Doc wore. "MOLLE didn't really come into use until after that. The uniform is old-time desert camo, but the G-3 isn't U.S. issue. Special Ops might carry it on mission that required it."

"What war?" Doc asked. "Desert Storm?"

"Could be," Eagle said. "Don't worry. For a lot of people, that was a lot of sit around and wait in the desert."

"You think I'm going someplace just to sit around and wait?" Doc asked.

"You got a point," Eagle said.

Roland indicated the rifle. "You got live ammo, so be careful where you point that thing. It makes a loud bang when it goes off. Remember, never fire on full auto unless you're pulling a Custer." He noted something about the uniform, or rather, the lack of something. "And, you're sterile."

"What?" Doc was confused.

"No name tag," Roland explained. "No shoulder patch. No U.S. Army patch. No flag. Nothing. Looks like a covert op, especially given the G-3. Most likely, you got that because it means you'll sound the same as whoever you're shooting at, which is an advantage if you're outnumbered. Every rifle has a different sound and—" Before Roland could give a dissertation on The Sound of Weapons, a door opened and Ivar entered, also in uniform, but of a very different era.

Ivar was dressed in gray upon gray: high-collared, long-sleeve tunic and wool slacks. The front of the gray coat was covered in brass buttons. He wore black boots and had a military cap tucked under his arm.

"Curious," Eagle said, looking Ivar over. "West Point. Mid-Twentieth Century."

"West Point?" Ivar was confused.

"Cadet gray," Eagle said. "In honor of General Winfield Scott's troops, who defeated the British near the end of the War of 1812."

"Why would I be going to West Point?"

"Why are any of us going anywhere?" Doc answered the question with a question.

Before they could speculate further, Mac entered.

"Whoa!" Roland said.

Mac was wearing OD green fatigues, World War II era, with the baggy pants used by paratroopers—which was validated by the large pile of gear he had in his arms: main parachute, reserve, Thompson submachine gun, and a kit bag full of other items.

"You're jumping in, dude!" Roland was excited and profoundly disappointed, the Naga staff being trumped by the parachute and Thompson sub. "I usually get the jumps. What gives?"

"You know how to rig this?" Mac asked, indicating the chute. "It's before my time."

"Before my time, too," Roland said, checking the parachute and harness. "But it's pretty much the same as the T-10. These four straps go around your legs and arms, and come together in the quick-release, which is in the middle of your chest, and—"

The jump school lesson halted as Moms entered.

"What the frak?" Roland exclaimed, distracted from the parachute.

Moms was covered in furs, roughly stitched together with animal sinew and held in place with ropes made of vines wrapped around her body. The furs were thick, and Moms was already sweating. She too, carried a Naga staff.

"Where the frak are you going?" Roland asked.

"No idea," Moms said, "but I have a feeling there's no running water or indoor plumbing. And it'll be cold." She saw Ivar. "Interesting. You're going to my Rockbound Highland Home, also known as Hudson High. The Military Academy." She almost sounded wistful. "Four of the worst years of my life were spent there. And you only get a day."

"Sounding better and better," Ivar said. He looked around at everyone else. "This is a weird assortment."

"Nature of the mission," Moms said.

"I wonder why both of you have the Naga," Scout said to Roland and Moms.

"Roland has one because it's very likely he's going to run into a monster," Dane said from the doorway. He went right to the blackboard. Edith Frobish slipped in behind him, closing the door.

She gave Eagle a quick smile, something the other team members noted, but she didn't notice they noticed, since Edith had the social acuity of, well, Edith.

Dane held the chalk poised over the board, but didn't write. "Anything we need to get out of the way before I get into the mission brief?"

Moms was getting used to wearing ridiculous outfits, from the short-skirted tennis outfit in North Carolina to the almost-sheer robes she'd worn on Ides, so she had no problem stepping forward in her animal skins. "Ivar said you confronted him about lying in the Black Tuesday debrief. But he's here, with us, ready to go on a mission. I assume, then, that bygones are bygones?"

Ivar appeared surprised that Moms was standing up for him, since he wasn't an original Nightstalker and had never really felt part of the team.

"We don't Sanction lying," Dane said. "I want to emphasize that who we are, what we do, must remain only with us."

"You didn't answer the question," Moms said."

"He gets a pass," Dane said. "This time. We were lucky. We probably won't be lucky again."

"All right," Moms said . "That's all I have. Anyone else?" She looked at each member of the team, giving them a chance to speak up.

No one did.

Moms joined the rest of the team at the table.

Dane turned back to the board and wrote the first, and most obvious, year down: *6 June, 1944 A.D., Normandy, France.*

"The Day of Days," Moms said as they all turned to Mac.

"I don't have a Screaming Eagle or All-American patch," Mac noted, indicating his left shoulder and referring to the two American airborne divisions that made the historic jump, the 101st and the 82nd.

"No, you don't," Dane replied. "You're infiltrating at the same time as the Pathfinders, first boots on the ground. Your drop zone is to the east of the invasion area, where you will link up with a French Resistance cell. Technically, you're from the OSS: Office of Strategic Services."

"Will there a be a Time Patrol agent from the era with the Resistance?" Mac asked.

"Reports from the agent of that era in the locale stopped suddenly," Dane said. "We're not sure what that means. We got enough from the agent and our analysts to pinpoint where the bubble will be. This Resistance cell's mission is to blow a key bridge; you'll get the target analysis and CARVER data in the download. In our history, the Resistance succeeded, and by doing so, delayed a Panzer division from making it to the beachhead in time to launch a counterattack. What data we have suggests the Shadow wants that bridge to remain intact. If those Panzers get to the beachhead any earlier than they did historically, it could turn the tide of the entire invasion."

"All right," Mac said. "Seems straightforward."

"As far as we can tell," Dane said, "it is. But that doesn't mean—"

"I know," Mac said. "Be prepared for the unexpected."

Dane nodded.

"I'd give my left nut to make that jump," Roland muttered.

"Neeley wouldn't be happy if you did that," Mac said.

"Don't worry," Dane said to Roland. "You have something significant also. Something most people consider a legend, but it was real."

Dane wrote: *6 June 452 A.D., Sjaelland Island, Denmark.*

"Beowulf," Eagle said.

"Who?" Roland was perplexed.

"Beowulf is a classic poem," Eagle explained. "In it, he fights a monster named Grendel and kills him."

Roland was caught up on the second part. "I'm going to fight a monster?"

"Technically, Beowulf fights the monster," Dane said. "We believe 6 June 452 is the day Beowulf confronts Grendel in the great hall of Heorot. At least that's the way the poem unfolds. What the reality is, we have no idea. The assumption among most people is that the poem is fiction, or perhaps reality, greatly distorted."

"What am I supposed to do?" Roland asked. "Why do I have the Naga?"

Dane gestured for Edith to take over. She reached into her satchel and removed a plastic-encased document. "This is the Nowell Codex, one of two manuscripts that make up the bound volume *Cotton Vitellius*, which is one of the four major Anglo-Saxon poetic manuscripts."

"Whoa!" Mac said, surprisingly coming to Roland's aid. "He'll get the nitty-gritty in his download. You're exploding *my* brain right now."

Edith nodded. "I'm sorry. This document dates back to about the turn of the first millennia. Around the time you went to England on the Black Tuesday mission. It contains the first known copy of Beowulf, which is the world's oldest English poem."

"I'm going back for a poem?" Roland was confused. "I thought there was a monster."

"The poem," Edith said, "was most likely composed for entertainment. But it has enough facts in it that can be verified that it's hard to tell where the line is between fact and fiction. No one is certain if Beowulf was a real person, or just based on a real person. The same with Grendel."

"Does it matter, Edith?" Eagle said. "If the Shadow is targeting the sixth of June in that year, in that place, then something is real."

"Indeed," Dane agreed with a curious glance at Edith, then at Eagle.

Edith pressed on. "Most would dismiss the concept of a monster like Grendel, but we know the Shadow has sent genetically modified creatures into our timeline. There are the kraken that are near the Gates when they open in the water."

"They're pretty badass," Roland said, having firsthand experience.

"That chimera I ran into was someone's bad idea of a monster," Scout said.

"Grendel sounds a bit like a yeti," Moms added from her own experience high in the Andes.

"Exactly," Edith said. "We can accept that the Shadow is capable of creating creatures that would be considered monsters in our legends."

"Thus, the Naga," Dane said. "We think many of what we call legends and myths are based on truths that have been lost in time. The biggest one of those, and the basis of what we do, is Atlantis. It *was* real. It *did* get destroyed."

Edith reached into her satchel, then pulled out a handful of photos and handed those to Roland. "Recent archeological excavations in Denmark have uncovered a hall built in the early- to mid-sixth century that closely resembles Hrothgar's great hall, Heorot, which Grendel terrorized. That's where you're going."

"So I help Beowulf kill Grendel?" Roland was trying to catch up.

"In the poem, Beowulf rips Grendel's arm off," Edith said.

"That's pretty wild," Roland said. "So what do I do? Just hang out and watch?"

"We don't know," Edith said.

"Roland." Moms's voice was sharp, and she shifted her admonition to the entire team. "Let's not get overconfident, people. Ivar barely made it back from Black Tuesday. And Doc escaped a firing squad by the width of his coat. Our luck won't hold like that."

Roland hung his head, and it was his turn to take on Edith's blush. "I'm sorry, Moms."

"Edith?" Eagle said.

"Yes?"

"Make sure you also give Roland the Cliff Notes version of the poem in the download. I think any of us would have a hard time understanding even the modern English version of Beowulf."

She nodded. "I'll do that."

Dane was already writing on the blackboard: *6 June 1998 A.D., Kala Chitta Range, Pakistan.*

"Pakistan's nukes," Doc said.

"On the sixth of April, 1998," Dane said, "Pakistan tested a medium-range missile capable of striking India, but because no one was absolutely certain until then if Pakistan had nuclear capability, it wasn't seen as a direct threat. More saber rattling ensued. The world knew India had nuclear capability—"

"Smiling Buddha, 1974," Doc said.

"Yes," Dane said. "But no one was quite sure in 1998 what was in the scabbard on the Pakistani side. On May eleventh, India detonated three nuclear weapons underground, making their own statement. In response, on May twenty-eighth, Pakistan proved without a doubt it was the seventh nation to have nuclear capability by detonating five bombs underground."

"Not much subtlety there," Mac noted.

"And after each country tested their weapons," Doc said, "the citizens went crazy. Dancing in the streets. Celebrating their ability to annihilate their foe, even though it most likely meant their own annihilation. I remember seeing film clips of the jubilation in India after Smiling Buddha was detonated. My parents were horrified that people could be so ecstatic over such a terrible thing."

Dane nodded. "People reacted the same in Pakistan. The twenty-eighth of May was signed into law as the Day of Greatness and National Science Day. They gave special medals to the scientists. Pakistanis celebrate it to this day."

"So what happened on the sixth of June?" Doc asked.

"Nothing," Dane said. "And that's the way it needs to stay."

"Where exactly am I going?" Doc asked.

"To join a special task force," Dane said.

"Task Force Kali," Moms said, finally understanding. "But that wasn't established until after Nine-Eleven."

"Kali was actually established in 1998," Dane said. "As these events were escalating."

"Explain, please." Doc said.

"Task Force Kali," Dane said, "was, and is, a forward-deployed Special Operations Force whose mission, should it be required, is to secure Pakistan's nuclear weapons stockpile."

"But it's based in Kandahar now," Moms said. "We weren't in the 'Stan back then."

"The FOB, Forward Operating Base, was set up in the United Arab Emirates in 1998, after the back-and-forth nuclear testing," Dane said.

"Wait," Doc said. "How did they propose to secure the Pakistani arsenal? And why?"

"To keep a nuclear war from starting," Dane said. "Once India and Pakistan started flexing their nuclear muscles, escalating the testing, people in power got worried. International Sanctions were imposed on both countries after the first test, but things appeared to be going off the rails, and neither India nor Pakistan paid much heed. There was too much national pride at stake. The situation was getting worse. When politicians get worried, they usually try to find a military solution to a problem they can't fix any other way. Kali's job was, and still is, to prevent the use of those weapons by infiltrating Pakistan and securing the warheads."

"That's a suicide mission," Doc said.

"It's viewed more as political leverage," Dane said. "The Pakistanis would have to kill American soldiers in order to get to the nukes."

"*If* the team can get to the nukes in the first place," Doc said. He wasn't buying the snake oil. "And, skipping over how these soldiers are going to infiltrate Pakistan and seize what is probably the most highly-guarded place in the country, do you actually think if Pakistan makes the decision to use those nuclear weapons, they're going to care about a handful of American soldiers?"

Dane shrugged. "I didn't make the plan. But you have to remember that a small American force in West Berlin kept the peace for a long time as a tripwire. The Berlin Brigade was always more a show of force than a reality of force."

"Okay," Doc said, trying to process all this. "I'm part of this task force based in the UAE. What happens on the sixth of June, 1998?"

"Told you." Dane spread his hands. "Nothing. At least, in our history that we can determine."

"That's brilliant," Doc said, his voice dripping sarcasm. "Just great."

"A null mission," Ivar said.

"Huh?" Roland said.

Ivar clarified. "Making sure nothing happens as opposed to doing something."

"Oh," Roland said. "Like mine. Let Beowulf kill Grendel."

"Don't assume you're on a null mission," Dane said. "Any of you." He paused. "Even though it seems most are shaping up that way."

Moms spoke up. "A null isn't a null. The Shadow will try something. It might not even be what we think. Any of *us* could be the target, just like Scout was on Black Tuesday. No matter what it is, each of us is going to have to do *something*."

"This FOB is a thousand miles from Pakistan," Doc noted. "What can I do from there?"

"We don't know what you're supposed to do," Dane said. "For all we know, the problem could be internal to the Task Force. It might not have anything to do with the warheads, or even Pakistan. The data is fuzzy with a lot of uncertainty."

"'The data is fuzzy'?" Doc repeated. "More than usual?"

"More than usual," Dane said.

"But it's the closest mission," Doc pointed out. "Time-wise."

"There is no such thing as 'close,'" Dane said, "when it comes to time travel. In fact, the less time that has passed, the *less* data we have, as the variables are more numerous. Something farther back in the past has fewer possibilities."

"That doesn't make sense," Moms said. "Seems it should be the opposite."

"Overall, among the multiverse, yes," Dane agreed. "But in just our timeline, no. The closer we are to it, the more possibilities."

Doc thought for a moment. "In 1998, all of Pakistan's nuclear material was consolidated, wasn't it?"

"The public stance," Dane said, "was that their nuclear weapons were demated. That means the warheads are kept separate from their fissile cores and the delivery systems. The Pakistanis claim that's still true, but no one really believes it. In '98, the fissile material, at the very least, was stored at a Depot in the Kala Chitta Range in northwest Pakistan. That was Task Force Kali's objective. The place was abandoned in the early part of this century. The good news is that because it was abandoned, Foreman's CIA contacts were able to gather the plans for the place, since no one considers it important anymore."

"Is the Shadow trying to get Pakistan to attack India on the sixth of June, 1998?" Moms asked.

"We don't know," Dane said. "Since 1947 when they divided, they've had four official wars, all of which Pakistan has lost. Add in a number of border skirmishes, and it's one of the tensest and most volatile places on the planet. An easy place to toss a match into." He turned to Doc. "You'll get everything about Task Force Kali, its plans, its personnel, all of it, in the download."

He ended that line of discussion by pointing the chalk at Ivar, who was running a finger around the tight collar of the dress gray coat, trying to make it wider even though he had a skinny neck.

6 June 1843 A.D., United States Military Academy, West Point, New York, Dane wrote. "The West Point class of 1843 is to graduate on the first of July," he said.

Everyone waited for him to continue, but he didn't.

"And...?" Ivar prompted.

"And we have no idea what's supposed to happen on the sixth of June," Dane said. "We just picked up the ripples from it. They were very widespread, but not specific. Whatever happened didn't have an immediate effect, but a lot of very large, long-term ripples years afterward. One that absolutely will become a Cascade if unchecked." He indicated Edith. "Give him some background."

"The West Point class of 1843," Edith began, "contained—"

"Ulysses S. Grant," Moms said.

"Yes," Edith said. "Researching that date and that location, he is the most historically significant person present at the Academy."

"What if the target is someone or something else?" Ivar asked.

"The target could be anything or anyone," Dane allowed.

"Stonewall Jackson and George Pickett are also there," Edith said. "They won't graduate until 1846. Pickett will be last in his class. And many of those West Pointers in that era affected history in different ways. Most of them fought in the Mexican War, the result of which greatly expanded the territory of the United States. And later, many were senior officers in the Civil War, on both sides."

"The target could be the Academy itself," Moms said. "There was a very strong movement at various times to dismantle it. Davy Crockett tried to pass a bill abolishing West Point. Grant himself wasn't too big on the Academy in later years. If you took out the Academy somehow, let's say by causing a great scandal instigating a demand for it to be shut down, think of all the people who won't have graduated and eventually gone into the positions they did: Grant, Lee, Eisenhower, MacArthur, Patton, Pershing. It's a long list."

"How much do you know about horses?" Edith asked Ivar.

"Horses?" Ivar shook his head. "They've got four legs."

"I can ride," Scout said.

"We know you can," Dane said. "And we'd love to have you go on this mission, but unfortunately, women weren't admitted into the Academy until 1976."

"Why do I need to know something about horses?" Ivar asked.

"Grant was a master horseman," Edith said. "At some point that month, he set an Academy record for jumping a horse that stood for over a quarter century. As near as I can pin it down, it might well have been on the sixth of June."

"I've never ridden a horse," Ivar said.

"Don't worry," Dane said. "Edith has made sure your download contains everything you need to know about that, and a lot more."

"That didn't work too good for me," Roland noted.

"Grant is the one who has to jump the horse, right?" Ivar said.

"Forget about it for now," Dane said. "It most likely won't come up as an issue for you. Just keep an eye on Grant."

"There's something else about Grant we should consider," Edith said.

"What?" Dane asked, a bit sharper than necessary, but he wanted to get on with the briefing.

"His best two subjects at the Academy were mathematics and art," Edith said. "That exemplifies a very unique mind, since those talents are in two different parts of the brain. He studied under the Romantic artist Robert Walter Wheeler while at the Academy. Given what's happening at the Met, that could have some significance. For all we know, Wheeler could be the target. He had many students, including James Whistler. He had a great influence on art in America."

"You'll get all the information you need in the download," Dane said, which was his fallback position, instead of saying they really didn't know what the Shadow had planned for each bubble. He wrote the fifth date on the board: *6 June 478 B.C. Pythia, Greece.*

"Only two years after my last mission," Scout said. "What's in Pythia? Another battle?"

"A sports and cultural festival," Edith said. "The Pythian Games were one of four in a series of Panhellenic Games. With the Olympics being held every fourth year, the Pythian games were two years after, and thus two years before, each Olympics. They were held in honor of Apollo."

Dane stirred, always pushing Edith to stay away from info dump, because they were soon going to get an extraordinary info dump prior to departing on their mission. But Edith plowed on, displaying more courage in the face of his obstinacy than ever. "The thing about these games is that unlike our modern Olympics, which focus only on athletics, they also featured art and dance. In fact, they might be considered the blossoming of various forms of art in the Western world."

As Dane began to say something, Edith cut him off again. "Given that we're seeing the art in the Met disappear, I think art is something that might factor into all the missions. In fact, the Pythian Games actually started with art and dance, and then the athletic competitions were brought in later. The legend is the Pythian Games were started after Apollo killed Python and established the Oracle at Delphi, which is where the games are held."

Dane held up a hand. "Lead with the headline, Edith."

She reached into her satchel then pulled out several photos. She passed them to Scout, who spread them out on the table so everyone could see.

"What are we looking at?" Scout asked.

Edith explained. "The Charioteer of Delphi is one of the best-known statues that still survives from Ancient Greece, and it dates directly back to the Pythian Games of 478. It's considered one of the finest examples of works in bronze. The statue commemorates a victory in the chariot races. It was a life-size representation of the chariot and driver. What's in the picture is the only part that was recovered and still exists."

"Existed," Dane corrected. "It's gone."

"Like the art in the Met?" Moms asked.

Dane shook his head. "No. Not like the art in the Met. This statue actually disappeared from the Delphi Archeological Museum yesterday. The public story is that it was stolen. The video footage from the security cameras shows it snapping out of existence. The Greeks, of course, have no clue what happened. Thus, the cover story."

"So, for real, disappeared?" Scout said.

Edith passed her another photo. "These are stills from the video. Note the time stamps."

"One second apart," Scout said. She held two photos side-by-side. "There, and not there."

"What about other museums?" Eagle asked. "Is art disappearing for real from them?"

Edith answered. "We don't know. Only those of us who are Time Patrol can see what's happening in the Met. A check of the database indicates that the Charioteer is the only significant piece of art that's really vanished."

"What that might mean," Dane said, "is that it's the first direct assault on art by the Shadow. Not the result of a ripple in time, which is what we're picking up in the Met."

"The Charioteer," Edith said, "is part of the beginning of art. And with its disappearance, we're seeing the beginning of the end of it."

"'*Now this is not the end*'," Eagle quoted. "'*It is not even the beginning of the end. But it is, perhaps, the end of the beginning*'. "

"Huh?" Roland said.

"Churchill," Eagle said. "A speech he made early in World War II, when things were looking pretty bleak."

Edith surprised everyone by quoting the same speech. "'*But in the end all the oppositions fell together, and all our foes submitted themselves to our will*'."

For once, Dane wasn't in a rush to move forward.

Moms finally broke the silence. "Good words to bear with us. We will prevail."

A low rumble of assent came from the rest of the team.

Scout pointed at the board. "478 is two years after Thermopylae. When I went back last time, I became a priestess of the Oracle of Delphi named Cyra. Will I inhabit her again?"

"We don't know," Dane said.

"What does Sin Fen say?" Scout asked, referring to the Time Patrol's seer.

"She advises you to seek counsel from the Oracle at Delphi as soon as you arrive."

"Right," Scout said. "Consult an Oracle. Why don't I consult with Sin Fen right now?"

"She's busy," Dane said.

"Doing what?" Moms asked.

"There are other timelines," Dane said. "And we maintain a presence in the Space Between."

Scout dismissed that and moved on. "What about Pandora? What's the mythology around Delphi and the Pythian Games?"

"Short version," Dane said to Edith.

Edith closed her eyes for a moment, then opened them. "Hera sent a serpent, Python, to chase the pregnant goddess Leto. But Leto escaped and gave birth to Artemis and Apollo."

"Hold on!" Moms said. "Artemis is the same as Diana in Roman mythology, right?"

Edith nodded. "Yes. A link to the woman Roland ran into. Apollo swore vengeance on Python, but the creature fled to Delphi and hid there, burying itself in the ground. Apollo tracked it down and killed it with his bow. Unfortunately, by doing so, he'd committed a crime, and Zeus told Apollo he'd have to make amends. So he founded the games."

Scout tapped the table as she said each name. "Apollo. Artemis. Zeus. Python. I'd say the odds are good that Pandora shows up. And we have no idea why I'm going there and then, other than this sculpture disappearing. But you said the statue was based on a victory in the games. So it actually wasn't created until *after* the sixth of June, 478 B.C., right?"

"I have a theory based on the information forwarded from the Time Patrol agent of the era." Edith gave a sideways glance at Dane. He nodded, giving her theory permission to be aired. "The person who sculpted the Charioteer of Delphi was Pythagoras of Samos."

"*The* Pythagoras?" Eagle said. "As in the Pythagorean theorem? The philosopher?"

"No math," Roland muttered. "Please. No math."

"Ditto on that," Scout said.

Edith's uncertainty was clear. "Whether Pythagoras the sculptor and Pythagoras the mathematician and philosopher are the same person is debated among historians. Most believe the mathematician lived earlier, roughly 570 to 495, which means he was dead by this time. Yet others believe those dates are off. They point to the fact that the mathematician was from Samos, and the sculptor signed his work Pythagoras of Samos. And the mathematician also dabbled in music and other arts."

"Please stop saying math," Roland muttered .

"Regardless," Edith said, "if it *is* the same man, he had a very powerful influence in both the sciences and philosophy. And art."

"Math and art," Ivar said. "Like Grant's two best subjects at West Point."

"Exactly," Edith said.

"You said the agent indicated they *might* be the same," Scout said.

"Yes," Edith said.

"And who is that?" Scout asked.

"The Oracle at Delphi," Edith said.

Scout nodded. "I'll keep an eye out for Pythagoras, then, and consult the Oracle. But I just find it way too much coincidence that with all of history for the Shadow to pick, this is only two years after my last mission. And I wonder—" She didn't finish her statement.

"Wonder what?" Dane asked.

"I made a promise to King Leonidas," Scout said. "He asked me—rather, he asked Cyra, who I was inhabiting—to go back to his wife and daughter and to teach his daughter."

"Teach her what?" Moms asked.

"To be like me," Scout said. "Rather, to be like Cyra. Apparently, she impressed him a lot during their journey from Delphi to Thermopylae."

"We have no idea whether his widow and child will be at the Games," Edith said. "Surely, there will be some Spartans competing."

"I don't see how such a personal thing would have the focus of the Shadow," Dane said. Which they all recognized was an excuse for him to move on.

Except he didn't write anything on the board. For the first time since the team had met him in the Space Between and he'd given them the choice to join the Time Patrol, he appeared uncertain.

"It's that bad?" Moms asked.

"It's unprecedented," Dane said. He sat at the table with the team and Edith, which was also unprecedented. He nodded toward the interior door, which led to the spiral deck overlooking the Possibility Palace. "When we look down into the spiral, we see the past. The time spiral goes down a long way, but not to the bottom of the Possibility Palace. We don't know where the bottom is."

"I wanted to ask about that," Doc said.

"Our first analyst desk begins with recorded history," Dane said. "The time spiral ends there. But when you look down from the edge at that point, the pit goes farther down. We can't see the bottom. It's almost like the view up, fading into a gray mist. Prehistory."

"Is there a bottom?" Eagle asked.

"We don't know," Dane said. "There certainly was a starting point for Earth, and for mankind. We'd have to assume one of those is the very bottom. The Alpha Point."

"So I'm going into prehistory," Moms said. "Before your first desk's time? How far?"

Dane nodded. "Thirty-two thousand, four-hundred and fifteen Before Present."

"That's a lot of numbers," Roland said.

Dane quickly explained what Before Present meant.

Scout spoke up. "What's the break point between history and prehistory?"

Edith took that. "Prehistory is when no written records exist. The break point isn't a clean one. The transition period is after a society has developed writing, but before the first historians started making notes. Essentially, this is around the fourth millennium B.C."

"I'm going back way before that," Moms said. "Were there humans? Neanderthals running around? What's the lay of the land?"

"The Neanderthals were extinct in Europe by then," Edith said. "There were humans."

"Where am I going?" Moms asked.

Dane got up and wrote on the board: *Chauvet Cave, Southern France, 6 June 32,415 Years BP (Before Present)*.

"The good news," Dane said, "is we're pretty sure what your mission is about."

"The cave drawings," Eagle said.

"Exactly," Dane said.

"The earliest drawings date from that time period," Edith said. She reached into her satchel then retrieved several images that she passed around to Moms.

"A caveman did these?" Roland asked as they went by him. "Pretty cool."

"Why do you assume it's a man?" Edith asked.

"Or cavewoman," Roland quickly amended.

"You'll get all the data and interpretations in the download," Edith said, "but the Chauvet drawings are among the first art ever discovered. They are unique even when compared with other, earlier cave drawings. There are some that were discovered in Indonesia recently, and Spain, which date several thousand years earlier, but the Chauvet drawings are much more advanced. They mark a distinct advance in conceptualizing and actual implementation.

"The artist, male or female, scraped the wall, smoothing and cleaning it, before painting. The backdrop for the drawings is lighter than the surrounding walls." She got up then walked around to stand behind Moms. She pointed. "Note there's a three-dimensional quality to the drawings. They even have a suggestion of motion. Of movement. That's incredibly hard to generate in a two-dimensional drawing."

"So, I'm going to a cave where somebody is drawing on the wall over thirty thousand years in the past," Moms said. "And...?"

"The vagaries of the variables," Dane said. "We don't know what happened in that cave. Who that person was. Why they decided to draw those images. All we know is that is one of the earliest pieces of human art we know of."

"Apparently, the Shadow knows of it, too," Moms said.

"Apparently," Dane agreed.

"Hold up," Doc interrupted. "I thought one of the limits of time travel was no traveling into the future, and no traveling before recorded history."

"That *was* what we thought were the parameters," Dane said. "We still can't go forward in time, because it doesn't exist yet. It hasn't been formed. We didn't think we could go back before recorded history because we thought the Gates needed to be able to latch onto something specific when they open. If we don't have a record of the time, we don't have that anchor. I guess no one thought to look back at something so far in the past that still exists, like these cave drawings."

"The Shadow did," Scout said.

"They're also the one creating the bubble," Dane said. "So they have the capability."

"When are we now?" Eagle asked, and it took a few moments for everyone to process the four words, except for Dane.

"The time and place of the Possibility Palace is the most closely-guarded secret we have," Dane said. "The last thing we want is for the Shadow to punch a Gate through to here and now. It would be devastating if they launched a direct attack on the Possibility Palace."

"The view outside my hospital room," Eagle said, "appears to me, at least, to be prehistory. I've seen no creatures, though. Nothing flying. Nothing living besides the grassland."

"Almost all of you have had a run-in with an agent of the Shadow," Dane said. "To be frank, you're the last people we're going to be sharing that secret with."

"Why are some cave drawings so important?" Moms asked, getting back on mission.

Dane glanced at Edith.

"The mind is what sets humans apart from other animals," Edith said. "It's evolved over the millennia. Tool making was mastered by various hominid species almost a million years ago. What really separated humans from the rest was our ability to think and plan for the future. To remember and learn from the past. To conceptualize. A higher order of consciousness.

"At some point, our brains became very different. Essentially a mutation. We could imagine. We had what is called symbolic thinking, allowing one thing to stand for another. Ancient art, the first art, is the marker for when this cognitive change occurred. Without this jump in evolution, none of this, none of who we are, what we are, as a species would have occurred."

Moms took a deep breath then expelled it. "All right. I get it. It's important."

"What about tokens?" Eagle asked, holding up the Badge of Merit he'd taken on his previous mission. "Any for these missions?"

"I tried to find things that might be helpful," Edith said. "But there was nothing useful."

"We need a moment," Moms said to Dane.

"We'll be waiting at the Gates," Dane said as he escorted Edith out of the room.

Moms stood up and looked around the table. "You've all heard the words before. There's no one going on their first mission here. But there was a reason Nada and I had this ritual. It's too easy to get complacent. To become jaded. Not just to the missions and even time travel, but to our purpose.

"Dane likes to mention the vagaries of the variables," Moms continued. "The problem being on the Time Patrol is there are way too many of them. And some of them can get us thinking. Wondering why we're doing what we're doing. Whether we're doing the right thing. Whether allowing people to die, whether it be Caesar or Anastasia Romanov"—She looked at Doc—"is the right thing.

"I'm going to make it simple for you. *It is.* It's our shared history. Our timeline. Our world. Our people. We are the ones who hold the line between the Shadow and our timeline. We are the ones who protect those who think time travel is just a neat concept, unaware that not only is it a reality, but that parallel worlds are, too. And there are some who mean us harm. We have to remember, we're not punching holes into anyone else's timeline and trying to alter their reality. Trying to wipe *their* timeline out. It's the Shadow who is attacking us."

She paused and took a deep breath. "We don't know why the Shadow is trying to destroy us. We may never know. All we have to know is we are the defenders of our timeline. The lives of billions have been placed in our trust."

She looked at Eagle.

He stood, wincing in pain from the injured shoulder. "We are here because the best of intentions can go horribly awry, and the worst of intentions can achieve exactly what it sets out to do. It is often the noblest scientific inquiry that can produce the end of us all. We are here because we are the last defense when the desire to do right turns into a wrong. We are here because mankind advances through trial and error. Because nothing man does is ever perfect. And we are ultimately here because there are things out there, beyond mankind's current knowledge level, which man must be guarded against until we can understand those things, as we finally understood the Rifts and the Fireflies and our role in that. We must finally understand the Shadow. We must remember this."

Moms finished. "Can we all live with that?"

The Missions Phase I

Normandy, France, 6 June 1944 A.D.

MAC WASN'T THERE, and then he was there, but he'd always sort of been there. It was the best way to explain how he arrived so abruptly, becoming part of this time and place. He was in the bubble of this day and this place, not before, and hopefully, he wouldn't be here afterward.

"Stand in the door!"

Mac barely had a chance to grip the metal frame around the opening in the side of the plane before he was slapped on the rump and the jumpmaster screamed, "Go!"

Mac went on pure instinct, throwing himself out of a perfectly good airplane, chin tucked, hands around the reserve across his belly. The airplane's prop blast immediately ripped away the leg bag containing the Thompson submachine gun and the blasting caps. Mac was automatically counting, "One thousand, two thousand, three thous—" then the opening shock of the parachute jerked him upright.

Getting to four thousand without the chute opening was bad for a static line jump.

After checking the canopy, he looked down. Darkness waited since the full moon was blocked by thick clouds. Feet and knees together, knees slightly bent; the regime of training and hundreds of subsequent jumps kept him on task. He checked the area, strangely quiet on the eve of the greatest invasion in history. He glanced down once more and saw the deeper black opening of the well directly below him.

Mac pulled on the risers, trying to 'slip' the canopy, but the ground was rushing up the way it always did in the last fifty feet of the jump, and there was movement to one side, and he saw the woman with the gun.

He had two seconds to process the terrain in the small opening amongst the trees: a farmhouse, some battered fences, a crumbling barn, and, of course, a well. All this flashed while he tried to direct himself away from the well. Seriously, what were the odds? He made himself small, because the woman was pointing the gun at him, but then he realized it wasn't a gun, it was a shovel, and she wasn't pointing it, she was standing next to a pile of dirt.

The ground rushed up, not like Mac was descending, but it was rising. Time was moving even slower as the adrenaline raced; every paratrooper knows time is a variable. Mac had to laugh out loud because he was sure he was going in that damn well, no matter what he did. He was being drawn into it. What was it Moms had said: the Fates?

They were giving him the finger.

He'd done so many dangerous missions, not just Time Patrol, but Nightstalkers before that, and all those IEDs he'd disarmed in Iraq and Afghanistan, and now, he was going to drown in a well on the most important mission of all, on the Day of Days.

It is 1944. A train stalls in a railway tunnel in Italy, and 521 choke to death; Casablanca *wins Best Picture at the Oscars; Louis Buchalter, leader of Murder Inc., is executed at Sing Sing; in Britain, the prohibition on married women working as teachers is lifted; the latest eruption of Mount Vesuvius kills twenty-six; Mohandas Gandhi is released from prison; 749 Americans die in a rehearsal for D-Day called Exercise Tiger; Hans Asperger publishes a paper on a syndrome; Rome falls on 4 June; also on 4 June, Enigma messages are decoded in real time after a man named Alan Turing, who possibly had Asperger's Syndrome, did some work on a thing called a computer; the first V-1 rocket hits London; at age fourteen, George Stinney becomes the youngest person ever executed in the United States after a three-hour trial in South Carolina; the "day the clowns cried" in Hartford when more than 100 children die in a circus tent fire; the first jet fighter becomes operational, the Messerschmitt 262; Paris is liberated; Henry Larsen becomes the first person to navigate the Northwest Passage in both directions; Rommel commits suicide; Franklin D. Roosevelt is re-elected, becoming the only four-term President; Olivier's film,* Henry V, *opens; Operation Market Garden goes* A Bridge Too Far; The Glass Menagerie *by Tennessee Williams premieres; General McAuliffe of the 101st Airborne replies "Nuts" to a request for surrender; the Red Cross wins the Nobel Prize for Peace in the midst of the greatest war mankind has ever waged.*

Mac was almost at ground level, and no matter what he did, the well was funneling him in.

Some things change; some don't.

The woman dropped the shovel and yelled, *"Merde!"* She sounded a bit disgusted, and Mac thought, *Hey, I'm the one going down the hole, lady.*

She ran toward him, but there was only absolute blackness as he dropped into the well. In that last split second, he was surprised Fate had zeroed it perfectly. He missed the surrounding wall as if he'd planned this. He tensed, drawing a deep breath, waiting for the inevitable water.

Feet and knees together, knees slightly bent, rotating elbows in as if for a tree landing (they hadn't covered well landing at Benning, so this was the next best solution he could come up with).

He decided this was a fitting ending, because he'd done enough bad things to deserve it, and maybe the reason he always imagined the other side of living to be nothingness was because if there were a heaven, then there was a hell. Those thoughts vanished as his feet hit hard dirt, and he felt the impact through his boots to his knees. He tried to collapse, but the space was limited, and he hit his head hard on the rock side of the well.

Darkness fell.

Sjaelland Island, Denmark, 6 June 452 A.D.

Famed was this Beowulf: far flew the boast of him,
son of Scyld, in the Scandian lands.
So becomes it a youth to quit him well
with his father's friends, by fee and gift,
that to aid him, aged, in after days,
come warriors willing, should war draw nigh,
liegemen loyal: by lauded deeds

Roland wasn't there, and then he was there, but he'd always sort of been there. It was the best way to explain how he arrived so abruptly, becoming part of this time and place. Without fanfare or excitement among those around him, not just bcause of the bubble, but also because everyone around him was passed out from drinking. He was in the bubble of this day and this place, not before, and hopefully he wouldn't be here afterward, especially since he was sitting on a bench, his head slumped forward on a plank table looking at (and smelling) puke drooling out of the mouth of the warrior whose head was next to him. There was also the matter of the guy having really, really bad breath.

Even Roland had limits.

It is 452 A.D. Attila doesn't sack Milan because the city bribes him with massive amounts of gold; Wen Cheng Di, only twelve years old, becomes the Emperor of Northern Wei; Pope Leo I helps convince Attila to not sack Rome and to withdraw from Italy; the City of Venice is founded by fugitives fleeing Attila's army; why else would someone build a city in a swamp?

Roland lifted his head and peered about the immediate area. Other than his head, he remained perfectly still, all his senses on alert, although his sense of smell had already been wiped out.

Hearing wasn't much more useful, as these guys had some major nasal problems, their snores cutting through the air as deeply as their smell.

Some things change; some don't.

Nada would have gone on a rampage and kicked some major butt. Not a single warrior was pulling security, never mind the requisite fifty percent awake as per Rogers Rules of Rangering. Of course, Robert Rogers had over 1,200 years before he'd be born and start making up rules.

Roland counted fifteen guys in armor, and one idiot who'd taken his armor off and was just in breeches and tunic. He was lying on top of one of the trestle tables on his back, arms folded on his chest, head resting on his rolled-up tunic.

Roland realized that idiot was Beowulf, since the poem indicated he'd boasted he could beat the monster on its own terms: *mano a mano,* or, more accurately, *mano a monster.* In the poem, he handed his sword to someone then stripped off his armor and shirt. Apparently, that part of the poem was true.

Never underestimate the power of human stupidity, Nada had said more than once. Roland considered that a Nada original, not knowing the now-deceased team sergeant had appropriated it from Robert Heinlein. Of course, it was such a basic truism, how could anyone lay claim to it?

Roland straightened up to get a better view of the entire place. The hall was fifty meters long by thirty wide. A large fire pit in the center held glowing embers and a few remaining flames, dimly lighting the interior. Thick beams arced overhead, and shadows flickered along the outer walls. Dual rows of trestle tables and benches lined the hall. At one end was a dais on which there was a large throne, with a lesser one next to it. There were shields, axes, and swords hung here and there, martial decorations that made the place feel like an oversized team room.

A manly-man sort of place; the ultimate man-cave.

Roland felt at home.

Continuing his scan, Roland adjusted his initial assessment. Everyone wasn't asleep. A man dressed in black pants and tunic, with a spear across his lap and a sword sheathed at his hip, was sitting cross-legged in the shadows, his back to one of the corners of the hall. Roland couldn't make out details, but there was no doubt *he* was watching everything.

And Beowulf's chest was moving too rapidly. Not the steady rhythm of slumber. The boast wasn't equal to the reality.

Roland got up, the Naga in hand, and did a physical recon. The watcher's eyes tracked him, and Roland saw that Beowulf cracked his eyelids to observe.

There were old bloodstains everywhere. There had indeed been a slaughter in this place a while back. Not twelve years, as the poem indicated. Probably a few months. Roland had a feeling that the poem exaggerated a lot of things, as stories always did the farther they got from the reality.

According to the poem, there'd been thirty killed during Grendel's last rampage. The bloodstains indicated that number might be accurate. The telling thing about Roland was that he could guesstimate a number of dead from old bloodstains.

There was movement, and Roland turned.

"What are you doing?" Beowulf demanded.

"Checking the perimeter," Roland said.

"You're one of King Hrothgar's hunters," Beowulf said. "It was brave of you and your comrade to volunteer to spend the night with my men and me."

What comrade? Roland could see a door behind the throne dais, but heavy bars had been laid across it and hammered into place .

Beowulf slid off the table. "A name, stranger?"

"I am Roland the Slayer." His earlier mission with the Vikings was coming in handy, although that had occurred four hundred and fifty years before now, or a few weeks ago, in Roland time. He hoped none of the others had already laid claim to the Slayer add-on, like one of the Vikings had. The reality was that Roland had slain quite a few in his own time; and other times.

"Well met, Roland the Slayer," Beowulf said.

There was an edge to the way he said it that bothered Roland. He ignored the feeling and continued to look around. The large, double wooden doors at the front of the hall had a bar carved out of a single, large tree across it, sealing the entrance. That would take several men to remove. Roland wondered if they had things like fire exits in these old halls, given that they used a real fire and they probably needed one. He was more concerned, though, with a monster breaking in, than getting out in case of fire.

"Why did you volunteer to join us?" Beowulf asked. "In all the excitement and ceremony, there was not time to talk."

A good question, Roland thought. For lack of a better answer, he said, "My God directed me to." He hoped Beowulf wasn't an atheist, but so far, the God thing had seemed pretty popular and much more literal in ancient times.

"Which God?" Beowulf asked.

Roland noticed that the watcher was scanning the room while also listening. The download throbbed in his head, trying to alert him to something. Reluctantly, he allowed it access. There were a couple of Christian references in the epic poem, but it was speculated they were added later. And Beowulf's question didn't seem to lend itself to the one God thing, whatever that was, and the download provided the term: monotheism.

Roland grabbed the first Norse god that popped up in the download. "Hel." Roland wanted to smack himself as soon as he uttered the name. *Seriously, Edith?*

"Why would Hel want you here?" Beowulf demanded of Roland.

"I don't question the ways of the gods," Roland said. "I do as I am bid."

Beowulf appraised him. "You appear to be a fierce warrior."

"I've done my share of"—Roland had to think, grasp, improvise—"warrioring." Not his forte.

"The monster is mine," Beowulf warned, "if it dares show. Do you understand?"

"I understand," Roland said.

"And what is your name?" Beowulf challenged the watcher, who had not spoken. "Are you a slayer, like your fellow hunter?"

The watcher uncrossed his legs and stood. He was tall and lean, with a narrow face. His eyes were sunk deep under thick eyebrows. His hair was dark, unevenly cut. Unlike Beowulf and the thanes, he didn't sport a beard, although dark stubble shadowed his face. "I am just a Jager. My name is unimportant."

Roland recognized the term without the help of the download: a Jager in his time was a member of a special operations unit for several different Northern European countries. Here and now, it meant Hunter.

"Most names *are* unimportant," Beowulf said. "But my name is well known." He walked forward toward Roland. "What have you heard of me?"

Now that Roland could see him better, Roland gave Beowulf some points. The guy had some serious size and muscle. And scars. He was Roland's height, not quite six and a half feet. He wore a pair of leather pants, boots, and that was all. Roland felt positively overdressed for this party with his Naga, leather tunic, and pants.

Roland accessed the poem to answer his question. "That you are the one who defeated Breca and slew the sea monsters."

Beowulf stood a little bit taller as he came up to Roland. "I did. I fought for three nights in the chill water. In the end, I dispatched five of the creatures with my sword."

Five nights and nine monsters in the poem. Reality was a bitch.

"And what have *you* done to earn the attention of the gods?" Beowulf challenged.

"I slew a prince of the Britons," Roland said, "when he was guarded by an elite force." Technically, Roland kept the prince from being conceived, but he was using poetic license, because, well, he could. "I killed the great warrior Ragnarok Bloodhand."

Beowulf cocked his head. "I have not heard of this Ragnarok Bloodhand." *Sort of.*

"It was a long time ago," Roland said. "I have also killed monsters. Some sea serpents." Roland still hadn't spotted an unsecured way of getting in or out of the hall other than the front doors. Breaking that wood bar would take quite an effort and cause a racket, which partially explained why the men were sleeping. "I have battled kraken," Roland expanded, feeling a smidge cocky since his tale wasn't an ancient poem embellished over the years, but hard reality. Plus, Beowulf was irritating him.

"I have heard of kraken," Beowulf grudgingly allowed.

"Fierce sea creatures with many tentacles," Jager said, staring at Roland, seeming to have no interest in Beowulf at all.

"And I've killed Valkyries," Roland said, then realized he had once more stretched past the limits of poetic, but now he focused on Jager.

"They take the bodies of the dead," Beowulf said. "Why would you fight one? You'd be fighting the will of the gods."

"It attacked me," Roland said.

"Then perhaps you should be dead," Beowulf said as if it were a real conundrum. "Perhaps you *are* already dead, which would explain why you do the bidding of the Goddess Hel."

The hair on the back of Roland's neck tingled, a warning he'd learned never to ignore. He looked at the double doors. "Is there another way in here?"

Beowulf shook his head. "Only the front can be opened from the inside. We sealed every other door."

Too late, Roland realized his mistake as the monster dropped from above and landed on the floor with a solid thud, right next to the fire pit, cracking the flagstone beneath.

Nobody ever looks up.

Roland spun to face the monster as it shredded two of Beowulf's thanes before they were awake, blood, viscera and flesh splattering about.

With his first glimpse of Grendel, Roland realized this was a lot worse than he had imagined it could be.

The monster was just that: twelve feet tall, humanoid, but with green scales covering his body. Massive hands ended in five fingers, with thick claws that came to a sharp point extending four inches. Grendel's eyes were set deep and far back in the sockets. They glittered with yellow malice as he searched for his next victims. He didn't appear to have a neck, just shoulders bulging with muscles, sloping up to the broad head that existed mainly to house a very wide mouth lined with razor-sharp teeth and four large fangs, two up, two down.

The better to kill you with.

Kala Chitta Range, Pakistan, 6 June 1998 A.D.

Doc wasn't there and then he was there, but he'd always sort of been there. Unfortunately. It was the best way to explain how he arrived, becoming part of his current time and place without fanfare or excitement or notice of the other man sharing the hide site with him. He was in the bubble of this day, not before, and hopefully he wouldn't be here afterward.

If the world made it to an afterward.

"Into the valley of death we go. Message decoded, sir."

TASK FORCE KALI A GO

VIA PRESIDENTIAL AUTHORIZATION

CODE FOUR KILO NINE NINE ECHO TERMINUS

REPEAT GO

VERIFY

CODE FOUR KILO NINE NINE ECHO TERMINUS

KALI WHEELS UP IN THREE ZERO MIKES

TIME ON TARGET FOUR HOURS ONE FIVE MIKES

INITIATE CLOCK AT MESSAGE TRANSMISSION DATE TIME STAMP

MAY GOD BE WITH YOU XXX

Lockhart ripped open his envelope containing the authorization code, checking it against the one in the message.

"Crap," he muttered. "Yours, sir?"

Doc retrieved his.

Identical.

"Ours is but to do and die," Lockhart said. "And I'd put my money on the dying part."

Doc wouldn't bet against that most likely possibility.

"I've already synced and started the clock," Lockhart said. "I'll get the drop zone beacons and laser designator ready."

"Hold on a second, Sergeant," Doc said. He was stalling, confused. He'd thought he'd appear at the Forward Operating Base in the Arab Emirates. Dane hadn't been exaggerating when he said there was no 'close' mission, and that they weren't too sure about the data.

It is 1998. The shuttle Endeavor launches with the first American component for the Unity Space Station; the genome of syphilis is sequenced (over half a millennia after Columbus' crew brought it to the Old World from the New World); the Second Congo War begins. It will claim

3.9 million lives before it ends five years later, making it the bloodiest war since World War II, and it barely makes a headline; Titanic *wins Best Picture at the Oscars (spoiler alert: Jack dies); in St. Petersburg, Nicholas II and his family are finally buried, eighty years after their deaths, which is where Doc visited them again about two decades from now.*

As if that isn't enough to confuse Doc.

Some things change; some don't.

Lockhart was peering out the observation slit. Doc noticed there was a bright glow out there, and he joined Lockhart, their shoulders pressed together in the tight space. Below and to the right, on the side of a tall mountain ridge, the area was bathed by bright searchlights, highlighting a road winding up from the valley and ending at a large tunnel opening: the Kala Chitta Nuclear Weapons Depot. In Doc's estimation, there was no way a handful of Special Forces soldiers was going to take that place.

Then he remembered Moms, Nada, Roland, Eagle, Mac, Scout, and the Nightstalker missions he'd gone on, and now, the Time Patrol missions, and he knew people like that didn't believe anything was impossible. The same for people like Sergeant Lockhart, and the Task Force loading out in the FOB, to attack on a mission they all knew was most likely a one-way trip.

They were coming, no matter what.

Doc slumped back, trying to organize his thoughts. The hide site was a seven-by-four-foot wide, six-foot deep hole, chipped, dug, and constructed out of the side of a steep mountain with the addition of PVC pipe and some tough sheets of shaped plastic. It was crowded with their gear: weapons, mission equipment, food (not much), and water (critical). Doc also saw several small baggies in one corner, and it took him a moment to realize they contained body waste.

Everything that came into the Hole came out of the Hole.

Doc knew Hole was a word to be capitalized in his thoughts because that's the way the men who rotated through on their fifteen-day shifts viewed it. It was their entire world for those long days and nights. They never left it, except at the end, to climb over the mountain to the landing zone on the other side, to meet the helicopter bringing their relief team.

Or, on certain evenings, to prepare the way into the Depot.

The download filled in other data: the Hole was at nine thousand feet, while the Depot was fifteen hundred feet below. The observation slit was four inches wide, just enough for a telescope and night vision devices. The Hole was covered with specially made camouflage netting and thermal blankets, in case the Pakistanis decided to take a look with heat-sensors.

"Sir?" Lockhart stared at him, puzzled and concerned.

"Sync the clock," Doc said, trying to buy time with time.

Lockhart held up his wrist, pressing a button on the side to light it up and show the countdown. "*I'm* already synced, sir. They're loading the Combat Talon at Al Dhafra right now. They'll be airborne in twenty-one minutes."

A modified C-130, the Talon was the Special Ops version of the venerable Hercules transport plane. The download laid out the plan: the Talon would be packed full of Special Operators who would implement the assault plan. The plane would fly wave-top level across the Gulf of Oman, go "dry" over southern Iran, continue NOE—nap of the Earth—across Iran, penetrate into Afghanistan airspace, and fly along the border with Pakistan. Then it would turn east, punching into Pakistan to deliver the troops via low-level parachute right on top of the facility.

Lot of ifs there: if the Iranians didn't spot it and shoot it down, ditto for what passed for a government in Afghanistan, and then, the much more capable Pakistani Air Force and Army awaited.

Then there was getting inside the most secure facility in Pakistan.

Which meant Doc and Lockhart had to go to down there and open the front door before the Task Force arrived.

That part of the plan was there, too, in questionable detail, a best-guess plan based on the available intelligence at the time.

It was supplemented in the download by the intelligence the Time Patrol had gathered two decades from now, which was much more extensive. That new intelligence indicated the current plan was doomed.

"You gotta be kidding me," Doc muttered as he realized what was expected. He looked out the slit, then checked his watch. It was just after dark, around ten P.M. local time. Given the Talon's air speed, the distance, the low-level route, and the requirement for an in-flight refueling, the countdown made sense; it would be over four hours before it arrived.

And in those four hours, he and Lockhart had to get from here, into there. Doc could see numerous guard posts facing the road. The download confirmed other observation points, motion detectors, trip wires, video cameras, night vision cameras, and a slew of anti-intrusion devices planted by the Pakistanis surrounding the entrance.

Lockhart was next to him. "Yeah, I know. Remember, nothing is impossible to the man who doesn't have to do it."

Doc was startled. "Nada used to say that all the time."

"Who's Nada?" Lockhart asked.

"Someone I served with," Doc said. "He was killed on a mission." *Years from now. In Afghanistan.*

"That sucks," Lockhart said. He pulled back, and Doc heard him organizing gear, getting ready to move out.

Doc closed his eyes, analyzing the infiltration plan, using what Mac had taught the team about the CARVER target analysis formula and his own scientific expertise. The download had data that the planners of the mission in 1998 hadn't had access to. Back then, they worked off satellite imagery, scant intelligence from the CIA, and the observations from the hide site and recon missions down the mountain to prepare the way. Intelligence after the fact was something every analyst would give anything for, and it was a critical advantage of the Time Patrol.

After September Eleventh, 2001, the United States had worked out a complicated arrangement with Pakistan regarding its nuclear materials. The fear was that Islamic fundamentalists would make an attempt to seize nuclear warheads, so the United States provided over $100 million in assistance a year to help secure them; in essence, bribery. But the Pakistanis refused the offer of PAL (Permissive Action Link) technology, which the U.S. and all other nuclear powers used. PAL was a system of sophisticated checks and balances on the release of nuclear weapons. Doc smiled grimly; the reason for the refusal had been obvious. The Pakistanis had been afraid the Americans would hide dead switches in the technology, insuring the weapons could never be activated.

They were most likely right in that fear, since it would be the logical thing for the U.S. to do. The U.S. had put worms in whatever computer gear they "gifted" the Pakistanis, and more intelligence had been gleaned from that. Through Foreman, their CIA contact, an urgent request for intelligence regarding this Depot, abandoned by Doc's time, had been sent out to the field. What came back had been included in the download.

"It's not going to work," Doc said.

"What?" Lockhart asked, looking up from the rucksack he was closing up.

"The plan," Doc said. "They didn't have all the intel."

"They never do." Lockhart was next to him.

"There's early warning radar on the other side of the ridge. It will pick up the Talon coming in from Afghanistan."

Lockhart frowned. "Satellite imagery doesn't show that. Intelligence didn't report any."

"Two arrays are positioned in caves, not visible to overhead imagery."

"How do you know that?"

"I know," Doc said.

"But if you knew it, why didn't you tell anyone before we came here?"

A good question that Doc couldn't answer.

Other problems were coming to the forefront as Doc compared the intelligence in the download from a couple of decades in the future to the plan based on the now, in 1998. One glaring problem was that here and now, no one had known the design of the interior of the complex. The Kali plan worked off of a best-guess as to how such a Depot *should* be designed, with a Containment Facility and a fissionable material Core deep inside.

Doc knew Nada had a saying about *should*.

Doc shook his head, not just over the impossible and suicidal plan, but for remembering Nada's sayings more often now than he had heeded them when he was alive.

Except Nada *was* alive now. Doc didn't want to pursue that line of thought.

Instead, he checked the design of the facility from the download, and it was more sophisticated than the plan had anticipated. Futile piled on top of futile. If they tried to implement Kali as planned, it would be a massacre of every member of the team.

"What the hell is going on?" Lockhart demanded with an edge of something else in his tone that Doc had heard before; a precursor to taking action, most likely of a violent nature. "We've got a lot of men inbound. We got to get down there and open the door."

"We won't be able to," Doc said. He turned around and found what must be his rucksack. The SOP packing list for this unit's backpacks was in the download, so he was able to get what he needed by feel.

He heard a slide pull back on a pistol and turned. Lockhart had his sidearm in hand, although he hadn't raised it. "Sir, we have to do our duty. The team is relying on us."

Doc gave his best impression of a confident smile. "Don't worry. We're going to. There's just some adjustments I have to make." He nodded toward the observation slit. "Let me show you."

Lockhart holstered the gun and joined Doc, peering out.

Doc pointed. "See that guard post to the left of the road, where it makes the S-turn?"

"Yes."

Doc slid the needle into Lockhart's neck with his other hand, pushing the plunger.

Lockhart reacted so quickly, the syringe was ripped from Doc's hand, and a gash was torn in Lockhart's neck. As the sergeant reached for his pistol, Doc clamped both his hands over the holster. They struggled for a moment, then the sedative took effect, and Lockhart slumped.

Doc quickly bandaged the small wound then positioned the unconscious man as comfortably as he could. Doc wrote a note, then pinned it to the front of Lockhart's jacket where he'd see it when he regained consciousness.

Doc closed his eyes once more and thought hard, envisioning what lay ahead and what would be needed. Because when he'd thought of the others on the team and how they wouldn't hesitate to implement the plan, for the first time, it struck home to him that he was one of them. He had been a Nightstalker, and now he was Time Patrol, and this was his duty.

Doc repacked his rucksack, appropriating some gear from Lockhart's. He went to the right front part of the hide site. Leveraging an entrenching tool, he pushed aside the thick piece of plastic that had been in place when Lockhart and whoever Doc was replacing had crawled in here. Doc slithered out. He put the plastic back, making sure the camouflage was intact.

The mountainside was steep. Doc thought of all those hours he'd spent in the silo with Eagle, forced to practice his climbing and rappelling, and wished he'd spent more time training and less time complaining. There was a path; well, not a path, but a way that had been used before.

Doc began to climb down the mountain toward the Kala Chitta Nuclear Weapons Depot to stop a nuclear war.

Delphi, Greece, 6 June 478 B.C.

Scout wasn't there and then she was there, but she'd always sort of been there. It was the best way to explain how she arrived, becoming part of her current time and place. She was in the bubble of this day, not before, and hopefully she wouldn't be here afterward.

And she was Scout, not occupying the priestess Cyra, as she had just two years previously, on her Ides mission. Two years in *now* time, only a few weeks in *Scout* time.

One small blessing that was immediately negated.

"You're too late."

The first thing Scout saw was the body lying in a pool of blood on the floor of the cave. Then a small fire. And on the other side of the fire, an old woman dressed in a white robe, with a heavy red cape over her shoulders. She was clutching the cape tight around her neck and had a purple veil over the lower part of her face.

"I'm too late?" Scout asked, trying to understand where she was, who was dead, and who the old woman was, although that answer popped up instantly: *the Oracle of Delphi.*

"Can't you see?" the Oracle asked bitterly, pointing at the body. She appeared to be very old, but that was relative in this era. She could be in her forties or her nineties. Her hair was white and surprisingly long, curling over her shoulders. Her eyes were pale blue, and something wasn't quite right about them. Cataracts, Scout realized, remembering her grandmother's eyes—her dear Nana, so different from her mother.

Scout looked more closely at the body. A man lay facedown, his white robe stained with blood. "Who is this? What happened?"

"That's Pythagoras," the Oracle said. Her voice wasn't seer-like at all, but like that crazy aunt who smoked too many cigarettes and drank too much bourbon. "The man you were supposed to save."

Scout knelt, but she knew dead, and he was dead. She checked anyway, her finger on his neck. No pulse, but the skin was warm. "Who did this?"

"I only caught a glimpse," the Oracle said. She nodded toward a narrow passageway deeper in the cave. "I was in there and came out just a few seconds before you arrived. But you're too late," she repeated.

It is 478 B.C. The first Parthenon was destroyed two years previously by the Persians, and it would be thirty-one years before construction would begin on the second one, which the modern world would know as THE Parthenon; Hiero I becomes Tyrant of Syracuse following the death of his brother Gelo; a Temple of Confucius is established in what becomes modern day Qufu; Aristides commands an Athenian fleet of thirty ships to free the Greek cities on Cyprus and capture Byzantium from the Persians.

The Oracle shook her head. "How can you travel so far, be so close, and yet fail?"

Good question, Scout thought.

Some things change; some don't.

The Oracle walked stiffly to a stone throne that looked very uncomfortable then sat in it. "Bring me—" She gestured as she pulled the veil away, revealing her face, lined with worry and age.

Scout saw a table on which an amphora and chalice rested. Scout poured wine into the chalice then brought it to the Oracle. The old woman's skeleton-like fingers curled around it.

"Who did you see?" Scout asked. "Who did this?"

"A woman with a dagger," the Oracle said. She drank from the chalice. "Tall. Her hair was different. Black. With a single white streak running from here"—The Oracle touched her own head above the left eye——"over the top to the back. She ran when she saw me come in."

Scout knew who that was. "Pandora."

United States Military Academy, West Point, New York, 6 June 1843 A.D.

Ivar wasn't there, and then he was there, but he'd always sort of been there. It was the best way to explain how he arrived so abruptly, becoming part of this time and place, without fanfare or excitement among those around him. He was in the bubble of this day and this place, not before, and hopefully he wouldn't be here afterward.

"To Sam, and perhaps his graduation!" someone shouted in a Southern accent. "Or as his family knew him, to Hiram."

Someone else chimed in. "Or, as the Army will forever know him, Lieutenant Ulysses S. Grant!"

Ivar was extremely uncomfortable for some reason, and relaxed his shoulders as he tried to get oriented to his new surroundings.

"Get your chin in, plebe!" Spittle sprayed Ivar's face, and he blinked at the large man screaming at him, trying to understand what could cause such rage. Looking past the red face, Ivar saw a half-dozen cadets standing around a wood plank table, hoisting mugs in honor of the toast. The mugs were all pointed at the man sitting at the end of the table, and Ivar realized he was looking at the future four-star General and President of the United States.

Grant's mug wasn't in his hand.

The others turned their backs to the table and away from each other and drank, which Ivar found odd, but Edith had found intriguing in the research for the download; it was tradition, based on practicality. The original purpose was that by turning their backs, the cadets could rightfully claim under the honor code that they had not seen each other imbibing alcohol, which was forbidden by regulations. These days, it was more form than substance, but West Point was big on tradition whether it made sense or not.

Ivar studied Grant. He made Ivar appear to be the epitome of physical fitness. Grant was short, slight, and Ivar doubted he weighed more than 120 pounds. He had thick, dark hair, imperfectly combed, and was clean-shaven. *One hundred fifteen pounds,* the download corrected him, just as the red-faced cadet slammed an open palm into Ivar's chest, pinning him against the log wall. "Eyes straight ahead, plebe."

Plebe, a member of the lowest class at the U.S. Military Academy, dating to 1833, most likely a shortened form of the Latin plebeian. Edith's download translated the term, which wasn't very useful, but Ivar did as ordered and stared straight ahead, tucking his chin in and wondering what the heck was going on, and what military purpose tucking his chin in accomplished—prevent it from getting shot off, perhaps?

"Gentlemen, spirits treat me ill," Grant said, an uncomfortable smile on his face. "I appreciate your fine gesture and best wishes, but I cannot partake further."

"When I make a toast, *I* take it ill to be rebuked," the Southern accent replied.

"You're in a foul mood today, George," someone else at the table said.

"We don't take slights lightly where I come from in Virginia," George said. "I toasted Mister Grant, and he refused to partake."

"Your family hasn't lived in Richmond in years," the same someone said. "You came here with an Illinois appointment, if I remember rightly."

Factoring George, Richmond, an Illinois appointment, and a total student body of less than 250 cadets (Ivar had always been good at sorting data), Ivar came up with the most likely suspect: George Pickett, West Point Class of 1846.

A chair fell to the floor, and even the cadet hazing Ivar turned about to see what was amiss. Pickett had knocked his over, and he was swaying drunkenly. His face was red, and his dark mustache twirled at the ends, ending in little spikes.

Grant laughed uneasily, taking a step back from the table. "I meant no offense."

"But you gave it," Pickett said. "You do not act as a gentleman, but what can be expected of those such as you?"

"Easy, George," someone else said.

Ivar chanced a look at his surroundings, and it took a moment to pin down the most likely location: Benny Havens Tavern. The dark windows and the flickering lanterns in the smoke-filled room indicated it was night outside.

Pickett pointed at the mug in front of Grant. "Pick it up, Hiram."

"I don't fancy that name." Grant had been born Hiram Ulysses Grant, but the Congressman who'd given Grant his appointment to the Academy had made a clerical error on the paperwork, listing his name as Ulysses S. Grant. Once the Army had something down in writing, it was practically impossible to get it changed. Friends called him Sam, and that suited him just fine.

A flicker crossed Grant's face. "Is it a heavy burden being the Immortal in all your sections, George?"

Immortal? Sections? Ivar realized he was going to be spending a lot of time sifting through the download if this kept up. *Immortal = last, academically; Sections = classes.*

"Is it a heavy burden, Hiram," Pickett said, the name dripping derision, "to be stepping in between myself and my lady?"

Grant was stunned. "What are you speaking of?"

"I saw you confiding with her this past weekend," Pickett said.

"I was merely being courteous," Grant said. "No confidences were passed."

Pickett slammed a short horsewhip onto the table, rattling the glasses. On the other side of the room, the proprietor, Benny Havens, had been resting his head on the wide wooden plank which served as bar. He started, lifted his head, then peered at the cadets. "None of that in here, lads."

Pickett ignored him. "I challenge you, sir, on your honor. Or lack of it."

"Easy, George," another cadet said. "There's no need for that. None at all. You've had too much spirits."

"My honor is not slighted so easily," Grant said. "And dueling is foolish and against regulations. I have been through too much here in these forlorn four years to be a fool now."

"Perhaps your honor isn't slighted so easily because you have none," Pickett pressed.

"It's late," Grant said. "It will be reveille in an hour, and there's a storm brewing outside as well as in here. I must be back to barracks. I can ill afford more demerits this close to graduation. I prefer not to spend any more time here at my Rockbound Highland Home than absolutely necessary." He looked at another cadet. "If you'd like, Thomas, I can ride York with you back to the stables. It was most kind of you to join us, as I know you rarely frequent this establishment."

A cadet who had not uttered a word and was sitting at the corner of the table looked up and nodded. "I'd appreciate that, Sam. It gave me a bit of trouble to ride York down here, but I wanted to test my mettle. It is clear to see why he has been dubbed the Hell-Beast." Thomas had long mutton chop sideburns, not quite making a beard, but getting close.

Hell-Beast? Ivar thought. Some creature from the Shadow? But then, Ivar shook his head. A horse. York. In fact, *the* horse on which Grant would make the jump that wrote him into the record books at the Academy.

Grant made for the door. The quiet cadet, Thomas, joined him, but Pickett wasn't done.

"That is all you will say in your defense, Hiram, whose middle initial, S., stands for nothing? And why are you so friendly with him, Jackson?" he demanded of Thomas. "You should associate with better, even though you are poor South."

Thomas Jackson? The name clicked in the download: Thomas, who would be better known as Stonewall two decades in the future.

Grant shook his head, but didn't say a word. He and Jackson went out into the darkness. Pickett followed, which caused the other cadets to scramble after, wanting to see how this would play.

Ivar needed to keep an eye on the most likely object of his mission. He went to the door then peered out. In the bright moonlight, Grant was unwrapping the reins of the largest horse Ivar had ever seen—not that he'd seen that many horses in person—from a hitching post.

York was a horse whose name had been written in history, mainly because of Grant riding it. A chestnut stallion, well-muscled and exceptionally tall, it had arrived at the Academy stables a few months previously and gained a reputation as intractable and unrideable, having thrown many a cadet. In this way, it had earned its moniker: Hell-Beast, a term Grant never used.

Pickett walked around Grant to the side of the horse. He snapped his short whip on the well-muscled flank of the mighty beast, and it tried to rear, but Grant held onto the bridle.

"Easy, York, easy," Grant said in a surprisingly calm voice, given the suddenness of the action. He placed a hand on the horse, and it immediately quieted down. Grant meticulously wound the reins around the post, then turned to Pickett. For the first time, Ivar saw anger, indeed rage, on Grant's face.

"A man does not beat an animal," Grant said. "Never!"

"An honorable man does not intrude between another man and his lady." Pickett stepped up to Grant, the horse on one side. He slapped Grant across the face. "On your honor, sir!"

Grant nodded. "Accepted!"

"One half-hour," Pickett said. "The river field with pistols. We will see who has honor. And courage."

It is 1843. Lord George Paulet occupies Hawaii in the name of Great Britain; the world doesn't end on the twenty-first of March as had been predicted by preacher William Miller; Tivoli opens in Copenhagen; the world's first computer program is translated and expanded by Ada Lovelace, using a sequence of Bernoulli numbers, although the computer hasn't been invented yet; Robert Todd Lincoln is born; Kierkegaard's Fear and Trembling *is published.*

One of the upperclassmen was worried about something else. The hazer hit Ivar on the shoulder. "Get some hot flips poured into a bottle, plebe, and bring it to the river field. This is going to be interesting."

Some things change; some don't.

Chauvet Cave, Southern France, 6 June 32,415 Years B.P. (Before Present)

Moms wasn't there, and then she was there, but she'd sort of always been there. It was the best way to explain how she arrived, becoming part of her current time and place without fanfare or excitement among those around her—if there had been anyone around her. She was in the bubble of this day, not before, and hopefully she wouldn't be here afterward, because if so, it would be a long time before she'd be able to take a hot shower again.

Moms staggered and had to kneel. She was light-headed, confused. Uncertain of where she was, when she was.

Time Patrol.

In time. "Way, way, way in the past," Moms whispered to herself, still kneeling, eyes squeezed tightly shut as she tried to gather herself.

In place. "South of France."

She opened her eyes then looked about. She was in a deep valley, stretching in both directions as far as she could see, which wasn't that far. A thin snow was falling, swirling about in a nasty, chill wind. The sun was muted behind low-hanging gray clouds. She realized there was dust mixed in with the snow and checked the download. At least she had the thick furs, because the south of France was much different from the tourist brochures of her present. This was near the end of the Last Glacial Maximum, the last ice age. Northern Europe was covered in ice, all the way down through Germany and most of Britain.

When she was stationed in Europe, she'd traveled to this area with someone on a walking trip of the Dordogne, a rare change of pace for her and not her idea, of course. It had been beautiful and green, and the land, even in modern days, wild and rough. Now, she could be on a different planet. The terrain was gray and appeared mostly dead. She was on the edge of a polar desert, with stunted trees trying to grow on the steep sides of the valley.

Moms tried to remember her companion on the trip. A man, another soldier, but she couldn't remember his name. She could picture him in her mind only vaguely, and remembered that he'd been killed in Afghanistan some years later. Another life, another person. Someone long gone in her memory, along with the person she had once been.

Moms squatted down, trying to clear her mind of distractions, not realizing the inability to retrieve memories was a distraction of its own.

It is 32,415 Years B.P. Three thousand years before this, Homo neanderthalensis *was extinct in Europe, and was currently becoming extinct everywhere as the world transitioned to the age of* Homo sapiens; *around this millennia,* Homo sapiens *populates Europe; ice sheets still cover the Great Lakes, the mouth of the Rhine, and most of the British Isles; no* Homo sapiens *are in the Americas; the wooly rhinoceros and cave bear wander Europe.*

Some things change; some don't.

Orienting herself to the terrain features of what would be called the Gorges of the Ardèche Valley, which were almost exactly the same in her time, she estimated she was about two kilometers from the target, the cave, which was farther up the Gorges. The Ardèche River coursed down the lowest part of the valley, about twenty feet from where Moms was, but it was almost completely covered with a thick layer of ice, the water pressing through underneath and opening into a narrow central channel. There were brush and stunted trees struggling for life on either side of the stream. Between her and the stream was the only sign of activity: a narrow trail, the dirt hard-packed, following the course of the water on this side.

The walls of the Gorges were too steep to climb in many places. Moms could see how a tribe would settle here if they could find a cave that could only be approached from below. She imagined there were several inhabited caves along the course of the river; not just by humans, but some by cave bears.

"Bears," Moms said, mimicking someone pretending to be frightened, someone on television a while ago, millennia in the future, but she couldn't remember who. It had been a joke, but if she ran into a cave bear, it wouldn't be funny. Males could weigh over a thousand pounds. This was their end, though, this last ice age. They'd be gone in a few thousand years.

Moms giggled. Just a few thousand years. As if that were nothing. A speck of time. And it was; she'd just crossed, what was it, 32,000 or so years, with one step? A step too far. Or was it A Bridge?

Moms slapped herself across the face.

"Pull yourself together!"

Then she slapped herself again for saying that out loud.

Moms stood. She'd preached to the team about being too complacent, but there was another aspect: a mission too vague to understand or plot a course of action. Should she just go to the Chauvet Cave, wander in, and say hi? According to the download, there was some sort of basic language now, but of course, the download had no record of it. So Moms couldn't even say hi. Scratch that.

She was *here*, and it was cold and miserable, and she had no clue what was *there*, in that cave. Dane always seemed so confident they'd figure it out once they got when and where they were going. Observe all the pieces, see how they fit, and see what doesn't fit, what the Shadow had planned that would upset what was supposed to happen.

Except what, exactly, was supposed to happen? Happened? It was history. It was now. Moms shivered, trying to think straight.

Moms had wanted to complain, to question the mission, but as team leader, it wasn't something that could be done in front of the others.

Nothing is impossible to the man (or woman) who doesn't have to do it.

One of Nada's favorite sayings, and one they'd only shared privately in the CP, Command Post, back at the Ranch. In front of the team, it had always been *No problem, can do*. Because that's what leaders did.

Why we are here? Moms had no frakking clue at the moment.

She heard movement to her left, farther downstream. Backing up, she lay down in the snow and dust, behind several uprooted trees that gave a modicum of concealment.

Figures appeared on the trail, bundled in thick furs. Seven bearded men. Two women shepherding children, a boy and a girl, pre-teen, but able to walk on their own.

Not much of a tribe, Moms thought. But this was pre-agriculture, and they survived by being hunter-gatherers, and that didn't allow for large groups in one place.

Two of the men had spears. The rest had wood, piled high on their backs with rudimentary carriers made of branches and animal sinews. They had clubs in their hands. Moms understood the need for firewood from her winter warfare training. Fire was as essential as water in this type of environment. It was needed to melt ice, cook food, keep predators away during the dark, and keep from freezing to death. Glancing up, she saw that the sun was lower, heading toward the west rim of the valley.

The last man passed, and though she was tempted to follow the party, she remained still. Another tactical lesson learned via the blood lessons from the history of combat. Plus, she knew where the cave was.

Her wait was rewarded.

Five warriors and a woman came down the trail. The men were not bearded. Not of this time. Besides the lack of beards, everything they wore or carried was from another era. The men were dressed in well-worn leather, layered on. The outermost layer was basic armor, pieces of protective metal woven into the fabric. They had swords at their sides and spears in one hand.

Moms placed them at some time during the Bronze era. Warriors, not just by their accouterment, but also the way they moved. One man was out front on point, five meters ahead of the main body. The rear man spent most of his time walking backward.

She remembered Roland speaking of meeting a Spartan whose timeline provided mercenaries for the Shadow. These were from some timeline that appeared to be in the same position. Perhaps early Spartans, before the red cloaks and the crested helmets and the chiseled pecs and—

Moms shook her head. That was a movie. Not real. This was real.

The sixth, the woman, was the outlier. She was dressed in black trousers and tunic, covered by a long coat. She had a pack on her back which appeared to be made out of a material like nylon, and a quiver of arrows was attached to its side. In her hands, she held a bow.

The point man raised a fist as he came abreast of Moms's position. The other five froze as he looked left, right. Moms had also gone still at the signal. She stopped breathing, her hands on the Naga, knowing that even with the weapon, these were very bad odds.

Seconds passed, an eternity, then the point man signaled for them to continue.

The female hesitated for a moment, and Moms felt the woman's gaze rake over the area where she was hidden. It was tangible, and it took everything Moms had not to stand up.

Then the woman moved on.

The intruders disappeared up the valley.

Moms took a deep breath and got to her knees, then stood. She estimated there was about an hour of daylight left.

They'd attack once their target was in the cave. The downside of an excellent defensive position was that it being a trap if there was no exit, and the download confirmed the Chauvet Cave had only one ground-level entrance .

Moms slipped through the brush to the trail.

She began following.

There was killing to be done.

The Present

Our Present.
Area 51

"RUSSIANS." COLONEL ORLANDO spit with the wind; his father had raised no fool. He watched the small plane on approach to the pitted concrete airstrip in the middle of nowhere, Nevada. The runway dated back to World War II when the Air Force decided Nevada was a pretty good place to teach hastily-trained pilots to drop bombs, since the many misses pretty much had the same effect as a hit: a lot of sand and rock blown up.

"You don't like Russians?" Eagle asked. "Ms. Jones was Russian."

"She was a Nightstalker," Orlando said. And that was the end of that, because Orlando had been a Nightstalker longer than anyone knew, which meant everyone alive had come after him, and he'd outlasted all his teammates. When he'd no longer been able to be an operative—the distinct odor of alcohol was his constant companion—Ms. Jones had made him the recruiter for the elite team.

Now she was gone, too.

Time takes all, Eagle thought. His shoulder ached with no painkiller, but he'd piloted the Snake here, and that had precluded taking any.

The plane touched down.

The Snake was behind them, a jet-engine tilt-rotor plane that, according to the Department of Defense, was still being computer simulated and not yet in production. Eagle had been flying one for four years for the Nightstalkers, and now, as a member of the Time Patrol, had access to it when needed.

"Who are the new Nightstalkers?" Eagle asked. It was a question that had been on the edge of his brain ever since being "recruited" into the Time Patrol.

"Bunch of yahoos," Orlando said. "Never be the same as you guys. Plus, without Rifts to shut, they spend most of their time cranking their yank. Or is it yanking their crank? Working routine stuff like stolen biological agents, nuke stuff, lab mishaps, containment failures. The usual dumb scientist stuff. Be glad you moved on. The scientists seem to be getting dumber." From the tone of his voice, it was clear he was not happy that Eagle and the others had moved on.

"The Ranch the same?" Eagle asked.

"Yeah," Orlando said. "The new Nightstalkers headquarter out of Area 51 for now. It's just as you guys left it."

"Good," Eagle said.

The plane decelerated. It was a twin-engine jet with a single blue stripe down the side. No tail number, no other markings. It didn't exist to the FAA. It didn't have a transponder. There were lumps under the wings that an observant man could tell housed anti-missile defenses and some offensive capability. Both Eagle and Orlando were observant men.

The plane halted fifty feet away. The front left door opened out and down, providing a short staircase. There was no one for almost ten seconds.

"Geez," Orlando complained. "You remember the Army, Eagle. Any time you get a tasking for warm bodies, you never send your best people. You send the folks you wanna get rid of."

Then a big man dressed in nondescript khakis was framed in the exit. He paused and peered about, saw Orlando and Eagle, then looked past them to the Snake. He looked over his shoulder and said something, then came down the steps with the swagger of, well, a big man, used to dominating whatever setting he was in.

He was followed by a woman, dressed the same. She was young, blond, blue-eyed, and beautiful in that not-quite-a-real-person, thin, tall, model sort of way. She also came down the stairs with the aura of one used to being watched at all times, for reasons different than that of the man.

"I think they sent her to the wrong place," Orlando muttered.

"Don't judge a book by the cover," Eagle said.

"I don't read books."

A Russian soldier came next, his hand on the shoulder of a young woman confined in a straitjacket. Her head was close-shaven, just a dark stubble. She was of average height, skinny to the point of anorexia, and seemed resigned to her fate.

"That's just great," Orlando said.

The big man walked up to Orlando and Eagle, not bothering to wait for the others. "I am—" he began in a Russian accent.

"You're nobody," Orlando cut him off. "No names. We do the naming. For now, you're Boris." The woman arrived, having heard the exchange. Before she could speak, Orlando also christened her. "And you're Princess. And you're"—He looked at the girl in the straightjacket—"Lara. Welcome to Area 51."

The Missions Phase II

MAC WOKE IN A PILE OF MUD, but he could see the moon above, so that meant he was alive. And not in the well, so the mud was okay. He had that moment every paratrooper savors, lying on the ground, alive, because it wasn't the jump that killed you, it was the ground, or the well, which made him wonder: How the hell did he get out of there?

Mac's face was burning, and the backs of his hands were skinned raw, but otherwise, he felt intact, nothing broken, as far as he could tell initially. He turned his head, wincing in pain, and looked about. The farmhouse was clearer now that the clouds weren't blocking the available light from the stars and moon. It had been a nice place once upon a time, but was rundown and appeared uninhabitable; five years of war will do that to a place.

There was the sound of artillery in the distance, but no nearby small arms fire, which was a relief. He heard a woman cursing in French and remembered his last vision. He looked the other way, and she was shoveling and muttering profanities, although it didn't sound bad in her language. There was a body next to her, and he suspected that had something to do with the cursing.

Mac was in his jump harness, and turning his head farther, he could see the risers leading to the suspension lines leading to the canopy—made of nylon, not silk—and Edith's download tried to jam in the information about a woman, Adeline Gray, being the first to jump the nylon, but really, there was a lot more important stuff Mac needed to know right now. He could see that the apex of the canopy, where all the suspension lines met, had a rope through it, and the rope was tied to a harness worn by the skinniest donkey Mac had ever seen.

The fact that both he and the donkey were in harness caused Mac to laugh, but it barely escaped his parched throat. He was so thirsty after being pulled out of a well. He searched for the cotter pin on the lanyard, his fingers burning, and he realized a couple of them were broken on his right hand. So much for intact. Using remaining fingers that seemed functional, he used the cotter pin to unlock the quick release. As he inserted the pin, it occurred to him to wonder who thought they needed a key on the quick release for the harness, thus negating the quick release aspect. Did they really think someone was going to hit their quick release while still in the air? And then the answer was there, courtesy of Edith Frobish's download: Yes, indeed. It had happened, so, like many things in life, it had been redesigned for the lowest common denominator, i.e., the stupid.

He hit the release, and the four straps popped free, and his body grew an extra inch. Mac rolled over, automatically feeling for the .45 pistol on his right hip. It was there, but his attempt to open the flap with two broken fingers didn't work. He knew Nada would be upset with him for not having checked the weapon before anything else, but...

Mac got to his knees.

Relieved of the strain on its own harness, the donkey gave a relieved bray and took a step, dragging Mac's muddy chute and harness a few feet before stopping in exhaustion.

Mac generated some moisture. "Can I get some water?"

French, the language of lovers, Mac thought. Too bad he'd lose it when he got back to the Possibility Palace. If he got back to the Palace. So far, this op wasn't going too well. Which reminded him he'd known Latin and Spanish on his last mission, but couldn't dredge either one up for the life of him right now. He figured his brain only had so much space for so many languages.

The woman stopped shoveling and cursing. She turned to face him. "Oh! Maybe I can get you some water from the well? How would you like that?"

Mac gestured to the canteen on his waist, jammed behind the pistol. "I've got some water if you help." He held up his bloody hands.

She just stared at him.

"Did you drag me out of the well with the donkey?" Mac asked, more to make conversation, since he knew it was a Roland-type question, but she seemed a bit standoffish. Granted, he'd just appeared out of the sky and landed in her well, and she was burying somebody, but...

She cursed and dropped the shovel. "Maurice is not a donkey! He is a mule."

The download was a smidge late on that critical piece of information: a mule is the offspring of a male donkey and a female horse, getting the best of both species, minus the ability to reproduce. Still, a bit picky, under the circumstances.

She wasn't done. "Maurice pulled you out. He hasn't had a decent meal in over a year, and I feared he would drop dead when he had you halfway up, but I gave him the last carrot. A single, stinking carrot, which he would have turned up his nose at before the war, unfit for Maurice, the best and most powerful mule for ten miles all about!"

Mac looked at Maurice's skinny flanks. "Thank you, Maurice."

She walked over. In the moonlight, she appeared old, haggard, and very dirty. Her hair was wrapped underneath a kerchief. She wore baggy pants and a loose blouse, both smeared with mud.

"Here," Mac said, indicating the canteen. "Please."

She reached down, unsnapped the holder's cover, then pulled the canteen out. She twisted the top off then held it out. Mac took it with his left hand, which was in better shape than his right. He drank greedily.

"Maybe some for Maurice?"

Mac felt a moment's shame, but also wondered why, of all the farms in Normandy, he'd been dropped into this well. He handed her the canteen, and she took it to the mule.

"How long was I out?" Mac asked, trying to get back on track with the mission.

"Not quite an hour, but I was not timing it." She was holding the canteen up, dribbling the contents into Maurice's mouth, not too picky about keeping the metal from the mule's lips, but her hand was cupped underneath, catching every missed drop, and she put her hand to her mouth, drinking and then licking up every bit of moisture.

There was still time to do the mission, or rather, make sure the mission was done. Mac got to his feet, a bit unsteady. He took a step, and right away knew he'd torn something in his knee. He remembered the day his older brother ripped his knee up, during the next to last game of his senior year. That had wiped out the football scholarship to the University of Texas. Not that his family couldn't afford to pay his brother's way through school; they had plenty of money. It was more the vanished glory of the future gridiron. Mac's father missed that more than his brother, and had taken it badly.

Not quite as badly as when the State Troopers showed up and informed the family he was dead, but the difference wasn't enough to make his father a decent human being.

Mac limped over. Maurice had dried foam around his mouth, and his hide was covered in dirt. Mac felt more shame as he realized what truly bad shape the mule was in. He probably could have climbed out of the well on his own if she'd waited until he'd regained consciousness, rather than hooking the rope to the top of the chute, which he assumed had come down draped over the edge of the well.

"I think he's done for," Mac said.

She whirled about to face him, spilling water in her sudden fury. "How do you say in English, *va te faire foutre*?"

"Close enough in French," Mac said. *Mission. Back on mission*, he reminded himself. He looked at the body. "Who is that?"

"A fool," she said. She looked him over. "American? Not British."

"American," Mac confirmed. "Was he Resistance?"

"Him and the two already covered," she said. She screwed the cap back on then handed him the canteen. She walked back to the small mound and picked up the shovel to finish the job he'd interrupted.

"Crap," Mac muttered, realizing they were most likely the ones he was supposed to find. It also explained the lack of a light on the drop zone. He followed her over. "Their supplies?"

"The Germans were waiting for them," she said. "At, what do you call it? The drop zone?" She nodded. "About two hundred meters that way. A field. Much better to land in than a well, is it not? But then, if you had landed over there, you would be dead, too. Would you not?"

"Are the Germans still there?"

She shrugged. "Who knows?" She waved a hand to the west, where the sound of artillery was thundering on the horizon. The Day of Days was beginning to live up to its billing. "Since that started, I imagine things have changed for the Germans."

"How did the bodies get from the drop zone to here?" Mac asked.

"Maurice can pull a cart with bodies more easily than an errant paratrooper out of a well."

Maurice is having a rough night, Mac thought. "Did you know them?"

She sighed, and now that he was closer, he realized she was younger than he'd first thought—late twenties, early thirties—but it was her war-thin figure which made her look as old as the mule. Her face was drawn, her eyes sunken. "I knew them."

"Were you with them? In the Resistance? I was supposed to meet a team. We have to blow a railroad bridge."

"I was with them, but not this evening."

"Where are the supplies? The demolitions?" Of course, his blasting caps had come off with the leg bag, but Mac could improvise. That was why the team had christened him "Mac," after the guy on the show *MacGyver*. He'd never had the heart to tell them he hated the name. The Nightstalkers didn't give you a choice once they brought you into your new life and gave you your new name. As if Ms. Jones shredding your personnel folder wiped out all memories of your past.

Mac wished it had.

The French woman had gone back to the mule without answering.

"We have to blow that bridge," Mac said. "It's the key to keeping the Panzers from counterattacking the beachhead." He knelt next to the uncovered body. The chest was torn apart from a burst of gunfire. He looked at her again.

She was holding Maurice's head, and tears were making vertical lines of clean skin on her face. *She'd* had a tough night, Mac realized. Burying men would wear anyone out. But she was also here. Alive.

Mac reached across his body then opened the flap on the .45. He drew it. He wasn't as good with it left-handed, but Nada had insisted everyone fire one hundred rounds off-hand every time they went to the range.

Why?

Because he was Nada.

"Why aren't *you* dead?" Mac asked, which probably wasn't nice since she'd saved him, so far, but there was the mission.

She looked at him, her head pressed against Maurice's. "You phrase it poorly. The better question is, Why am I alive?" She let go of Maurice then came up to him, stopping just a few feet away, peering at him in the moonlight. She noted the .45 in his hand. "And you? Traveler from the sky. Traveler in time. Why are you still alive?"

She could be a Shadow agent, Mac reminded himself. It would explain why the rest of the Resistance team was dead. "Where are the demolitions?"

"Is that all you care about? The demolitions? The mission? Since you've been sent here, I must assume it is most important, eh? Critical?"

"It is."

"Tell me this, traveler. I have had years to think on things. Is it worth it?"

"It is," Mac said without much conviction.

"Worth this?" She indicated the body and the mound. She took another step toward him, grabbed his hand holding the gun, lifted it, then pressed the muzzle against the center of her forehead. "This would be easy. You asked me if I knew them. My father, who lies at our feet? My two younger brothers, already covered with dirt? Louis was only twelve, but the German shot him in the back of the head after he surrendered. I watched hidden in the trees with Maurice. He laughed. The SS officer. He laughed when he pulled the trigger. Are you going to laugh now when you pull the trigger?"

Sjaelland Island, Denmark, 6 June 452 A.D.

… the other, warped
in the shape of a man, moves beyond the pale
bigger than any man, an unnatural birth
called Grendel by the country people
in former days.

If Grendel hadn't paused to dine, he probably could have taken out all the thanes before they mounted any sort of defense, but the monster tore a chunk of meat off the thigh of one of the dead. He wolfed it down as the surviving warriors scrambled awake.

One of Beowulf's thanes charged him, more courage than smarts, leaping off the top of a table, axe raised for a mighty blow which Grendel didn't even try to stop. The axe thudded into the side of the monster's head, and the weapon pinged back, flying out of the thane's hand as if he'd struck a stone.

The man didn't have time to reflect on that as Grendel swiped with one paw, slicing through leather armor, skin, tendons, and bone with equal ease, eviscerating the man.

"Back!" Beowulf ordered the surviving thanes. "He's mine."

Roland sighed. The guy told a good tale, but there was no way he was going to—

Beowulf jumped, higher than any man Roland had ever seen jump outside of the Olympics. He went over Grendel's head, twisting in the air like a gymnast and landing on the beast's back. Beowulf slid an arm around, trying to get a chokehold.

Bad move, since it appeared that, unlike Roland, Beowulf hadn't focused on the "no neck" part of the creature's anatomy. Beowulf's arm slid up across the face, Grendel's fangs slashing his flesh as the arm went by the huge mouth, and then the warrior had nothing.

Not quite correct. Before he could fall off, Beowulf gripped hold of Grendel's forearm as the beast reached to rip the irritant off its back. Beowulf didn't let go of Grendel's arm. Beowulf had grabbed the proverbial wolf by the ears—by holding onto the arm, he kept the claws on that hand at bay, while it had to fight off the others with its free hand. The beast shook the arm, trying to dislodge Beowulf's grip as the surviving thanes attacked.

This distracted Grendel from chomping down on Beowulf. Grendel used his one free hand to fight, and he began to dispatch warriors in disconcertingly quick order.

Roland took a step closer, uncertain how to proceed. The poem was Beowulf's, not Roland the Slayer's. Pieces and parts were coming true. If this went according to script, or rather poem, Beowulf would rip the arm off, and Grendel would run away to his lair and bleed out.

The other thanes hadn't read the poem, nor were they obeying orders as they charged forward, spears, axes, and swords flailing away. Metal bounced off Grendel's scales. The scene would almost have been comedic: Beowulf hanging like a doll from one of Grendel's arms, shaken about while the beast fought the thanes with its other.

Except for all the blood flying about, and the screams, and the bodies being torn apart and dropping to the stone floor, never to rise again.

Roland was twitching; he'd never been one to hold back from a fight. It didn't appear that Beowulf was making any progress on getting that arm off. In fact, it became apparent as Grendel spun, arm extended, and slammed Beowulf's back into a wood post, that the warrior wasn't going to last much longer.

There was only one man left, Jager, and he was also holding back.

Who are you? Roland wondered.

Jager glanced at Roland. "We charge together?"

What's this 'we' stuff? Roland didn't answer. He charged by himself. Rather than going for a fatal blow, he aimed the point of the Naga staff toward Grendel's shoulder.

Instead of penetrating, the point slid up and then over the scales on the shoulder. Roland stumbled forward, having put all his effort into what should have been a severing thrust through the scales with the Atlantean metal.

This isn't good, Roland thought. He saw Grendel swinging Beowulf in circles, and he belatedly realized the monster was going to use the warrior as a club.

Beowulf slammed into Roland.

Roland was knocked the ground, the Naga falling from his hand. Dazed, he looked up. Beowulf, unbelievably, was still hanging onto the arm, but it was obvious he was almost done. With no more thanes attacking, Grendel reached with his free hand for the Danish prince.

Roland grasped for the Naga, trying to get back into the fight, but he was too slow as Jager dove forward and grabbed the weapon. He rolled under Grendel's swipe then jabbed the point of the Naga upward into Grendel's unarmored armpit. The blade slid in, and Grendel emitted a howl that shook the hall.

Jager held onto the Naga staff, straining with all his might, levering the blade in the beast's flesh, cutting through flesh and bone.

Grendel screamed again as Beowulf made one last effort, and the half-severed arm ripped free. Black blood spurted from the socket.

Beowulf fell to the floor, clutching the monster's arm. Jager stood fast, the Naga at the ready. Roland got to his feet, grabbing a nearby battle axe. Grendel staggered back several steps and howled once more, while looking at where its arm had been as if confirming what the pain was informing it.

Then it ran for the main doors.

None of the three survivors pursued it.

Grendel grabbed the beam securing the doors with his one hand and tossed it aside. It pulled the doors asunder and was gone into the darkness. There was another howl of pain, but this one was moving away.

Roland looked back.

Jager sat down on the closest bench, putting the Naga down. And Beowulf?

Beowulf was holding Grendel's arm above his head, muscles quivering with the effort. The prince let out his own howl, this one of triumph.

Kala Chitta Range, Pakistan, 6 June 1998 A.D.

Gravity works. It was one law of physics everyone on the Time Patrol agreed upon. Even Roland, the master parachutist, implicitly understood that rule.

Doc was making good time down the mountain. The download had given him a route he would have never been able to find in daylight, never mind at night wearing night vision goggles. According to the information implanted in his brain, Task Force Kali had begun working on a way to get into the Depot as soon as they were set in the Hole. The first rotation simply trekked over the mountain and dug in and built the Hole. That took a week, working at night, going back over the mountain to hide each day, then back over to build, until it was done.

Then the next rotation worked on charting out a path from the hide site to the Depot and finding a way in, other than the front door, making notes of all security and anti-intrusion devices along the route, and how they could be avoided or defeated. This was the path he was following.

It took Doc an hour and a half to descend to a level two hundred feet above the entrance to the Depot. There was still a deep valley between him and it, but now he could go horizontal, to the right, edging around where the mountain met the ridgeline. The "path" he was on could barely be called that, narrowing to just a few inches in places. If the download didn't insist that it had been traversed by other members of Kali, Doc probably would have turned back in places.

But he pressed forward, knowing time was of the essence.

The world around Doc was two-dimensional in the green glow of the pre-twenty-first century night vision goggles. He paused as he came to the first obstacle noted by the earlier teams: a trip wire hooked to a flare. Practically invisible, even with the goggles. Doc carefully stepped over it, clinging to the side of the mountain, the rock cold under his hands.

The trail began curving back to the left, meaning he'd left the mountain and was now on the ridgeline. He arrived at the second obstacle. A motion sensor. Doc reached into a side pocket on the rucksack then pulled out a small transmitter. He placed it on the narrow ledge then turned it on. It emitted a frequency that neutralized the motion sensor.

He left the transmitter, and then the sensor, behind. The trail widened into what could be called a path.

Doc halted, realizing his hands were shaking. He knelt, trying to regain his equilibrium, which took a few minutes. The trail edged around a spur of rock, and the download warned that a guard post in the form of a pillbox was ten meters past there. It was oriented not just to cover the path, but also overlooked the road from the valley up to the Depot. It was supposed to be manned by two soldiers, but the reports from the three Kali team members who'd made this journey before Doc to prepare the way, indicated that on the three occasions, the post had been manned only once, and then just by a single soldier who'd been sleeping.

Doc began to crawl forward on his hands and knees. He reached the spur then peered around it. He could see the concrete pillbox, with the snout of a heavy machine gun poking out of a portal toward the road below, and found a small comfort that it wasn't aimed at him.

Doc crawled forward, expecting a burst of machine gun fire and bullets to tear through his body. Inch by inch, he crept toward the post. He reached it, flattening himself even more, then crawled underneath the muzzle of the gun. He made it past, continuing to crawl, until he was around another bend in the path and out of sight of the post.

Doc stood, closed his eyes, and envisioned the rest of the way until he got to a ventilation shaft. It was clear of warning devices and—

"Who are you?"

The question was in Urdu, but the download immediately translated it.

What was surprising, to Doc as much as the soldier asking the question, was Doc's instinctive reaction, the result of years of special operations training bursting forth at the moment it was needed. Doc spun about, saw the Pakistani soldier eight feet away, his own G-3 rifle in his hands but not aimed, and Doc charged, drawing his knife as he did so. As the Pakistani began to bring the muzzle up, it was too late as Doc swung the blade, the razor-sharp edge slicing through the front of the neck.

Blood spurted forth, pumped by a young and powerful heart, drenching Doc. The soldier was blinking, confused, stunned, his brain trying to process his accelerating death. He dropped to his knees, mouth moving, trying to say something, and then collapsed forward, head hitting Doc's knees, and then the body slowly rolled to the side.

Doc looked down, the blood a dark green in the night vision goggles.

There was no doubt the man was dead. *Not a man,* Doc thought, staring at the smooth face of a teenager who probably shaved once a week. The eyes were wide and blank.

Doc looked at the knife in his hand and then at the boy-soldier, as if by doing so he could make a true connection between his action and the result.

For all his time on the Nightstalkers, and now in the Time Patrol, this was the first time Doc had killed.

It changes a person.

"'Pandora?'" The Oracle shook her head. "Their kind have not walked the Earth for many years, but..."

"I met Pandora before," Scout said. "At Thermopylae."

She'd failed even before she had a chance to succeed. It made no sense. If she were in the Shadow's bubble, how had the Shadow acted before—then Scout remembered Pandora killing the Valkyrie, claiming to not be part of the Shadow. It made no sense.

But Pandora had lied about other things, so what was the truth?

"You're the traveler in time who went into Cyra two years ago at Thermopylae," the Oracle said. "She told me what happened. That she was supplanted for a day, the final day of the battle. She retains only the vaguest memories of what occurred." The Oracle shook her head. "That I should live to see such things." She looked at the body. "Why would Pandora kill him? He was here on commission to prepare some sculptures."

"The art," Scout said. "And the math and the philosophy."

The Oracle finished the chalice then held it out.

Scout indicated the body. "What was he doing here?"

"To hear a prophecy, of course."

"Did you talk to him?"

"She killed him as I walked in," the Oracle said. "And then you appeared. out of thin air. I don't know *who*, exactly, you are. I just know *what* you are. You come here from the future."

Scout spun about as she sensed a presence in the entrance to the cave. A priestess came in, then halted abruptly. She was tall, with red hair just like Scout's. She was also older, with wrinkles etched around her eyes indicating years passed outside in the sun and wind, in addition to a lot of worrying. She had a white robe like Scout's, with a red belt. A ceremonial dagger, the scabbard encrusted with jewels, was tucked into the belt.

"Mother! Are you all right?"

The Oracle waggled the chalice, and the priestess walked past Scout, giving her a curious glance, then topped off the drink. "I'm fine," the Oracle said. "Him, not so much."

The priestess shifted her attention to Scout. "I know you."

Scout nodded. "You're Cyra."

"And you're Scout," Cyra said. "I was there, but not there, when you took over my body. I was you, but not you. And you were me, and not me." She shook her head. "Very confusing, and I'm still not sure what to make of it. Nor was my mother."

"Me, neither," Scout said. "Sorry for—" she wasn't sure what to say. Borrowing your consciousness and body? She didn't think there *was* a protocol for this.

"But what happened?" Cyra asked, indicating the body. "Who is this?"

"Pythagoras of Samos," the Oracle said.

"The sculptor?" Cyra frowned. "How did he get in here? He didn't pass the priestesses at the Spring."

"I was in the back," the Oracle said. "I don't know how he got in."

"Who did it?" Cyra asked.

"I only caught a glimpse," the Oracle said, but she tipped the edge of the chalice toward Scout. "She says it was Pandora."

Cyra's eyes widened. "From Thermopylae? I have some memory of you, of us, meeting her. Why would she do this? Why would she come here?"

"I think she is an agent of the—" Scout paused, uncertain how much to say, not sure who, exactly, the Oracle or her daughter were. Was the Oracle a Time Patrol agent? It seemed so. But how was Cyra part of this? Another agent, to follow in her mother's footsteps?

"The Shadow?" The Oracle finished the sentence. She nodded at Scout. "Yes, I am the one you are to meet. I sent the warning into time to get help. But you are too late."

"Why did you send a warning?" Scout asked.

"I sensed trouble looming," the Oracle said. She lifted a finger off the chalice and pointed at the body. "I was right, of course."

"But this violates the Sacred Truce of Hierominia," Cyra said. "All of Greece will hunt her down."

"*I'll* hunt her down," Scout said. "If she's still here."

"Who is this Pandora?" Cyra asked, but she directed the question toward her mother.

"She's like us, but not one of us," the Oracle said. "There is much I have to teach you."

"And this Shadow," Cyra said. "What is that? How can you send a warning in time?"

Scout glanced at the Oracle, but the old woman didn't answer her daughter's questions. Scout could see where one could get a reputation as a psychic with such answers and lack of answers.

"She said we were sisters when I met her at Thermopylae," Scout said.

"Pandora has the Sight," the Oracle said. "I can sense you have it," she said to Scout. "I have it. But there's a divergence on how powerful the Sight is in each of us." She tipped the cup toward Cyra. "She's my daughter, and she has it, and I believe hers will grow more powerful than my own one day. She'll sit in this blasted chair and have her ass rubbed raw, listening to every stupid question one could possibly imagine. Telling fools what they want to hear, and every once in a while, telling someone special something important."

Scout opened her mouth to ask a question, but the Oracle wasn't done, addressing both Scout and her daughter. "We are descended from the original priestesses of Atlantis. A place only we know of. The word means nothing to the world. Other than visions I get at times, *I* don't know much of Atlantis. I know it was destroyed by the Shadow a long, long time ago, and some of its priestesses, our ancestors, escaped and scattered around the world. Tell me, girl," she asked Scout. "In your time, what is known of Atlantis?"

"It's only a legend," Scout said. She accessed the download. "The first mention, and really the only source, is from a man named Plato. He—" She paused, realizing Plato hadn't been born yet.

The Oracle leaned forward. "Yes?"

"It's just a legend in my time."

"You were going to say more."

"There are things I cannot speak of," Scout said.

"But we are sisters," the Oracle said.

"That's what Pandora says, too," Scout noted.

The Oracle seemed to take it as an insult. "One must be careful, I suppose. Pandora is like us, but not one of us." She gestured, and Cyra picked up the amphora, carried it over, then poured a generous portion into the chalice. Scout noticed the Oracle's hand was shaking. Topped off, the Oracle took a deep drink before resting her hand, and the cup, on the arm of the throne.

"You must hold the secrets you must hold," the Oracle said, sounding none too pleased about it. "I make it easy for those who come in here. I tell them we are descended from Helen. They know of her from Homer. That our line goes back farther than that, to Thera. That is far enough for those who need to be impressed. They know of Thera, and that it was struck with a great disaster a long time ago which wiped out that kingdom. Close enough. And that our priestesses traveled from there to Knossos on a ship with Apollo. And from there, to here. That's a pedigree to impress even kings."

"But Pandora," Cyra said. "She is spoken of as a Goddess."

"No," the Oracle said. "She is human. Not a Goddess. According to legend, she was the first human woman created by the Gods, molded out of earth, designed to be a punishment for humanity after Prometheus stole the secret of fire. The Gods conspired together, and each contributed a gift, a seductive gift, to her constitution."

"They also gave her a *pithos* full of evils," Scout said.

"Which she loosed upon the world," the Oracle said. "She is why there *is* evil in the world. She brought it. She sows it."

"By killing Pythagoras, she has already changed"—Scout paused—"the future."

My past, Scout thought. *I've failed.*

"Perhaps you can redeem yourself." The Oracle finally put the chalice down and pointed toward the cave entrance. "I can sense her. Pandora is still here. You must find her. Finish her. Finish her evil."

United States Military Academy, West Point, New York, 6 June 1843 A.D.

"Dueling is forbidden," Benny Havens said as he mixed together some ungodly concoction.

Ivar watched in disbelief as the barkeep added rum, beaten eggs, sugar, and a variety of spices into a blackened kettle on the bar. Havens pulled a red-hot poker out of the fireplace, then shoved it in and stirred. Ivar could see ashes from the poker float to the surface.

Havens was a big man, solidly built, with close-cropped salt-and-pepper hair and a craggy face. The download confirmed that a "hot flip" was Havens' hangover specialty, a favorite among cadets, although Ivar thought that was more wishful thinking than reality. It was drinking over drunk, which every college student tried, even cadets at West Point in the mid-nineteenth century.

Ivar also now knew that he—or whoever they thought he was—had been brought down here to Havens' bar to be the lackey, since every group needed a lackey. That was true in every college, as far as Ivar could remember from his undergraduate and even more numerous graduate student years.

If he'd been more introspective, Ivar might also have realized *he'd* been the lackey in all those colleges, so it might be ironic that he was one on a Time Patrol mission. But Ivar shied from introspection, because when he went too deep, he went back to the Fun in North Carolina, when he'd been duplicated a half-dozen times. Ever since, he'd never been quite sure if he were the original Ivar, or one of the duplicates.

Havens looked up, satisfied with his mixing skills. "The Superintendent finds out, they'll both be booted from the Corps." He lifted the kettle. "Hold that empty bottle for me, lad."

Ivar did as requested, and Havens carefully filled it. For someone who was objecting to dueling, he didn't seem deterred from providing refreshments for the event.

"What if one of them gets shot?" Ivar asked, focusing on more mundane matters.

"Pickett's a hothead," Havens said. "He's challenged twice before, but it's always come to naught. It's a Southern thing, mostly. I'm surprised at Sam, though. He's always been one of the calmest lads I've ever seen, but he was right in that he can't imbibe. One draught, and he can't see straight. Some men have that curse. Another bottle, lad." He corked the first one.

"Sam can't get shot or kicked out," Ivar said.

Havens raised an eyebrow. "And why is that?"

"It just is. He's a good man." Ivar thought that was weak, but Havens nodded.

"He has that sense about him," Havens said. "I can tell you from my time in service in the war, that a good leader is one who can keep his head when things are getting hot."

The download confirmed that Havens had served in the War of 1812, which Ivar figured was *the* war to this point, although a couple loomed on the horizon for the class of '43.

"But," Havens said, "Sam did have two mugs of ale earlier. And he has a button when someone hurts a horse. Something to do with his father running a tanning mill. Horrible place."

Ivar didn't get the connection, but that wasn't important right now. "What can I do?" Ivar asked as he held out a second bottle, and Havens finished pouring the rest of the hot flip into it.

"Only one fella could cool Sam down." Havens put a cork in the second bottle.

"Who's that?"

"Jim Longstreet," Havens said, "but he graduated last year and is stationed out west at Jefferson Barracks."

"Who *here* can calm him down?" Ivar asked, a warm bottle in each hand, hearing the voices of the cadets outside moving away.

Havens folded his arms and looked at Ivar. "Why not you, lad? You seem an odd sort, but I've seen the like before." He smiled. "I remember when Poe used to come in. Edgar was a troubled lad with far too much imagination, and the Academy was no place for him. Imagination doesn't flourish on the Plain. He also had a tendency toward the morbid. We had many a long talk through the night until we agreed he should depart for other things."

"*You* got Edgar Allan Poe to resign?" The voices were almost out of earshot.

"Oh, I didn't get him to do nothing," Havens said. "And he didn't resign. He got kicked out. I hear he's spreading a tale that he showed up for formation in just his crossbelts, under arms with his musket, and nary a stitch of clothing, but the reality is, he just stopped going to class. Can't do that for long without something happening. And"— Havens nodded toward the door—"can't be dueling without something happening. I agree with you. I don't think Sam should get kicked out of the Academy. Perhaps you best go do something about that."

"I'd like to talk to you later," Ivar said as he hustled to the door.

"I'm sure you would, but you better be hurrying."

Ivar ran out of the tavern. There was a hint of dawn over the Hudson River along with the rumble of thunder in the distance. Ivar paused for a moment to get oriented. He assumed "River Field" was by the river, and he cocked his head and listened. He could hear excited voices, and he headed that way, a bottle in each hand, taking care not to stumble on the narrow path in the dark.

"Took you long enough," the cadet who'd been hazing Ivar said when he appeared at a clearing on the bank of the Hudson River.

"Give him a break, McClelland," another cadet said.

At first, Ivar thought the name was McClellan, future General of the Army of the Potomac, who was here at the Academy right now, class of '46, but the download indicated he needed to add the D at the end, and it was Grant's classmate, George C. McClelland. Ivar nodded to himself as he took in the data: McClelland graduated thirty-eighth in his class of thirty-eight, the "goat," and his listing was short in the Academy's register of graduates.: *Brief and patchy career, dismissed for conduct unbecoming and drunkenness, four years after graduating; in civilian life, a merchant and farmer*.

As McClelland uncorked the bottle then drank deeply, Ivar could see the young man's future plainly laid out.

He turned his attention to the field. It was roughly forty feet long by ten wide, framed by thick trees on three sides and the river on the fourth. A marvelous weeping willow was on the north end, and a large, flat rock on the south.

Pickett stood next to the rock, another cadet with him. The two were arguing.

Grant was alone under the willow, arms folded, as still as the trunk of the tree. Jackson had the Hell-Beast off to the side, holding onto the bridle.

McClelland and two other cadets were observing off to the edge, not committed to either side of this altercation. "Here." McClelland finally offered the bottle to the other two. He glanced at Ivar, seemed about to say something, then turned his attention back to the field, finding something more interesting than abusing a new cadet.

Pickett brusquely pushed aside the cadet who'd been arguing with him and strode a third of the way across the field toward Grant, who was looking off to the left. "Where is Powell with the pistols?" Pickett called out.

The three observers focused on the bottles rather than Pickett's question. The Virginian looked at Grant, who had not moved. "You can apologize, Hiram, and we can forego this."

He just lost, Ivar realized in a flash of understanding, having spent enough time around Moms, Nada, and the team to understand combat. Pickett had lost without a shot fired, because he'd given up control of the situation.

Grant didn't say anything, allowing enough time for the victory to resonate, then he unfolded his arms. "It will be dawn and reveille soon. We"—" He stopped as a rider galloped up and slid out of the saddle, a wooden box in hands.

"'Bout time, Hill," one of the cadets with a bottle said.

Ivar connected the two names in the download: Ambrose Powell Hill, known in history at A.P. Hill, but to his friends as Powell.

"Had to skirt the Duty Officer," Hill said. He walked to the flat stone and opened the lid. "I'll charge the pieces. I request that both party observe."

Pickett looked from Hill to Grant, waiting for the latter to speak up, but Grant wasn't going to yield so easily, not when he already held the upper hand. Pickett stiffened then turned watch Hill, although he was sobering up fast.

Hill was quickly done with his task, placing the pistols back into the box. He faced the field. "Gentlemen, please take your pieces."

"Shouldn't there be seconds?" Ivar called out, surprising everyone.

A.P. Hill nodded. "To be true, there should be seconds."

"I'll second Pickett," McClelland said, staggering over.

Grant looked about, but neither cadet on the sidelines stepped forward.

"I'll—" Jackson began, but Ivar beat him to it.

"I will stand with you, sir."

Grant nodded.

Hill was back on course, rather eager for this to occur. "Since Mister Pickett issued the challenge, the choice is his. His second will select." McClelland looked into the box, then drew out a pistol. He brought it to Pickett.

Ivar glanced at Grant to his side. "Want me to, sir?"

"It's what we're here for," Grant said.

Ivar walked the thirty feet across the field, withdrew the remaining pistol, and brought it back to Grant, but he didn't offer it to the cadet. Instead, he faced the others. "Did you know," Ivar said in a loud voice that all could hear, "that the first duel in America took place at Plymouth Rock in 1621?"

McClelland glared at Ivar. "Shut up, plebe."

Ivar ignored him. "I read that in Paris, some time back, there were these two Frenchmen who got into a row over a woman. She was a famous dancer, and the lover of one and the mistress of the other."

A slight smile cracked Grant's face, and with that, Ivar could tell his anger was gone. "Not even a wife to either?" Grant asked.

"No, sir," Ivar said. "One challenged the other to a duel. But not just any old duel. They both believed they were more intelligent than other men. And they needed to duel in a way that befitted their superior intellect. So they agreed to have what they called an 'elevated duel' to match their elevated minds. Each got into a balloon with his second. A large crowd gathered to watch. The balloons floated up, above all the buildings. Maybe a thousand feet. They were about one hundred feet apart."

"Rather far for a pistol shot," Grant observed.

Pickett was still holding the pistol at his side. His face showed his complete befuddlement at this turn of events. Ivar was quite grateful to Edith for her love of the arcane. Ivar saw someone come out of the tree line in his peripheral vision, but he kept his focus on Grant and Pickett. "They were using blunderbusses."

"Ah," Grant nodded. "I have an idea where this might be headed."

"One fired at the other dueler and missed. The second man did not aim at his opponent."

"He fired at his balloon," Grant said.

Something finally got through to Pickett. "Why, that lacks honor!"

"But shows some smarts," Grant observed.

"Yes," Ivar said, "the other dueler did indeed fire at his opponent's balloon, a much more opportune target."

"What happened?" Jackson asked from his position with the Hell-Beast.

"Oh," Ivar said, "the balloon collapsed, and the first dueler and his second fell headfirst to the ground and died."

"Despicable," Pickett said. "No gentlemen would—"

"If you be gentlemen," a voice called out, "then you best be getting back to the Academy."

Benny Havens held an old flintlock pistol in his meaty grip.

Ivar could see rays of sunlight piercing the clouds over the hills on the far side of the river. But there was also the flicker of lightning approaching from the north.

Grant faced Pickett. "Perhaps you should ride York back to the stables, George, since you like to use your whip on him. I'm sure he'll transport you quite safely."

"Put the gun back in the case, Mister Pickett," Havens said, waving his pistol thus giving the cadet a way out while saving some face.

Pickett did so, placing his pistol back in it and snapping the lid shut in frustration. A.P. Hill picked it up.

Just in time, as a pair of riders galloped up.

Ivar recognized the man in the lead from his painting: Major Delafield, the Superintendent of the Academy, his horse barely holding his portly weight. A cadet was with him, wearing a red sash and outfitted with a saber—the duty officer. A.P. Hill quickly shoved the box into a saddle bag then hid it on the other side of the rock. Ivar stuffed the pistol, not an easy task, into the back of his pants, wondering how, exactly, the damn thing worked, because even though he'd had extensive firearms training upon joining the Nightstalkers and Time Patrol, flintlock pistols had not been on the training schedule. An accidental discharge right now would not be opportune.

"Gentlemen," Delafield called out, surveying the field in the growing light of dawn. "What are we about this morning?"

Surprisingly, it was Jackson who spoke up. "I wanted my friends to join me in praising our Most Holy Father as the glory of His day begins, Major. And what better place than here in the midst of His glorious nature?"

Delafield stared at Jackson for a moment. "A better place would be within limits, in your rooms, in the barracks, getting ready for reveille formation. You have been very studious of late, Mister Jackson, and have improved your class standing greatly. We wouldn't want that hard work to go to waste." He glanced over. "Good morning, Mister Havens. Were you protecting these worshipping cadets from wild beasts?"

Havens tucked the pistol in his belt. "Indeed, sir, indeed. I thought I heard me some wolves howling in the forest."

Delafield remained still for a few more moments. He looked across the river and nodded. "It is indeed a splendid sunrise, worthy of praise. But there is also a storm coming, so I suggest all return to barracks before it breaks upon us."

Then he rode off with the duty officer.

The cadets began to disperse.

Ivar half-expected to be pulled back, his mission done, although he knew it was never this easy. A fellow could hope.

"Plebe." Grant was beckoning to him.

Ivar walked over.

"You show an aptitude for battlefield tactics," Grant said. "How many days ago did you arrive, as I have not seen you prior to this evening?"

Ivar had no clue, although the download informed him that the new class of '47 would straggle into the Academy all summer. "This past week, sir."

"You handle yourself well, Mister...?"

"Ivar, sir."

"Mister Ivar." Grant nodded. "It's a steep walk up to the Academy, and you might not be familiar with the way, since Mister McClelland saw fit to have you accompany him with a hood over your head; a foolish tradition for a plebe's first visit to Benny Havens. Why don't you ride with Mister Jackson and me? York can easily carry all three of us, since even combined, we weigh less than Major Delafield."

"Yes, sir," Ivar said. He looked over, and the only person left besides Jackson with the horse, was Benny Havens, who looked very old and very tired in the dawn light.

The innkeeper caught Ivar's eye and nodded. "Good job, lad. But keep your eyes open."

Chauvet Cave, Southern France, 6 June 32,415 Years B.P. (Before Present)

"'Hello darkness, my old friend'," Moms whispered, lying on her belly and peering down from the western slope of the valley.

Night vision goggles would be nice, but there was just enough visibility for her to see what she needed to. The glow from the fire lit up the entrance. What had taken her a while to determine was the location of the five warriors and the woman. They were in a cleft on the valley wall, about two hundred meters from the cave. One of them had overwatch, with observation on the cave. The others were hunkered down, hidden from the cave by a spur of rock. Waiting.

The woman was a little distance from the men, leaning back on her pack, the classic rucksack flop, so still, she might have been part of the rock.

Moms could hear the echo of voices from the mouth of the cave, but it was nothing she could process. It sounded like grunts and groans, but there was a pattern underneath it, something that tingled her consciousness.

They can speak, but they cannot read, because they cannot write, Moms thought. The art. She remembered how the Time Patrol used a form of hieroglyphics as its written language, spanning all the eras. Images as words. Edith was right. The art was important. The art was the important part of getting concepts from one person's mind into the minds of others beyond direct conversation.

Moms rubbed her eyes. The mission.

As long as there were voices, Moms figured the intruders wouldn't attack. But once silence came and the fire died down, it didn't take much imagination to figure out what would happen.

Moms slid out of position and began to crawl along the side of the valley, using every technique she'd learned over the years to remain unseen and, more importantly, unheard.

It took two hours for her to get within ten meters of the intruders' position. The noise from the cave had died down to an occasional grunt, mainly from two distinct voices. Discussing caveman philosophy? Quantum physics? Moms stifled a giggle. The fire was still going, although not as brightly as before. Moms had the intruders directly between her position and the cave.

The woman would have to go first. After that, Moms knew it would be a free-for-all. The range of the Naga was a bit more than that of the spears the warriors carried. And it would slice through their weapons, another advantage.

But one couldn't argue numbers.

Six to one.

That was reality.

Moms waited, poised for any advantage.

One of the warriors got up and walked past the woman. Her head swiveled to follow him, then turned back toward the man on watch. The man was unfastening his pants so he could urinate.

Moms took his head off with a swipe of the Naga. Before the head hit the ground, she jabbed at the woman's chest, and that's when Murphy came into play. The tip of the Naga skidded on some sort of armor underneath the woman's tunic, going to the right, slashing into the woman's arm and then away.

Moms didn't have time to correct her first mistake as the warriors charged. She spun, the Naga level, and gutted the fastest two with one sweep of the blade. She kept moving, charging, staying on the offensive, seeing the woman doing something in the corner of her eye, but focused on the next two warriors as they simultaneously jabbed with their spears.

Moms blocked one, tried to duck the other, then felt the sear of pain on her right arm as the point of the spear sliced her flesh.

She jabbed the point of the Naga into the neck of the warrior on the left and was rewarded with a blossom of blood from the jugular (should have done that to the woman, a small part of Moms's brain chastised). Moms rolled forward, bringing the Naga up.

The next warrior had his spear over his head for a thrust, but his momentum was his downfall as he was spitted on the Naga.

Moms twisted the Naga, trying to get his body off the blade. She finally got the blade free then faced the last warrior who'd been on overwatch, knowing she was running out of time since the woman was only wounded.

The last warrior thrust with his spear. Moms blocked, slicing through the spear two feet from the tip. He dropped it, then drew his sword. Moms took advantage, jabbing him in the gut, rewarded with the solid thump of metal into flesh. He grunted, the first sound anyone had made, and staggered back, dropping his sword.

Moms was slammed in the back of the left shoulder. She whirled about. The woman was notching another arrow, and Moms knew the first was in the back of her shoulder, but there was no time for that now. Moms charged, aiming the tip of the Naga for the bow, not the person.

It was the right move as the woman released, the tip of the arrow hitting the Naga blade, ricocheting away. Moms didn't slow down, slamming the point directly into the woman's face, then through it, pinning her to the rock wall behind her.

Moms tried to pull the Naga back, but it was stuck, so she went to one knee, spinning about, hands raised defensively, because the overwatch was still alive.

He wasn't there. Four warrior bodies. The overwatch was gone.

Moms stood and walked to where she'd wounded him. A copious blood trail headed away.

He was gutted, Moms knew. She'd seen it before.

He was a dead man crawling.

She was wounded, too, but it wasn't fatal.

First things first.

She turned back to the woman pinned to the rock wall.

The Present

EAGLE GLANCED ACROSS the cockpit at Orlando. "Are you sure?"

Orlando shrugged. "What's the worst that can happen?"

"Someone dies."

"People die every day."

"We could *all* die," Eagle said.

"That's the whole point of the test." Orlando pulled an oversized flask out of his pocket, unscrewed the lid, took a deep drink, then offered it to Eagle.

"I'm flying," Eagle said. He had the Snake at 10,000 feet altitude, having taken off as soon as the three Russians boarded. Orlando had unbuckled the arms of the young woman's straitjacket, then directed all three to go up the ramp into the cargo bay. Eagle had then flown the Snake, almost vertical, gaining altitude and circling, but not moving away from the position over the airfield.

"In the old days," Orlando said, "pilots had balls. Big brass ones. A little drink wouldn't have scared them. Hell, they were supposed to drink."

"My shoulder is killing me," Eagle said. "I should be on painkillers, but I'm not. You think I'm going to take a drink if I can't take something for the pain?"

"You *could* take something for the pain," Orlando pointed out, waggling the flask. "You *choose* not to."

Eagle shook his head.

"It's always about choice," Orlando said. "Remember that. And hell, this thing can fly itself on autopilot." He stood up from the co-pilot's seat, which reminded Eagle he'd never buckled in on takeoff or put on his parachute as per SOP.

Eagle sighed and flipped on the autopilot.

Orlando stood in the passageway between the cockpit and the cargo hold. "Yo!" he yelled to be heard over the sound of the two jet engines. "Listen up."

Boris, Princess, and Lara were on the red web jump seats along the outer edge of the bay. Boris and Princess sat on the same side, but with enough distance between them to indicate they wanted nothing to do with each other. Lara sat on the other, cross-legged, eyes closed. She didn't open them at Orlando's shout. The harness was still around her body even though her hands were free. She seemed used to it.

"Why are we here?" Boris shouted back.

"They didn't tell you?" Orlando said. "Oh, that's right. They weren't supposed to tell you. You've all volunteered to try out for the most super-secret, best of the best, covert unit in the world."

"I did not volunteer," Princess complained.

"Who does?" Orlando said. "If you really were volunteers, we wouldn't want you. It would mean you're stupid. We don't do stupid here."

"Where is here?" Boris demanded. "What is this Area 51?"

"Now, thirty years ago," Orlando said, "that question might be sorta legit. But seriously, son. You don't follow the news? You didn't see *Independence Day*? The original or the sequel? I hate sequels, although *Aliens* was pretty good. And the second Godfather. That was good too. Maybe better, but it's debatable." Orlando pointed. "That way is the Nevada Test Site. Seven-hundred and thirty-nine—"

"Seven-hundred and forty," Eagle corrected him, remembering their last Nightstalker mission, after the *Cluster-Frak in Nebraska* .

"Seven-hundred and forty nuclear weapons have gone off there," Orlando said. "Pretty good barrier. Area 51 is just about below us. Groom Lake. Big runway. Air Force and NASA test their high-speed stuff out here since it's pretty far from anywhere. Vegas is that way," Orlando pointed in a different direction, and Eagle didn't have the heart to tell him he was off. It really didn't matter. "I have a theory," Orlando said. "People go to L.A., to suffer, and Vegas to die."

Boris and Princess exchanged confused glances. Lara still hadn't opened her eyes or indicate she heard any of this.

"Y'all want to go to Vegas?" Orlando asked. "Or do you want to go to L.A.?"

Boris stood up. "I do not like this."

"I was just joking," Orlando said. "You're not going to either place." He looked at Boris. "And no one gives a rat's ass what you like or don't like." He reached up and hit a button.

The noise level in the cargo bay increased dramatically as a crack appeared in the back. The ramp lowered, while the top portion went up into the tail section. Both moved until the ramp was level and locked in place.

Boris looked at that, then back at Eagle and Orlando. "What is this?" he yelled.

Princess edged away from the ramp toward the cockpit. One of her hands was tight to her side.

"She's got a knife," Eagle yelled into Orlando's ear, the equivalent of a whisper.

"I know," Orlando said. "Saw her take it off Lara's guard. Idiot didn't even know she lifted it."

Orlando pulled a grenade out of his pocket then held it up so they could all see it. "Choices!" he yelled, then he pulled the pin, knelt, and rolled it to the center of the cargo bay.

Everyone was frozen for a moment.

Princess ran for the cockpit, away from the grenade. Boris was frozen, eyes wide, staring at it, less than five feet in front of him.

Lara darted forward, scooped it up, then continued her run and swan-dived off the back ramp, grenade in hand.

"That was different," Orlando said, reaching for his flask.

The Missions Phase III

Normandy France, 6 June 1944 A.D.

AFTER HOLSTERING THE .45, Mac discovered a chocolate bar in one of the bulging pockets on his fatigue shirt. It was broken, but edible. "I found breakfast."

She was sitting next to the shovel, staring at the body of her father.

He offered it to her. She looked at it blankly, then took it. She broke it in half and held the rest up for him. "We have not had chocolate in five years."

"You keep it," Mac said.

She stuffed the rest into a pocket. Mac took that as a positive sign, that she felt there was a future when she would eat it. The most positive sign he'd noted since appearing here.

"What is your name, *madame*?"

"Mademoiselle," she corrected. "My name is Brigit."

"Hey, Bridget. I'm Mac."

"No. *Bree-geet.*"

"Right. Brigit." Mac sat next to her, trying to ignore the ticking clock of the mission and the passing darkness. "Do you know what time it is?"

She leaned forward and reached into her father's vest, retrieving a pocket watch. "I would have forgotten it. I never liked the watch much. He was always living according to it, making us live our lives according to it. Does time matter to him now?" Nevertheless, she angled the surface so she could see in the moonlight. "Two and a half hours past midnight."

Several hours of darkness left. The download tried to intrude with the exact time the mission should be done, but Mac was finding it easy to block the information intrusions. This mission was off the rails, pun intended, and he was going to have to do a lot of improvising. From what he'd seen of Edith Frobish, improvising wasn't one of her fortes, so the download was less of a priority.

Brigit put the watch back into her father's vest. "Mac? Short for something?"

"No. Just Mac," he said. "How come the Germans didn't get you?"

"Because I was hiding in the trees," Brigit said as if explaining to an idiot. She had a vacant stare, although her eyes were on her father's body, as she murmured: *"Wound my heart with a monotonous languor.'"*

It sounded so much better in French, Mac thought. The stanza of poetry by Paul Verlaine that was broadcast to let the Resistance know the invasion would begin within twenty-four hours. He repeated it, feeling the words roll off his tongue. *"Blessent mon cœur d'une langueur monotone."*

"What does that even mean?" Brigit asked. "I told my father not to go after he heard the transmission. But he took out his watch, and with that, I knew he would go. I begged him not to take Louis. But Louis insisted. It was his chance to be in the war. To be a hero. You men, fooling yourselves with talk of heroism and bravery and honor. Isn't every war like that? Talk of bravery and heroism and ending in dirt? Now, Louis will become dirt, become part of the farm that he should have had one day. Raised a family on. Now, there is only me."

"Why did you tell them not to go?" Mac asked.

She turned to him. "I am not a coward. I have been part of seven raids. I have placed the explosives myself. Because of that, I have killed. Not just the Germans on the trains, but the French who work them. That is another great lie men tell. That war is black-and-white. That things are clear-cut. We are all dirty. We have killed men who were just trying to earn a paycheck so their families could eat. But this time? I felt we should not go."

"What did you feel?"

"Danger. A trap. I cannot explain it. Just a woman's feeling. Not something that a man like my father would pay attention to. I begged Louis." A single tear, all her body could spare, slid down the clean pathway the previous tears had cleared. "I went but stayed in the trees with Maurice and the cart. There were too many soldiers. Nothing I could do. So, here I am. Alive. Alone. With the last mule. And I have to finish burying my father with my brothers, because they, too, believed the lie that all would be well."

Mac looked at the barn with the roof half-collapsed. A bomb had landed behind the house, collapsing a wall and blasting the interior. Probably from the air raids that had been conducted all along the coast of France in preparation for the invasion. Not just here in Normandy, but everywhere, so the Germans wouldn't know where it was coming. Civilians were killed, their houses destroyed, just to keep the Germans guessing.

"*'In wartime, truth is so precious she should always be attended by a bodyguard of lies'*," Mac quoted. "Churchill said that."

"Churchill would say that," Brigit said. "Men like him always find wonderful things to say to make it appear they are doing something good while others do the dying."

"When the bombing started, why did you stay here?" Mac asked. "Why not move inland?"

"I was here waiting to get you out of the well," Brigit said, and she finally cracked a smile, which transformed her face for a moment, making her much younger.

She'd been beautiful once, Mac thought.

"Besides, Papa would never leave. And now, he won't. This land has been in our family as long we can trace back. There is a Bible in the house with pages and pages of the family tree. Sometimes, I think my family were here when the Romans came through. The Germans are only the latest of armies to come and go. And now, the Americans and the British and the Canadians will come. And they will go, and the land will still be here, and now Papa and Charles and Louis will always be here."

Suddenly, Maurice made a strangled noise, and his front legs gave out. He went to his knees as Mac and Brigit jumped to their feet and ran to him. His back gave, and he was lying in the mud.

"Oh!" Brigit cried out as she sat next to her mule, putting his large head on her lap.

What else could go wrong? Mac wondered.

Brigit stroked the soft spot between his ears, humming something to him. Maurice was looking up at her with big eyes full of sadness and regret for leaving her alone. His breathing grew quicker and shorter, and then he died.

Mac was surprised to feel a tear on his cheek. "I'm sorry."

She spoke in the monotone the bereaved often reverted to. "Maurice was a good mule. I raised him. I used to braid flowers and make a wreath for his sweet head. Before."

A quick barrage of artillery thundered to the west. Mac assumed they were German guns firing at planes and the main airborne assault.

"Surely, your father had the demolitions?"

He expected her to get angry, but instead, she carefully laid Maurice's head on the ground then stood. "We must bury Maurice."

Mac blinked. Maurice might have been starving, but he was still a mule.

"Yes," Brigit said, as if finally registering his question. "My father had the pod he recovered from the airdrop three weeks ago. And we already had explosives from earlier drops. We've plenty of explosives."

"Blasting caps? Where are the caps? Did the Germans get them?"

She started to walk toward the barn. "I must wash up."

Mac was having trouble following her thinking. "You've got water?"

"No. I wash in mud." She smiled just a bit, looking over her shoulder to let him know she was joking.

Mac followed her. "How can you live here? Where do you sleep?"

She pointed at the barn. "I live there."

As they got closer, all Mac could see were rocks, splintered wood, and rusted, old farm gear.

She paused as she reached the edge of the barn, where stones from the old wall had collapsed in a large pile. "We must bury Maurice."

You're going to end up having to eat Maurice, Mac thought, but he didn't say it.

Brigit grabbed a shaft of rusting metal attached to a mule-drawn plow then pulled. A trap door, covered with rocks, easily lifted up, revealing a set of stairs descending into the ground. It reminded him of the entrance to the Den underneath the decrepit filling station at the Ranch outside Area 51.

"How did you do that?" Mac asked.

"Not real rocks, of course."

Mac touched one, and he could feel that it was hollow. "They look real."

"I was a theater designer before the war. In Paris. I got away from here when I was seventeen."

"Why did you come back?" Mac asked as she began to take the stairs. He followed her into the darkness.

"Family. Close the door, please."

Mac saw a lever on the inside and pulled it. The door was not only expertly camouflaged, it was perfectly balanced. It shut with a slight thud.

A match flared, and Brigit lit an oil lamp. "I won awards for my sets in Paris. But this is my greatest achievement. My home for four years, ever since the German tanks destroyed the house in 1940. I did manage to talk my father out of rebuilding it. I knew it would only get destroyed again since the war was not over."

The space was surprisingly large, twenty feet long by fifteen wide. Old wood beams crossed the ceiling.

"It was a root cellar," Brigit said, "but it had stopped being used many, many years ago. It was full of rocks and dirt. When we were children, my brother Charles and I would hide in here, and my father would get very, very angry. He told us it was dangerous. He did not understand what real danger is."

There were wood shelves along all the sides. Some held glass jars and cans and sacks of potatoes and onions. Not much, but the result of careful rationing of sparse harvests.

"I knew the war was coming long before my friends," Brigit said. She went to a tin tub, which looked like a trough for animals, then turned on a spigot. A trickle of clear water flowed, and she filled a pitcher, and then turned the spigot off. She poured two glasses, and offered one to Mac, who took it gratefully.

"When I came back home each year to visit, I began working on clearing this out, and fixing it up." She frowned. "I started in '35."

"You did see the future," Mac said.

"It was not hard if one was open to the reality." She drank the entire glass. "I made this place because I knew my family would need it. I, myself, made plans to go to London. I had friends in the theater. They told me I could easily get a job. All I had to do was get on the ferry and go across the Channel. I did, several times, but I always came back to France."

"Why?"

"I am French." She nodded at the space around them. "My father thought I was foolish to spend so much time working down here. That there were other things I could do that would be more useful." She pointed at the spigot. "I dug the water line and laid the pipe from the stream." She pointed up. "I put in ventilation, spreading it so the smoke would not be seen in daytime. When the war came, I returned home. Papa and my brothers hid in here with me when the Germans came. They were mad at me because I brought Maurice down here with us. They were not so mad when we went back up after the Germans had passed, and there were no cows or goats or chickens left. They were all taken. All we had was Maurice.

"But after the fighting stopped, they went back up and lived in the house. Worked the farm. I stayed down here. Maurice and I."

Mac realized that Maurice had been her companion, more than her father and brothers, for the entire war. And she'd sacrificed Maurice to get him out of a well. She wouldn't be eating him, he knew that.

"Are you the only one they sent?" Brigit asked as she turned the spigot on once more then began filling the trough.

"Yes."

"The explosives are there." She pointed to a dark corner. She removed the kerchief from her head, revealing short, black hair, poorly cut.

Mac found the supplies. Enough C-4, det cord. Antique for him, but cutting edge for now. Enough to do the job. Almost.

"What about the fuses?"

"Papa said you were to bring them. Whoever parachuted in."

Mac thought about all the field-expedient ways to detonate C-4.

Brigit interrupted. "But my other brother, Charles, had some from the other missions. He kept them with him all the time. Said they were important."

"Where are they?"

"As I said. With him."

Brigit began to pull off her clothes as if he weren't there. He figured modesty was a trait that had also been blown away by the war. He could see the bones of her spine, and her hips jutted out. Her skin, though, was still toned, a smooth, light brown. Her breasts were flat above her narrow waist. She stepped into the tub then sat down in the water, which immediately turned dirty. She leaned forward, dipping her hair under the thin flow. She cleaned it as best she could, ignoring him as if she were completely alone, or he were just Maurice standing there.

He realized she'd probably prefer that he were Maurice, and that made him sad.

"There is soup on the grate," she said, her voice partly muffled. "It is cold, but that is the way the fancy restaurants in Paris often served it. You can pretend you are in Paris."

Mac knew he'd be back at the Possibility Palace before he got hungry. "I'm going back up."

She lathered her hair. "This is the last of the soap."

Mac opened the trapdoor and heard her yell "Light!" so he hustled up and quickly shut it behind him.

Mac walked to the mound of dirt. She hadn't buried her brothers very deeply. Then again, she hadn't had much time. He used his hands to pull the dirt off the bodies. He paused when he saw Louis's young face, half of it blown away by the exit wound from the bullet to the back of the skull, his jaw and broken teeth exposed on one side.

"Sonofabitch," Mac muttered. He'd seen so many bodies like this. Especially in Iraq: men, women, children, hands tied behind their backs, forced to kneel, then the bullet to the back of the head.

He cleared the dirt off Charles. He'd gone down fighting, his body torn by too many bullet holes to count. But the fuses were safe in an inside pocket, in a wooden case. Mac opened the case and checked. Enough.

He stood. Took a breath. Looked at the two boys. The old man. The mule.

He cursed in French, which sounded so much better than English. He took off his field jacket and laid it over Louis' mangled face.

He grabbed the shovel and began to expand the grave. He ignored the pain from his two broken fingers.

Digging took precious time, but it was still dark. The bridge was only three kilometers away. Mac knew how quickly he could rig what was needed.

The old Mac would have been excited at the thought of blowing up a bridge, every demo man's wet dream.

Right now, this was needed. He laid Papa next to his sons. Then he went over to Maurice. He unhooked his chute from the harness, then grabbed two of the leads and dragged the mule to the grave. Maurice wasn't very heavy; the war had wasted him down. Mac laid the animal across the bodies. It was cheating, but it was a good metaphor for how Maurice had ranked in Brigit's life and how much he had contributed. The dead weren't going to complain. They'd all end up being the same.

As he shoveled dirt on top, Mac imagined Maurice with a garland of wild flowers on his head. As he tossed a shovel-full on top the mule's head, covering the vacant eye, he said, "Thanks, Maurice. You were a good guy."

The grave was inadequate, but there wasn't time to do it right. There really wasn't time to do it at all.

Mac assumed the Shadow had somehow tipped off the Germans about the drop zone, an easy enough task. The fact that Brigit had stayed hidden and not been killed with the rest of her family was the wild card. Along with Mac landing here, although that one might also be due to the Germans moving too soon. They should have allowed Papa and the boys to put out the marking lights and then rolled everyone up, but the other drops, the Pathfinders at the same time to mark the drop zones for the main airborne forces, must have rattled the Germans.

By now the 82nd, 101st, and British glider forces were on the ground. Mac knew the history, and Nada would have summed up what was developing in the dark succinctly: a cluster-frak. Few troops were arriving according to plan, but given that one of the primary missions of the

Airborne was to wreak havoc, the scattering was actually achieving an important goal. It would confuse the Germans as much as if the plan had gone correctly.

This one-rail line was key, though, because in history, it had been blown, and that had delayed a Panzer division for ten days. Without those ten days—

Mac froze at the sound of a rifle bolt being worked. He reached for the .45.

"Please do not." The voice had a German accent in French, which was weird, and even though he had the download, Mac took a moment to decipher what was said. It was amazing how much a bad accent could screw up a beautiful language.

Mac turned. A German officer and three soldiers stood there, spread out tactically. The officer had a field cap with the skull and crossbones, along with the lightning SS on the collar tab. Nothing subtle about that.

"You killed the boy," Mac said.

"Unfortunately, I did not have the honor. That was my *oberführer*."

The three soldiers had bolt-action rifles pointed at Mac. It occurred to him, one of many strange thoughts at strange times in his life, that Nada would have approved of those rifles. They would never waste ammunition firing on automatic. They had to make every shot count. The officer had a pistol in a holster. He wore a long, gray coat and gloves despite the warm June night.

Mac kept his hands at his sides, but far enough away from the pistol to not draw a nervous shot from one of the riflemen.

"Why did he kill the boy?" Mac asked. "He shot him in the back of the head, from the trajectory, while he was kneeling. That means he'd given up."

The officer considered the question as if there were some hidden context to it he didn't understand. "*Why*? He was a terrorist. Not a uniformed combatant. The Führer has ordered that terrorists be summarily executed. How does *your* country deal with terrorists?"

Mac sensed there was more to that question than the surface of it.

"*My* question," the officer said, "is how did the bodies get here? We killed them two hundred meters from here. Your parachute is there." He pointed. "We followed cart tracks back here once we finished a sweep of the immediate area. So, I must assume there was another party involved. Who else is here?"

"No one," Mac said.

"Answered too quickly." The officer took several steps closer, the soldiers flanking him. "I am *Hauptsturmführer* Procles. And whom do I have the pleasure of addressing? American, I assume."

"Procles? That doesn't sound German."

"And your name?"

"Mac."

"And your rank?"

"Sergeant First Class."

"An enlisted man." Procles nodded. "But I will treat you as an equal, given the nature of your mission. My *oberführer* would like to speak with you. He will not treat you as an equal."

"I'd like to kill him," Mac said. "And I will." The download kicked in. "Procles. One of the Heracleidae, great-great-great-grandson of Hercules. Founder of the Eurypontid dynasty of the Kings of Sparta."

"It is not an uncommon name in my"—Procles paused—"the area I come from. I would love to chat, truly I would, as I am sure you have some interesting stories, but those are for my *oberführer*."

"How can you wear that uniform?" Mac asked. "Knowing what it represents."

Procles indicated for the three riflemen to stay in place. He walked up to Mac, close enough so that his comrades couldn't hear. "This army is one of the most efficient I've had the experience of serving in. If I am to fight, I prefer fighting with the best. I do as I'm ordered, Sergeant Mac. As I'm sure you do. I would highly recommend you tell my *oberführer* whatever he wishes to know. Your death will be much easier and pain-free."

"I thought Spartans stood for something," Mac said as he slipped the switchblade down from inside his sleeve into the palm of his hand. "You're just whores for the Shadow."

Procles stepped forward in anger, reaching for his pistol. As he flipped up the clasp on the holster for the Luger, Mac slammed his switchblade into the officer's stomach, slashing upward.

Procles's eyes went wide in surprise. Mac slapped Procles's hand aside, then drew the Luger as he also jerked the blade to the side, gutting the SS officer-slash-timeline mercenary.

One of the privates realized something was wrong and yelled a question in German. Mac let go of the knife, wrapping that arm around Procles's neck, keeping him as a shield while he fired the Luger.

His first round hit the rifleman who'd called out in the center of the forehead, snapping the head back and dropping him dead.

The other two fired, missing. Even bolt action didn't help bad shooting, and a second soldier died with a headshot. The third threw down his rifle and tried to run. Mac shot him twice in the back.

Then he let go of Procles, letting him fall to the ground. Mac wasn't even breathing hard as he watched Procles crumble into himself, leaving only dust behind.

Sjaelland Island, Denmark, 6 June 452 A.D.

Every nail, claw-scale, and spur, every spike
and welt on the hand of that heathen brute
was like barbed steel. Everybody said
there was no honed iron hard enough
to pierce him through, no time-proofed blade
that could cut his brutal blood-caked claw

Roland was drenched in blood. He recognized the copper smell, and he could feel it all over his skin, soaking into his leather garments. There was no texture quite like it. He sat next to Jager, not sure of his next move. Jager was also saturated with Grendel's blood.

"This is a fine blade."

Roland looked to his left. Beowulf was holding the Naga staff in one hand. In the other, he had Grendel's hand. The rest of the arm stretched to the floor, where the severed shoulder lay.

There was a shivering howl in the far distance, and Roland looked toward the sound, which echoed through the front entrance of Heorot.

"He ran," Beowulf said. "It is a shame I could not finish him here."

"He won't last the wound," Jager said. "There is too much blood."

"This is true," Beowulf said. "Still, I wanted to present the queen with the body."

"You have a worthy trophy," Jager added, indicating the arm.

Beowulf smiled. "True, also."

Roland stood and held his hand out. Beowulf reluctantly passed the Naga staff to him. There were voices outside the hall, human voices, but they weren't coming any closer.

Beowulf shook Grendel's massive arm. "I must take this to the king and queen."

He staggered toward the door, pulling his prize.

Roland watched him. Daylight was beginning to show outside. Beowulf was framed in the entrance as he posed there and once more held the trophy over his head.

A roar from a crowd greeted him, the locals having spent the night uncertain who or what would be coming out of Heorot this morning.

Roland glanced at Jager. "That was smart."

Jager shrugged. "I took the opportunity."

"That's how the arm came off," Roland said. "You weakened it, yet he acts as if he tore it off by himself."

Jager shrugged. "It is what it is."

"He said you and I were comrades," Roland said.

"He did say that," Jager allowed. "But you are new to me, and I am new to you." He looked about. "You're not the man who fell asleep after the feasting and drinking."

So much for wasn't there, and then was there, but always sort of been there.

Roland made a mental leap that would have stunned Mac and impressed Moms. It was like the painting fading out. Only those who'd been through Gates saw it. Regular people, everyone else around, couldn't.

"Who are you?" Roland asked, his hand tightening around the staff of the Naga.

"Jager."

Several people had joined Beowulf at the entrance to the hall, the voices loud and boisterous.

"Have you faced many monsters like Grendel?" Roland asked.

"You said you killed monsters," Jager said by way of not answering.

"True. But I've never seen anything like that. Are we sure it's dead? It opened those doors with one arm."

Jager was staring at the figures in the entrance. "It was pouring blood. It will die. The wound is too grievous to close."

The crowd entered, led by a man and woman, each wearing a crown, flanking Beowulf.

"King Hrothgar," Jager said. "And his queen. They were in here before the darkness came, and the hall was closed and the doors barred."

Beowulf was carrying the arm and making light of it, but the sweat on his forehead and the quiver in his arms indicated he was straining. Roland checked the download. Yep: King Hrothgar and Queen Wealhtheow.

"Your warriors can mount the trophy, my king," Beowulf said, finally dumping the arm in front of the dais as the royals took their seats so they could look down on everyone.

Hrothgar signaled, and a cluster of men hurried forward to do exactly that.

"I am sorry, my king," Beowulf said in a loud voice, "that the rest of the body is not here. My plan was to hold his arm and strangle the beast, but I couldn't find purchase on his neck." Beowulf raised his own arm and showed where the fangs had slashed through flesh.

"My maidens will bind that," Queen Wealhtheow ordered.

"Let us give glory to God!" Hrothgar cried out. He pointed at Beowulf. "From henceforth, he will be as a son to me."

"The scales of the creature were impenetrable," Beowulf said, directed toward the king, but in a loud enough voice to be heard throughout the hall. Two maidens were ripping linen from their dresses to bind his wounds.

"No weapon could have penetrated," Beowulf continued. "Using my bare hands was the only way to defeat the monster."

Roland glanced at Jager, who just shrugged. Roland noticed a trickle of blood coming from the bottom of Jager's tunic.

"It was difficult," Beowulf continued. "I had to battle the beast alone after it killed my men. And then—"

Roland stepped out of the shadows. "This man was wounded by the beast. He requires assistance. He fought bravely. All were not killed."

"Not smart," Jager said .

A hush fell over the hall as everyone turned to see who dared interrupt the hero's story.

"How did you survive Grendel?" Hrothgar asked Roland.

Feeling Beowulf's glare directed his way, knowing that the story had to hold in order to become the epic, Roland lowered his head.

Jager stood. "He was taking me out of harm's way, King. By the time he could return to the battle, mighty Beowulf had already torn off the beast's arm."

Hrothgar waved a hand, dismissing Roland and Jager from his attention, and turned back to Beowulf. "Continue."

A single maiden came over to tend Jager's wound.

Roland tuned out the boasting. Jager had a nasty gash along his right side.

"It's just a scratch," Jager said. "There's no need for assistance."

"The mark of the beast," the maiden said, giving Jager a look which was so blatant that even Roland was astute enough to understand the intent. "It must be cleaned, or it will rot." She jerked aside his tunic.

Roland saw the scars and knew Jager wasn't joking when he said he considered it just a scratch. He also cared nothing for the maiden.

Roland sat close to Jager on the side away from the wound. He pressed the tip of his dagger against the skin over Jager's liver and asked, "Who are you?"

Kala Chitta Range, Pakistan, 6 June 1998 A.D.

The chatter of helicopters shook Doc out of his killing stupor. Looking over the valley, he saw a pair of helicopters, lights flashing, flying toward a landing pad near the entrance to the Depot. Looking past those, he could see a long line of headlights entering the valley from the main road that went south into the rest of Pakistan.

Confused, immediately wondering how they knew he'd killed the soldier, Doc realized this had nothing to do with him and everything to do with Task Force Kali being alerted and implemented for some reason. Pakistan was sending the trucks and helicopters to retrieve and deploy the warheads.

What was causing Pakistan to retrieve and deploy its nuclear weapons was the big question. Doc wondered what the Shadow had done to push the Pakistanis to decide to initiate nuclear conflict, but remembering his childhood in India before his parents emigrated to the United States, he knew it wouldn't have taken much.

Once all part of British India, Pakistan had been partitioned off in 1947 to establish a Muslim state separate from India. It was one of the ideas that looked good on paper, and caused bloodshed and death in reality. A third of Indian Muslims were left in India, and violence erupted between Hindus, Sikhs, and Muslims, resulting in anywhere from a half-million to a million deaths.

Now, there was another death.

Doc took one last look at the young soldier.

Doc spun about and ran, following the directions from the download. In a hundred yards, he skidded to a halt and looked right. Without the goggles, he wouldn't have seen it, and without the download, he'd never have known it was there: a grate set into the side of the ridgeline, camouflaged to look like part of the rock. He could feel the air blowing out of it.

The download informed him it had taken two of those trips for this grate to be prepared just right. He reached up and pulled. Nothing. He pulled harder, and the grate separated, bolts breaking free, severed just below the heads.

Doc didn't stop to marvel at the fortitude of those men who'd done this, sawing slowly and silently all thru the night, stopping with just enough time before dawn to make it back to the hide site.

He pulled a length of climbing rope out of the ruck, tied it off on the center of the grate, then tossed the other end into the darkness. He stepped up to the edge. As he looked down, the night vision goggles couldn't penetrate the absolute darkness of however deep this ventilation shaft was.

One hundred and eighty-two feet, the download told him. One of the men who'd sawed so patiently had dropped a small lead bob on fishing wire through the grate, unreeling it until he got slack.

But no one had gone in.

Doc had two hundred feet of rope. And once he went down, he knew it was doubtful he'd be able to climb back up the rope. He put one leg over the edge, then pivoted, putting the other leg into the void, sitting on the edge. He reached behind then pulled the grate up, kitty-corner. The grate was larger than the inlet, so it would hold. Unless it went exactly wrong, angled diagonally, and went straight through.

They'd even calculated that, and the risk was acceptable.

Nothing was impossible to the man who didn't have to do it.

He pulled up some slack, then snapped the rope through the carabineer attached to the harness and looped it correctly. He double-checked.

Doc took a deep breath. He twisted as he shoved himself outward into the void. He had his brake hand tight to his chest. He dropped eight feet then came to an abrupt halt as the grate clanged against the opening, anchoring.

Doc began long rappel bounds down the shaft. It occurred to him that he hadn't done one of Eagle's safety precautions: tied a knot at the end of the rope, so he wouldn't rappel into free fall.

But he had to trust the download, the lead weight, the fishing line, and damn luck.

He kept bounding, shoving out with his legs from wall, releasing his brake hand, slowly bringing it in to hit the wall again then shove back out.

Until, as he swung back toward the wall once more, his feet skidded on concrete, and his goggles finally came alive with a dim, green glow from behind.

Doc unclipped and turned toward the light.

The Time Patrol had paid a million dollars for the plans for this facility. Doc imagined some Pakistani architect was living the good life on some beach somewhere, wondering why someone wanted plans for an old facility which had been abandoned years ago.

Doc crawled forward, the light growing stronger until he could take the goggles off.

The shaft became a tunnel. Doc could feel the air pushing past him, indicating positive pressure maintained inside the facility. Following the information from the download, Doc began to run, making turns as indicated. He briefly wondered how the two Task Force Kali soldiers would have blindly found their way through this maze without the blueprint.

He came to a grate through which bright light flowed, and could hear voices speaking Urdu. Doc pulled the automatic weapon off his shoulder, made sure there was a round in chamber, finally trusting all that training, and kicked the grate out.

He jumped, landing on his feet, his knees absorbing the impact.

Two men in white coats were walking by. They were surprised to see him, turned, and ran. Doc walked up to a glass case then used the butt of the weapon to break it. There were two levers inside, one red and one yellow. He pulled the yellow one.

A shrill chirping noise reverberated through the tunnels of the Depot.

The red was the alarm for a security breach.

The yellow represented something much worse, a radiation breach from Containment.

Doc ran deeper into the facility. He passed a few dozen scientists and workers, all scurrying to get out. They gave him puzzled and confused glances, but no one challenged him. Who was going to confront a man covered in blood with a rifle in his hand? All the security for the Depot was on the outside, to prevent someone from coming in. Once you were in—

Also, the workers and scientists were all too concerned with getting out and away from the Containment at the center of the Depot, because they knew what the chirping alarm meant.

Doc made the last turn into the deepest part of the facility. A man in a white coat was standing at a keyboard set into a gray wall, typing a command. A massive vault door was wide open next to him, the entrance to Containment.

Doc shot him.

Doc slipped inside, then typed on the corresponding keyboard on the interior. The code words flowed through his fingers (cost: $250,000) and the vault door began to rotate ponderously inward on hydraulic arms.

"No! Wait!"

Doc turned, leveling the weapon at the man who'd cried out. An elderly scientist, his white coat flapping about him, was limping forward, using a cane. Doc's finger twitched, but he didn't fire.

The door shut with a whoosh of air and a very solid thud.

There was the sound of thick locking pins sliding into place.

Doc typed in the command to lock the door from the interior, with no external override possible, securing himself inside the Containment facility.

Delphi, Greece, 6 June 478 B.C.

Scout and Cyra walked down the slope of Mount Parnassus past the Castilian Spring. There was a cluster of people purifying themselves in the water before lining up in hope of being invited to consult with the Oracle. Scout paused, seeing about fifty supplicants, separated from the entrance to a cave by a half-dozen priestesses dressed in the same white robes that Cyra wore. They had red cloaks and garlands of flowers on their heads. They stood as still as the trees that flanked the cave, serene and calm.

"My fellow priestesses," Cyra said, indicating the women. "The supplicants try, even though it is well known my mother will see hardly anyone during the games."

"Then why was Pythagoras there?" Scout asked.

"Exceptions are always made," Cyra said, but there was an edge of uncertainty in her voice. She was rattled, but trying to hide it. She signaled, and two of the priestesses came to her. She ordered them to go to the cave to attend to her mother and dispose of 'another issue.' She also told them to speak nothing of what they saw in the cave.

"Sounds like the mob," Scout muttered.

"What?" Cyra was distracted.

"Nothing," Scout said. "Do they have the sight also?"

"No," Cyra said. "It is passed in blood. I received mine from my mother, and she from her mother before her, down through the ages."

"I'm pretty sure I didn't get mine from my mother," Scout said. "But—"

"What?" Cyra asked.

"Pandora said I needed to find out who my true mother is. So, who knows?" They continued down the mountain, toward the fields where the Pythian games were opening.

Scout was running the summary of information about the Oracle and her setup through her consciousness. The priestess chosen to be the next Oracle surrendered her name when she assumed the position, which sounded familiar to Scout, who rarely thought of the name her parents had bestowed on her. Nada had named her Scout from the very first meeting during the *Fun in North Carolina*, and that had been her name from then on, as far as she was concerned.

The Oracle had been around since the 8th Century B.C., and was so renowned for her prophecies that Edith had noted she was the most powerful woman in the classical world. No war with a state outside Greece, no expedition mounted, no major political decision was made without consulting an oracle, and the Oracle at Delphi was *the* one. Gaining an audience was a major coup, and Scout realized her mob analogy wasn't too far off, since it seemed those who offered the largest "tribute" seemed to get to the front of the line.

Edith had also included various modern theories as to the source of the Oracle's ability to prophesize: ethylene gas seeping up through the cracks in the floor of the cave; hallucinogenic hydrocarbon in the water of the Kerna Spring, upstream from the cave and reserved for the Oracle; extract from the *Nerium oleander*, which was poisonous, but might cause visions if imbibed in small quantities; even the possibility of snake venom (a sort of church tent revival). All were interesting, but didn't take into account the simplest, but strangest and truest, explanation: the Oracles were descendants of the priestesses of Atlantis.

Scout knew the history from the download, but it also gave her the future. At least, the future as it stood now. Eventually, the Christians decided the cause of the prophecies had to be demons, always a convenient explanation, and they destroyed the temple and eliminated the Oracle in 390 A.D. in the name of their religion.

As they continued down the path, Scout saw several warriors, their shields and uniforms striking a familiar chord. "Did you go to King Leonidas's wife and daughter after the battle?" Scout asked.

Cyra nodded. "Yes. I spent several months with them. I fulfilled the promise you made. But I would have made the same promise to the king. He was a noble man and a great king. He saved Greece, and his name will always be remembered."

"'Go tell the Spartans'," Scout quoted, "'stranger passing by, that here, obedient to their laws, we lie'." She was surprised to feel a tear sliding down her cheek as she remembered Leonidas and his warriors.

Cyra reached out then gently took the tear with the tip of one finger. "You have seen too much for someone so young."

Scout swallowed hard. "Do you have any sense of Pandora? Her presence?"

Cyra shook her head. "Like my mother, I felt something. I still feel it. But it's not specific. How about your Sight? You've met her face-to-face. You would be closer to her than either of us."

They stopped near the base of the mountain. There were thousands of people scattered about the plain in front of them. Groups gathered around various events from races to musicians performing. Tents were set up, food was being cooked, and the atmosphere was in sharp contrast to the darkness in the Corycian Cave.

Scout closed her eyes, reaching out, remembering being in Pandora's presence at Thermopylae. She could sense the people, a sea of emotions, mostly positive, a few spots that weren't; some red with anger, rage, even a few that were black as death, representing despair. A spectrum of humanity.

She reached farther out over the crowd, and thus, it was a complete shock when a low voice came from behind her and Cyra. "This is where the Earth-Mother, Gaia, was supplanted," Pandora said. "As you go around the world, it is fascinating, and disconcerting, how, in almost every culture, the worship of the Earth-Mother was twisted into a new religion or simply obliterated. In the beginning, all worshipped her. Now, such practice is hidden in the darkness, slowly dying away."

Scout had frozen at the touch of the tip of a blade against the base of her spine. She slowly turned her head.

Pandora was taller than Scout, slender, dark-haired except for a single streak of white starting above one eye and through the hair to the end of the locks on the back of her shoulder. She did not have a Naga staff, like she had last time Scout had run into her. But neither did Scout, so that evened out. But she did have a dagger in each hand, one pressed against Scout's back, the other against Cyra's.

"You're both poor priestesses," Pandora said, "letting me get this close to you. Makes me despair for the younger generation."

"You lied to me," Scout said.

"'Lied?'" Pandora seemed amused. "About what?"

"You wanted the map," Scout said. "That was your mission at Thermopylae."

"Oh, no," Pandora said, offended, or feigning it very well. "That was a target of opportunity. One rarely sees a Gate map. Few and far between, they are. Very valuable. I knew you were up to something, so I just hung around for it to develop. As I told you then, my mission was complete before you even arrived. And, might I ask, why are you back?"

"Why are you back?"

"What makes you think I ever left? Are you here to save someone?" Pandora smiled. "Ah, that's it. A rescue mission."

"Get out of my head," Scout said.

Pandora shifted her focus. "Cyra, daughter of the Oracle. How is your mother these days? Still extorting the nobles of Greece for her words of wisdom?"

"You just saw her." Cyra's voice was tight. "You were in the Corycian Cave. You murdered a man there. If I call out, the crowd will be on you. If you stab either of us, you violate the Truce of Hierominia. You'll be torn limb from limb. You'll be tried and executed anyway, for the murder."

"'Murder?'" Pandora laughed. "Speaking of murder, watch."

A bell rang in a field, just in front of them and about ten meters lower. A line of men bolted forward, racing barefoot across the packed dirt.

"Men compete with each other so directly," Pandora said. "They are such simple creatures. Yet they've managed to take over everything. That reflects very poorly on us women."

The crowd cheered as the runners crossed the finish line, a tall, muscular young man managing to lean forward at the very end to take the victory.

"What does that have to do with murder?" Scout asked. She considered options, countermeasures she'd been taught in the sawdust pits at Camp Mackall to disarm someone armed with a knife. She could—

"You'll be dead if you make any move," Pandora said, "along with your friend here. And that would be a waste of two such talented young women. There are so few of us, we really can't go around killing each other. Not unless absolutely necessary."

Pandora moved forward, between Scout and Cyra, the daggers still pressing against their flesh. "The young man who just won.."

Scout waited. "And...?"

"The baby I saved two years ago?"

"Yes?"

"The child is his son, which makes it the great-great-grandfather of Alexander, who will become known as the Great. Which makes that man the great-great-great-grandfather. It is hard sometimes to keep track of such family trees, especially royal ones."

"And...?" Scout asked again, noting that the point of the dagger was perfectly steady, no tremor, no increase or decrease of pressure. Pandora *would* kill both of them in an instant, if she desired.

"Did you go to the Temple here?" Pandora asked, reverting to her standard of answering questions by asking questions.

"No," Scout said.

"Ah. You should go before you depart. If you depart. Note what is carved in the stone on either side of the entrance. One is very applicable to you."

Scout accessed the download. "*Gnothi seauton.* And *Meden agan.*" Edith had kindly included the translation. *Know thyself. Nothing in excess* .

"I told you the last time we met," Pandora said, "that you had little clue who you are. What your power is. You still don't, or we wouldn't be wasting time having this conversation. Neither of you really understands. Your mother is a poor teacher," Pandora said to Cyra, "but that is to be expected."

"Easy," Scout said, sensing the priestess's surge of anger.

"My dear Scout," Pandora said. "Do you remember, at least, the stages of awareness as I told you?"

"I do."

Pandora pressed the blade a little bit harder against the base of Scout's spine. "Speak them."

"Awareness of self," Scout said, her voice tight. "Awareness of others. Awareness of the world. And fourth, awareness beyond the world."

"But you are so unaware," Pandora said. "Both of you. You were looking for me, but couldn't see me."

Another race was lining up, the men's bodies oiled and sleekly muscled.

"Note that no women are racing," Pandora said. "This was once the center of worship for Gaia, and now look. Men have taken it all over."

"That seems to bother you," Scout said.

"It should bother you also," Pandora said, "since you are a woman."

"My mother is honored here," Cyra said.

"Your mother is used here," Pandora said. "It is well known that the Oracle dies young. Used up by the supplicants, all male, who come to her with their pathetic need for advice."

"Why did you kill him?" Scout asked, trying to focus in the face of Pandora's apparent ramblings, which Scout knew had a purpose. She was afraid of what that purpose might be.

"Kill who?" Pandora didn't wait for an answer. She was watching the winner of the last race as he walked away, surrounded by a small entourage, including a woman and a very young boy, barely able to walk. "An assassin is going to try and kill the man and the child today," Pandora said. "I'd prefer that not to happen."

"Why should I believe you?" Scout asked.

"Because I think that same assassin is going to kill whoever it is you're here to save."

"A fine story you spin," Cyra said, "since you're the assassin."

"You've already killed who I was supposed to protect," Scout said.

"Really?" Pandora said. "That explains your bad mood. And who have I killed?"

"Pythagoras," Scout said.

"Who?" Pandora said.

"Pythagoras of Samos," Scout said.

"The painter and statuary?" Pandora asked.

"And mathematician and philosopher," Scout said. "He founded an entire school of—"

Pandora cut her off. "Yes, yes, he's dead."

"And you killed him," Cyra said.

"Such ignorance for two who have the Sight and are sisters is appalling." Pandora laughed. "Pythagoras of the Theorem has been dead for almost twenty years."

United States Military Academy, West Point, New York, 6 June 1843 A.D.

Roland wouldn't have fit on board, was Ivar's first thought as Jackson helped him onto York. The three cadets, weighing less than 350 pounds combined, didn't seem to bother the horse at all as Grant, in the front, twitched the reins. They began the long climb from the Hudson River toward the Academy, or rather York did, and the three did their best to remain aboard, Ivar hanging on to Jackson, who had his hands clasped around Grant's midsection, who had his thighs tight around the beast and his rear firmly in the saddle.

They passed McClelland and his two comrades, who were working hard to keep from falling off the trail and tumbling down to the river.

"I'll be keeping an eye on you," McClelland said to Ivar, but Grant nudged York, and they quickly left the walking cadets behind.

Halfway up, the storm broke, unleashing torrents of water so thick, Ivar could barely see the head of the horse when he looked around Jackson.

"Hang on," Grant shouted.

As if I had other options, Ivar thought as the horse reached a particularly steep section of the path. It felt as if they were going vertical for a little bit, the rain pelting him in the face, but then they leveled out. Grant had the horse on a dirt road, and York picked up the pace.

"Superintendent's somewhere ahead," Grant shouted over his shoulder. "Let's beat him back to the stables."

"Let's not," Ivar muttered.

Jackson had no comment on the matter.

Grant directed York off the road into the woods on the left.

"Why take a road when there's a forest?" Ivar wondered out loud.

"Never take the expected way," Grant said, "unless you have the advantage of numbers."

"Right," Ivar said.

"Did you forget about the bridge?" Jackson asked.

The rain had lightened slightly. No longer a Biblical deluge, it was more a shower.

"I did not forget about the bridge," Grant said.

"What bridge?" Ivar asked.

"The one on which the road crosses the stream ahead of us," Jackson said, "and that we *won't* be going across if we aren't on the road."

"We're wet already," Grant reasoned.

"But we're not drowned," Ivar said.

"Not yet," Grant said with a laugh. "But we're about to find out how strong York really is."

Ivar leaned to one side and peered ahead, water dripping down his face. "Let's take the bridge, sir."

The stream was now a torrent of water, cutting across their path.

"Just think," Grant said, halting York for the moment, twenty feet short of the stream. "That water came from the sky, flowed off the sides of the mountains, into the stream, which descends to the Hudson, where it flows out past New York City, eventually into the Atlantic Ocean. What a journey for a drop of water."

"Fascinating," Ivar muttered, his wool clothes chafing, and the ridge of York's spine not the most comfortable perch he'd ever experienced.

"We'll jump it," Grant decided.

"We might end up in the Atlantic," Ivar cautioned. "Eventually, you know."

"Perhaps back to the road," Jackson suggested.

"This is the path I've chosen," Grant said. "You are both free to walk back to the road and across the bridge to the Academy. You'll probably run into Mister McClelland and friends."

Ivar considered it, but he hesitated a moment too long as Grant leaned forward and whispered into York's ear.

The horse bolted forward, the three cadets simply appendages. It reached the near side of the creek, jumped, and cleared the distance with room to spare.

"Easy enough," Grant said.

They set off at a gallop for the Academy then rode through the front gate. As if ordained, the rain stopped, and the sun punched through a break in the clouds.

"The Lord smiles on us," Jackson said. "The storm has passed."

Ivar didn't see a connection between the two statements, but he could tell Jackson was certain there was. Ivar had to admit there was a degree of glory in the rays of sun slanting through the clouds and the mist rising from the ground, with the Plain of West Point ahead, the looming bulk of Storm King mountain beyond to the left, and the Hudson River meandering north directly ahead.

Grant halted the horse on the hard-packed road. Ivar slid off the back, glad the other two couldn't see his discomfort. Jackson dismounted, then Grant.

"It's been a most interesting morning," Grant understated as he led York toward a large building, perched on the edge of the plateau overlooking the Hudson River.

Despite having the data in the download, actually seeing the Academy and the terrain on which it perched was rather impressive to Ivar. He allowed Edith's notes into his consciousness as they walked toward the stables.

The name West Point came from the fact that it stood on a point of land on the west side of the river, where the Hudson narrows and makes a sharp turn to the west, a strategic position for control of the river and the boat traffic on it. During the Revolution, both the Americans and the British saw the value of occupying it. The Americans got there first, before the British could do so and cut the troublesome New England colonies from the rest.

A ship passing up or down the river had to slow to negotiate the bend, and given this was prior to steam engines, it entailed a complicated maneuver for sailing vessels. The colonists built a fort at West Point and extended a massive chain across the river, kept afloat by log rafts. Then they designed positions for gun batteries to cover the river on either side of the chain. Finally, to protect the batteries, redoubts were built inland all around West Point.

There was a lot in the download on Benedict Arnold and his attempt to betray the place to the British during the Revolution, but Ivar skipped that as they entered the stables.

"Whoa," Ivar said as they entered. "It stinks."

Both Grant and Jackson looked at him in surprise.

"I've never—" Ivar began, but realized saying he'd never ridden a horse or been in a stable was like saying he'd never been in a car back in his time.

"If you want a place that smells horrible," Grant said, "try a tannery. My father owned one, and if I never come across that odor again, it will be too soon." He smiled as he checked the stalls. "We arrived before the Superintendent." He nodded at Jackson and Ivar. "Thank you for your amiable company, gentlemen. It's best if you return to the barracks, especially you, Mister Ivar, before some upperclassmen finds you out of limits. I'll put York up."

Jackson gave a short bow toward Grant. "The pleasure was mine." He nodded toward Ivar, then headed toward the Plain and the barracks beyond.

Ivar wanted to stay near Grant, but the dismissal had been clear. "Good day, sir," he said, not sure what the protocol was. "Oh," he added. "You might give this back to Cadet Hill." He pulled the pistol out of his waistband then handed it over.

Grant looked at it. "I appreciate you seconding me. Do you know you rode with this loaded and primed the entire time?"

"No, sir."

Grant was examining the firing mechanism. "You have a lot to learn here, but the powder is most likely wet from the storm, so I doubt it would have gone off." Grant tucked it in his belt. "Thank you."

Ivar walked out of the stable, making a mental note for flintlock firearms training. He paused, then went around to the side, looking for a window from which to keep an eye on Grant. There was nothing on this side. He went toward the river side of the building, and as he turned the corner, an axe handle caught Ivar in the midsection, doubling him over and knocking his forage cap off.

As he gasped for breath, a hand grabbed his hair and pulled his face up so the handle could smash into his nose. Ivar heard the bone crack, and the sharp sting of pain brought tears.

Ivar staggered back, trying to blink the tears away to see who was attacking him.

"You're off limits, plebe."

Ivar recognized the voice and the large form: McClelland. He had the axe handle ready to strike once more. He swung.

Ivar surprised McClelland, and himself, by parrying it with a sweep of his left forearm. The blow stung the arm, but prevented it from hitting his head, where it had been aimed.

They take this hazing thing a bit too seriously, Ivar thought, shaking his head to clear it, blood flying from his broken nose. McClelland swung again, and Ivar hopped back, the handle whooshing by, just missing.

All those hours in the sand pits during training at Camp Mackall were finally paying off. Ivar adjusted his stance, legs the correct distance apart, right slightly forward, hands raised, ready to attack or defend.

McClelland swung again. Ivar ducked under the axe handle and threw two quick jabs into the larger cadet's ample gut. McClelland retreated a step, and Ivar knew he could take him. Pressing the attack, Ivar moved forward, tripped over a rock, and tumbled to the ground at McClelland's feet.

"Your luck has run out," McClelland said, and raised the axe handle over his head.

"McClelland!" The voice was sharp with command.

The cadet froze. "Grant. This is none of your business."

"He stood for me," Grant said. "Makes it my business."

Ivar looked up, the blood dribbling down his face. McClelland glanced at him, back at Grant, then down once more, as if calculating what to do next.

"You're drunk," Grant said. "You've assaulted another cadet. If I report you to the duty officer, you won't graduate, not that the Army will miss you."

Ivar wanted to say that he didn't get the impression McClelland cared that much, and this was more than an assault.

McClelland lowered the axe handle, then tossed it aside. "We'll meet again." He walked past Grant, toward the barracks.

"Was he talking to you or me when he said we'll meet again?" Ivar asked, as Grant knelt next to him and helped him sit up.

"Ignore him," Grant said. "He imbibes too much, and he's the goat of the class. He's barely scored high enough to graduate. Let me take you to the surgeon."

Ivar forced himself to stand. He gingerly touched his nose. It moved, and for a moment, Ivar thought he might throw up.

"No. No surgeon," Ivar said, figuring he could live with it for however long he had left here and get someone with a bit more expertise to realign the bones, rather than spend the rest of his life looking like a boxer with a bad career. Then again, that might make him look tougher. But his nose had always been too big, Ivar thought, and this could be a good time for a little reduction via a visit to a plastic surgeon when he got back.

"Look at me," Grant said.

Ivar turned to him. A nose job was something Ivar had always considered and—

Grant reached, and before Ivar could object, placed a hand on either side of the nose then pressed. With an agonizing crack, the nose was set.

So much for plastic surgery.

"I think McClelland is dangerous," Ivar said.

"He's just drunk." Grant took Ivar's elbow, and led him toward the Plain and back toward the barracks. "I have to jump York later today. I need to relax. I believe some time in Kosciuszko's Garden is appropriate."

I think McClelland is from the Shadow, Ivar really wanted to say, but he didn't think that would go over well.

Chauvet Cave, Southern France, 6 June 32,415 Years B.P. (Before Present)

Was she the Shadow's version of Moms? An agent who led a team? Were these her men? Who she was responsible for?

Moms stared at the woman. Her face was bisected by the blade of the Naga staff. The eyes on either side of the wound were vacant.

Moms grabbed the haft of the staff then rocked it back and forth, pulling. It took a few seconds, but it began to move, and she was able to pull it out of rock, flesh, bone, and brains.

The body tumbled to the snow and dust.

Moms flipped open the backpack and found a half-dozen silver metal tubes, cradled in some soft material. On the end of each was a blue light, with a button next to it. The technology was different, but Moms had no doubt what they were: explosives, to destroy the cave and the art.

Would destroying those paintings have destroyed art? Surely someone, somewhere, would do the same?

She began to check the corpse, ignoring the pain in her shoulder as best she could, but as she did so, the body crumbled inward to dust. Looking about, she noted the rest of the bodies were also gone.

Moms sighed and sat down. She reached over her left shoulder and felt the shaft of the arrow. This was going to hurt, she thought, but then the arrow also disintegrated into dust. A small blessing.

But now, blood was flowing out of the wound. Moms took a piece of fur, reached back, and jammed it as hard as she could into the wound to staunch the flow.

And then she passed out.

The Present

"JERK," EAGLE YELLED AT ORLANDO as he ran to the ramp then dove out.

He spread his legs and arms akimbo, getting stable and oriented. He saw Lara tumbling in the air. He pulled his arms into his sides, clamped his legs together, and dove, angled straight down.

Using just his hands, like fins for direction, he accelerated toward her.

This is Roland's gig, Eagle thought. He began making up the distance between the two of them, losing altitude the entire way.

Six thousand feet, the altimeter warned via his earpiece.

He saw her arm move, tossing the grenade away.

Five thousand feet.

Eagle was stunned when the grenade exploded, a brief flash, the sound lost in the air rushing by.

"Double Jerk, Orlando!" Eagle screamed as he adjusted his track slightly.

Four thousand feet. She was fifty feet below.

Eagle blinked as he realized she was slowing her spin. She was experimenting, thrusting an arm this way, tucking a leg that way. Why, when she had no chute?

Three thousand feet.

Ten feet away.

She was looking at him, no longer tumbling. She'd assumed an odd position. Legs together, arms spread wide above her head. Feet straight down toward the rapidly approaching desert.

She looks like an angel, Eagle thought, apropos of nothing of importance at the moment because they were both going to splat in about *two thousand feet*.

Eagle over-adjusted then bumped into her, chest-to-chest.

She smiled at him.

One thousand feet.

Eagle only had time to clip a single snap link from his lowering line into her straitjacket harness, then he jerked the ripcord.

His parachute blossomed.

Eagle was jerked upright, and then he felt the abrupt tightening of his harness as she hit the end of the fifteen-foot lowering line. He barely had time to look down before she struck the ground, then he was down, hitting hard, feet on either side of her body. He collapsed to his knees, straddling her.

"Frak me," Eagle muttered. He glanced down at the young woman lying between his legs. Now that he was this close, he noticed the poorly healed scars underneath the hair struggling to grow back on her scalp. A jigsaw puzzle of them.

Lara was still smiling. "He is a crazy man."

"He is," Eagle agreed. She had an American accent, not Russian. Who exactly was she?

"I like him."

"I don't."

The Missions Phase IV

Normandy France, 6 June 1944 A.D.

MAC CHECKED THE BODIES of the three soldiers, ensuring they were dead by putting an extra round in each man's head. When he turned back to the barn, he saw Brigit standing on the top step, wrapped in a towel, a Sten submachine gun in her hands.

Mac waved, and she simply turned and went back down the stairs, leaving the trapdoor open. Mac figured she wasn't worried about light discipline at the moment. He walked to the door and down the stairs, making sure to close the trap behind him.

Brigit was under the blankets on the bed. The Sten was leaning against the rock wall behind the bed.

"You buried Maurice," she said.

Of all the things she'd just observed, Mac thought. "Yes."

"Was the officer the one who killed Louis?"

"No."

"Ah," she sighed. "Then that one is still out there."

"Yes."

"You must wash."

Mac looked down. The front of his shirt was drenched with Procles's blood.

"There is a spare field uniform on a hook to your right," Brigit said. "Charles took it from one of the pods even though I told him keeping a British uniform was a bad idea. He looked forward to the day he could wear it in the open and fight the Germans."

Mac pulled off his fatigue shirt.

"I left you the water," Brigit added.

Mac looked at the muddy water in the trough. *When in Rome,* he thought.

Mac glanced over at Brigit. She had her back to him, her head buried inside the blanket, curled into a tight ball. He peeled off the rest of his uniform and stepped into the chilly and dirty water. He tried not to use too much of her last bar of soap. He noticed there were now streaks of red in the brown water.

Not sure he was much cleaner than when he'd gone into the tub, Mac stepped out. He used a small rag hanging next to some onions to try to dry himself.

"You Americans are so well fed," she said.

Mac felt his face burn in embarrassment because she was looking at him. She lifted the blanket. "Come here."

"The mission," Mac said.

"The mission will happen. You just killed four men. What happened to the officer's body? I have never seen that."

"He didn't belong here," Mac said.

"Neither do you."

"I think I do," Mac said. He could see her naked body, curled up so tight her knees seemed to be in her chest.

"I will help you with your mission," she said. "I know the fastest way to the bridge, but sometimes, there are more important things. I need you now." She straightened out, and he could see her breasts and the dark triangle between her legs. He felt foolish, standing there naked, with just a rag.

"Are you a good man, Mac?"

It seemed an odd question coming from someone who'd just seen him kill four men, shooting one in the back, then firing a coup-de-grace into their heads afterward to make sure.

"I don't know," Mac answered. He realized that was the truth.

"I think you are a good man."

"You don't know me."

"You can spend a lifetime with someone and not know them," Brigit said. "Minutes of life and death are different than a lifetime of nothingness."

Mac thought of the other guys who would have happily jumped into her bed. She was actually quite pretty with the dirt mostly gone and her hair looking softer.

"Mac. The last man inside me was a very mean German."

Mac went over to the bed and sat next to her. "What happened?"

"He hurt me. I waited until he was done, and then cut his throat with his own knife. He bled all over me. The blood was very warm, and it was a very cold night, so that was one good thing about it, but the blood turned cold very fast. He was a mean man, but also a stupid man. I buried him in the field."

Mac wondered how someone could be capable of hurting this woman, with eyes so blue. "I'm so sorry."

"That is why I need your warmth, Mac. Not the other."

Mac slid under the blanket, pulling her close, feeling her shiver. "You are cold."

"Oh, Mac."

He buried his face in her hair and held her tight in his arms. She was so thin. He could feel the strong beat of her heart against his chest. He held her in silence, the lamp flickering long shadows on the stone walls. He sensed her body warming. Her breathing slowed down, and her muscles relaxed.

She was asleep.

The bridge must come down. Mac tried to slide out, hoping she would remain asleep.

"Is it time?" Brigit murmured.

"Yes."

"I will come with you."

"You should stay here," Mac said.

"I can't." Brigit sat up, and he could see the ribs in her back, the arch of her spine. There were poorly-healed scars on her back, and he didn't want to ask. "I can't be here all alone." She got up, grabbed her pants and began putting them on.

Mac donned his uniform, including the British fatigue shirt that Charles had saved and dreamed of wearing.

When he turned back to her, she was also dressed, but the look on her face caused his heart to ache. It was a look he'd seen before. She was done, finished.

"The war will be over soon," Mac said. "I can promise you that."

"By Christmas?" she asked with a sad smile. "It seems every war will be over by Christmas."

Mac thought about this Christmas and the Battle of the Bulge, and how many would die so needlessly in the Third Reich's last spasm, a futile attempt at victory when the war was already lost. "No. Not by this Christmas, but in the Spring after."

"The war will never be finished for me, my dear Mac."

He knew then that there had been other mean Germans.

He walked around the small bed and cupped her face in his hands. "Brigit. You'll forget all of this one day and have a real life, and a husband and babies."

"I had a husband and a baby. In Paris." Her eyes filled with tears. "The war will never be finished for me, and now you are a part of me. You are here inside my sanctum with me. Thank you."

Mac held her face, looking into her wet eyes, and he sensed that he wasn't going home.

She wrapped her arms around him., He didn't think about it at all. He held her tight and knew that he'd never be alone again, and he felt weak with the comfort of it.

Sjaelland Island, Denmark, 6 June 452 A.D.

Now, Beowulf, thee,
of heroes best, I shall heartily love
as mine own, my son; preserve thou ever
this kinship new: thou shalt never lack
wealth of the world that I wield as mine!
Full oft for less have I largess showered,
my precious hoard, on a punier man,
less stout in struggle. Thyself hast now
fulfilled such deeds, that thy fame shall endure
through all the ages. As ever he did,
well may the Wielder reward thee still!

"Who are *you*?" Jager replied, unfazed by the dagger. "Sent by Hel to help the mighty Beowulf? Tell me, Roland the Slayer."

They were interrupted when a party of warriors came in through the ruined doors. The leader announced they had tracked the blood, and Grendel's footprints, as far as possible.

"Across the moor, sire," the leader said, "and then they ended at the edge of a blood-stained pool. We circled it, and there was no sign of the monster leaving. It is down there, rotting and being eaten by fish."

"Optimism," Jager said in a low voice to Roland. "How quaint."

The maiden tending to him was confused. "What are you speaking of?"

King Hrothgar stood, chalice in hand. "All praise mighty Beowulf. Slayer of Grendel. Bravest of brave." He emptied the chalice. "I will compensate you and the families of the men who died so bravely," Hrothgar continued. "I will pay gold."

"How much are you worth?" Jager asked Roland in a low voice. "How much is any man's life worth?"

"It's worth what we believe in," Roland said.

"A life is worth only the lives it can take," Jager said.

The maiden's hands were shaking, but she continued to clean the wound. Roland gave her points for that. He wished they'd sent someone like Moms or Mac on this mission. Someone who could chat with this guy and figure this out.

Roland looked toward the front of the hall. Beowulf was being showered with gifts. Seated between the king and queen, he had just donned a new armor breastplate, the metal shiny and bright in the light from the roaring fireplace.

"You didn't answer my question," Roland said, focusing his attention on Jager and giving a little extra pressure to the knife.

The maiden had finished her bandaging. Her earlier come-hither attitude was gone. "Fare well, sir," she said, and then scurried away.

"She was frightened so easily," Jager said.

"Most people are frightened by what they don't understand," Roland said.

"So you're frightened right now? Is that what you're saying?"

Roland shrugged. "I don't have to understand a lot of things. I just have to be able to kill what I need to kill."

Jager nodded. "Spoken like a true Jager—a true Hunter."

"How did you know you could penetrate into the armpit?" Roland asked.

"A Grendel only has a few vulnerable spots," Jager said. He was watching the hall. Food was being brought in. The wine and ale were flowing, voices raised loud in relief and victory. "Armpit works, but isn't fatal. Directly into the mouth, and then the brain, is fatal, but requires going into the beast's attack. There is a spot on the back of head, right at the base. It's a hard spot to get an angle on. But it is instantly fatal. That's the best place."

"You've fought its like before," Roland said.

"I have."

"And the scales can defeat Naga steel," Roland wondered aloud.

"Look at my spear," Jager said, nodding toward where it leaned against a beam. "And please, remove the dagger. It is not needed."

Roland knew he shouldn't, but he did. He slid the dagger back into the sheath, got up, and retrieved the spear. The haft was wood, the tip a piece of dull iron a foot long, widening to a four-inch base.

"The weight is off," Roland said, hefting it in his hand.

Jager held his hand out. Roland handed the weapon over, ignoring the voice of Nada screaming at him in his brain.

"Your weapon," Jager said, "which you call a Naga?"

Roland nodded.

"It's at the core of this blade, covered in iron. We used scraps, whatever we could find, to make our weapons. The scales on the first Grendels *could* be penetrated by Naga steel, as you call it. Then the beast's scales were improved. But that is not the worst thing about Grendels," Jager added.

"What is?" Roland asked.

Jager slanted his head so he could look at Roland out of the corner of his eye. "You know nothing of them? This was the first you've met?"

Roland nodded.

"Good," Jager said. "That is good." But he didn't answer Roland's question, which seemed to be as much his forte as fighting.

"You still have not told me who you are or where you come from," Roland said. "Or how you know of these Grendels."

"Nor have you answered my question," Jager replied.

Roland sighed. He got up and grabbed two large flagons of ale that had just been placed in front of a couple of thanes sitting at the closest trestle. The men glared at him, thought about it, then grabbed a serving girl to get them more.

Roland brought the ale back, handing one to Jager.

"Thank you," Jager said. He raised it. "To glory and death in the Hunt!" He took a deep draft, draining half the large cup.

Roland did the same. They set the cups down.

"Jager means 'hunter' in my world," Jager said, "but it will do for here. My old name is gone. It is the name I will die with. Are you indeed Roland?"

"My old name is gone, too," Roland said. "When I joined my team, I gave it up. They gave me the name Roland."

"It's a good name," Jager said. "They could have chosen worse."

"They could have," Roland agreed, thinking back to some of the suggestions that had been written on the board in the Den, back at the Ranch, so many years ago when he was recruited into the Nightstalkers.

"It was chosen by comrades," Jager said. "That is good also. And you've faced kraken. I hate them. Nasty things. Easier to kill than a Grendel, though. But if they get you into the water, then the odds turn against you."

"Where are you from?" Roland was getting frustrated, knowing he was far down a slippery slope. Was Jager from the Shadow? But then, why had he fought Grendel, if Grendel was the Shadow's creature? But the first rule of Time Patrol was not to talk about Time Patrol.

"A place far from here," Jager said.

Roland wanted to hit something or someone. He drained the rest of his cup. Then he grabbed two more from in front of the toughest-looking of Hrothgar's thanes. Once more, they didn't dispute him. Apparently, being covered in black blood from Grendel gave one some carte blanche.

He brought the cups back, putting one next to Jager. "Speak to me. I came here with the directive to make sure all develops as it should in the poem."

"'Poem?'" Jager snorted. "What does a poem have to do with any of this?"

Roland was flustered. "The poem of Beowulf's heroics"—Jager snorted again—"will be—" Roland didn't know what to say.

Jager shook his head. "But his supposed heroics just happened. Other than the things he's claimed. You speak as if you know what *will* be written is *already* written."

The first rule of Time Patrol. The first rule of Time Patrol. Roland repeated that mantra in his head.

Jager was staring off into the distance, his forehead furrowed. "There were some who thought..." He fell silent. "You *are* from *this* world, aren't you?"

Roland considered the question, saw no breaking of the First Rule, and answered, "Yes."

"Yet you speak of a poem that is already written of events that are just occurring."

Frak, Roland thought.

"So you are from this world"—Jager was speaking slowly, thinking out loud—"but not of this time."

Double frak.

"You are from the future of this world," Jager concluded. "Why are you here?" He didn't wait for an answer. "To make sure your world survives." He nodded. "Yes. Yes. That makes sense. Why you would be here in this place. Now. Because your world *does* lie in the balance today."

He fell silent, and Roland sensed the mood, so he waited.

"If we could have done that," Jager finally said, "things might have turned out differently. We could have saved our world. Some did think the Darkness was able to travel not only between worlds, but also in time."

"The 'Darkness?'"

"It makes the monsters."

"We call it the Shadow," Roland said.

Jager nodded. "The same. It goes by different names in different worlds."

"So you do not work for it?"

Jager turned and finally gave Roland his full focus, his eyes dark. "It killed us. Destroyed our world. There are, were, only a handful of us left. The Jagers. I might be the last, for all I know. And I will never find out any different. This world is where I will end. It was a one-way journey. This is my final Hunt."

"'Hunt?'" But Roland had seen the lack in that stare. There was nothing behind those eyes that was the essence of what most considered human anymore, no empathy, no love, no fear, no emotion at all, nothing other than revenge.

"We fought the Darkness for generations," Jager said. His voice was so low that in the hall filled with revelry, Roland had to lean forward to hear. "It sent its monsters into our world over and over again. Each generation, they were harder to fight." He laughed bitterly. "Kraken? We could kill them. The—" He paused. "It doesn't matter, what the others were. Finally, the Grendels came through the doors into our world. Many good Jagers died learning their weaknesses. But once we did, we killed them, almost as fast as they were coming through. Almost."

Jager fell silent.

Roland began to reach for his second mug, but noticed that Jager hadn't taken another drink from his first mug. Roland pulled his hand back. Waited.

"Tell me," Jager said, "where do these people think this Grendel came from if they have never seen its like before?"

Roland accessed the download. "*'They are fatherless creatures, and their whole ancestry is hidden',*" he quoted. "It's believed they are descended from Cain."

Jager's blank look indicated that name meant nothing to him, so Roland accessed the download once more because, honestly, the name didn't mean much to him, either. "Cain was the first human born to the first humans created by God, Adam and Eve. He had a brother, Abel. He killed Abel out of jealousy and anger."

Jager pondered that. "The first human born. A murderer. We had legends, too. The fatherless thing, that comes from the poem?"

"Yes."

"Fatherless. Interesting. I suppose, in a way, the Grendels are fatherless. And you are here to make sure the poem remains true?"

"Yes, and—" Roland paused. Was that his mission? "I don't know what my mission is. I have only twenty-four hours to make sure nothing is changed."

Jager arched an eyebrow. "Perhaps I have changed things. Perhaps I am why you are here. Perhaps you should stop me."

Roland shook his head. "I don't think so. In the poem, Grendel's arm *is* ripped off. He goes to the water hole and dies. Beowulf would never have done that without you. So, you are part of this."

"Interesting," Jager said. "Can you tell me how the poem goes?"

"I have rules," Roland said. "I cannot speak ahead of the time."

"That's fine." Jager shrugged. "Knowledge can be dangerous. I have wondered if we grew overconfident," he added, as much to himself as Roland. "If we'd lost sight of everything beyond the Hunt. Our world was focused on supporting the Jagers. Everything was built around that. The older ones told me there used to be more to living than Hunting. That there were songs—" He nodded toward the front of the hall, where a bard was providing entertainment. "That there was happiness before the Darkness attacked. That a child was looked at as more than just another possible Jager or, if not Jager potential, one who would spend all their life working to provide food and shelter for Jagers. We'd given up so much. Sometimes I think the Darkness had already won, before it finally won."

Roland wasn't quite following, but he remained silent.

"We'd learned *how* to kill Grendels," Jager said, "but we hadn't learned *what* the Grendels really were. When we finally realized, it was too late." Jager sighed and sat back against a pillar of the hall. "Those of us who were left near the end, the last Jagers, made a vow to prevent what happened to our world from happening to other worlds. Perhaps the Darkness was overconfident, too. It was beginning to pull some of the Grendels back through the doors. We feared they were being sent to other worlds, so we infiltrated their lair. The Valkyries who were running it *were* overconfident. They did not guard the doors. They saw no need. Every chance we got, we sent a Hunter through the door after Grendels went through."

Jager picked up his first cup. Drained it. He indicated the second cup Roland had bought over. "I thank you, but I must have my wits about me. My skills."

"Of course."

"Then it was my turn," Jager said. "And I went through. And here I am."

"Is it really dead?" Roland asked.

Jager nodded. "Yes."

"Then your Hunt has been successful," Roland said.

"Is that what your poem says?" Jager asked.

Roland checked. "Grendel is dead."

"And that's the end?"

"No."

"No," Jager agreed. "Because that wasn't the only one that I followed through the door of the Valkyries. There was another. This will be the beginning of the end if I do not complete my Hunt." He grabbed Roland's hand. "But you do come here from the future?"

Roland didn't know how to answer a blatant First Rule question.

Jager saw the hesitation. He let go of Roland's hand. "If only we could have done that. Gone back." He closed his eyes. "But." He opened his eyes. "You know from this poem how it is *supposed* to happen, right?"

Roland broke First Rule by giving the slightest nod.

"But you're here to make sure that it happens as it is supposed to," Jager said. "So nothing is certain."

Roland rubbed his forehead. He was from the future, but behind Jager's dissection of the current situation.

"If you fail," Jager said, "the poem will not be written. If I fail, the poem will not be written. Of course, it's about more than the poem, correct?"

Roland nodded. He'd lost track of the First Rule.

Jager looked out over Heorot. "Another monster comes tonight in your poem?"

"His mother comes to avenge him."

There was a spark in Jager's eyes. "The mother? What happens?"

"She grabs a thane of the king along with Grendel's arm." Roland indicated the grisly trophy that had been mounted. "Drags both back to her lair. Beowulf goes after her in the morning. Kills her."

"Not likely," Jager muttered, staring at an obviously inebriated Beowulf sitting between two maidens. He brightened. "But the mother will come. That is good. Very good."

"Why is that good?"

"She's the dangerous one," Jager said. "She's the one that will destroy your world."

"How?"

"She's pregnant," Jager said. "That's what we missed. We focused so much on the ones that fought us, we ignored the ones that went into hiding. The mothers."

"We have to kill a baby Grendel, too?" Roland asked.

"If she spawns," Jager said, "there won't be *a* baby Grendel. There will be thousands of eggs that hatch all at the same time, tens of thousands. Do you think they"—He indicated the hall—"could defeat ten thousand Grendels?"

Kala Chitta Range, Pakistan, 6 June 1998 A.D.

"What have you done, you fool?" the old man demanded.

Apparently, Doc having an automatic weapon and being covered in blood didn't bother this guy.

Doc walked past him, ignoring his questions. They were in a room thirty feet wide that curved away in each direction: the buffer and observation room outside the Core of the Containment Center of the Depot, where the fissile material was stored. A thick glass window beckoned to the interior. Doc peered through. The weapons were arranged in clusters according to the platforms they'd be deployed in: bomb, missile, mine.

"Who are you?" The old man was next to him. He had short white hair, a clipped beard, and deep shadows under his eyes. He wore baggy white pants and a white shirt, and leaned heavily on the cane.

"So, the fissile material isn't demated?" Doc stated the obvious, more to himself.

The elderly scientist blinked. "Who are you? What are you doing here?"

"My name is Doctor Ghatar." Doc held out his hand, aware that it was stained with blood.

The old man had his own ingrained instincts. He shook Doc's hand. "I am Doctor Hamid."

Doc nodded toward the weapons. "Publicly, your country has claimed the fissile material is demated from the warheads. This is not true, obviously."

Hamid peered at him. "Why have you locked us in here? There is no way out, other than the door you just shut."

A klaxon went off, adding to the chirping, to produce a very irritating cacophony of alerts.

"The Containment Core is not breached," Hamid said, tapping the radiation badge clipped to his shirt, undeterred by Doc's lack of reply. "I suspected there was no breach when everyone began running like scared children. My running days are long past. I also suspect that you triggered that alarm. And I suspect that whoever's blood you are wearing has been found, and that has triggered the second alarm."

"You suspect a lot," Doc said.

"You look Indian, but your accent says you are American." It was not a question. It was, of course, followed by a question. "Why are you here?"

"To keep your country from starting a nuclear war," Doc said.

Hamid shook his head. "By doing what? The vault door is indeed very thick, but they will get through it eventually. And then?"

"And then, whatever crisis that caused your country to decide to load out the nukes today will have passed," Doc said. "What has happened, by the way?"

"It is in the news," Hamid said. "An Indian commando team attacked Prime Minister Shari's motorcade, and he was assassinated. That is an act of war."

"Are you certain this happened?"

"There are pictures in the news," Hamid said. "I've seen them myself. This occurred just hours ago. And perhaps, even though you sound American, you, too, are an Indian commando, sent to render us defenseless while your country launches its own weapons."

"If India was going to launch," Doc said, "they would have already, and this place would be a smoking hole in the ground. My parents were Indian, but I left there as youngster, and we moved to the United States. I am American."

Hamid shook his head. "We suspected the Americans were spying on us. They are not our friends. They are the friends of India. I think you are conspiring with the Indians."

"I'm not conspiring with anyone," Doc said patiently. "I'm here to stop your country from throwing nuclear warheads at India and starting a conflict neither country will survive."

Hamid shrugged, a gesture Doc had seen more times than he cared to remember. "It is what it will be."

"Not anymore."

Hamid shook his head. "They will get in here. And then what will happen to you?"

"I'm not worried about that."

"And what about all the nuclear weapons your wonderful United States has?" Hamid asked. He was surprisingly calm, given the circumstances. "Should you not break into your own Depots and secure them?"

"They are secure," Doc said.

"Ah, Americans." Hamid said the word as if it were a curse. "You rant about other countries having the terrible weapons you invented, and which only you have ever used on other humans. How hypocritical! You have more nuclear weapons than any other country, yet you act like the bully on the playground the moment another acquires one."

Doc was more than ready to get snatched back the Possibility Palace. This guy reminded him of his father and his way of looping logic to win every argument. The secret was if the immediate point was not winnable, to change it to something that was.

The sudden silence was as startling as the alarms going off. Doc glanced at Hamid. "What happened?"

"I believe someone outside has figured out what I just figured out. That you are in here. That there was no breach of Containment. That the vault door is locked from the inside."

A phone rang, the sound echoing on the curved walls. Hamid walked to it without asking permission.

For a moment, Doc considered telling him not to answer, but by the time he could have made a decision, it was too late.

"Yes?" Hamid said into the phone. "This is Doctor Hamid. There is a man named Doctor Ghatar in here with a weapon. He says he was born in India but is an American now. He has locked the vault door control from the interior, which means it can only be opened from in here." He listened, then held out the receiver toward Doc. "General Raju wishes to speak with you. He is most upset."

Doc took the phone. "Hello?"

"This is an act of war," General Raju yelled, so loudly that Doc had to hold the receiver away form his ear.

"I've done this to prevent war," Doc said. "Not just between your country and India, but your country and the United States."

"And how would that happen?" Raju demanded. "There is already a state of war between my country and India."

"There's a Task Force of American Special Forces heading toward this facility right now," Doc said. "I need access to a Satcom link to order them to turn around. Otherwise, they will penetrate your airspace. It is likely you will shoot them down. But in doing so, you will escalate the potential for conflict between your country and the United States. I don't think you want that on your hands."

There was a long silence on the other end.

"*You* have created an act of war between our countries," the general finally said. "Now you say there will be a further act of war perpetrated. Why should I do what you ask?"

"Because I'm in here and you're out there," Doc said. "And you want what's in here."

"Your name is Doctor Ghatar?"

"Yes."

"Ghatar is Indian, is it not?"

"I'm American."

"So you say."

"General, is there anyone else listening on this line?"

"No."

Doc checked the download. "You've been skimming funds from the Pakistan Atomic Energy Commission. You've already accumulated over ten million U.S. dollars in a secret bank account in the Cayman Islands."

Doc could hear harsh breathing coming out of the receiver. Hamid was staring at him, finally surprised by something.

"You lie," Raju finally said.

"Perhaps," Doc said. "But if you don't get me the Satcom link, that will become public knowledge."

"Wait." The phone clicked off.

Doc checked his watch. Task Force Kali was out of Iranian Airspace now and over Afghanistan, less than an hour out.

Which spurred a thought. Doc wondered where Osama Bin Laden was right now and, of course, it was in the download, a footnote appended to Afghanistan. In February 1998, Bin Laden signed a fatwā declaring the killing of North Americans the duty of every Muslim, and proclaimed that Americans were very easy targets.

The Kali team could divert, then parachute into Afghanistan right on top of—

Doc stopped the train of thought.

"It is what it is," he muttered to himself, waiting for Raju to call back.

"What is?" Hamid asked.

Doc had almost forgotten about the old man. "What do you do here?"

Hamid shrugged. "I am just an administrative man."

"You're lying," Doc said. "You graduated from the Government College University in Lahore with a degree in Applied Physics."

"How do you know this? How did you know about General Raju skimming funds?"

"I know many things," Doc said.

"Your CIA is very dangerous," Hamid said.

The phone rang, and Doc answered. "Yes?"

General Raju did not sound pleased. "Get Hamid on the line. We must do this through the computer. Your satellite link will be text only."

Doc gestured, and Hamid took the handset. The conversation was swift and one-sided, with Hamid's contribution consisting of uttering "Yes, sir," several times, then hanging up.

"Come," he said to Doc, leading him to a control console holding a large computer display and keyboard.

Hamid typed in a command, and the screen went blank, then came back with just a cursor.

"You must enter the coordinates for the satellite dish to orient," Hamid said.

Doc knew he was giving the Pakistanis access to a U.S. military satellite, but he had little choice. He typed in the coordinates from the download, then hit Enter.

The screen flickered, then coalesced.

>*ACCESSING*

Doc waited, Hamid looking over his shoulder.

>SATELLITE ACQUIRED

Doc typed in the authorization code for the mission, then waited for a response from the inbound Task Force.

The seconds passed. Then a minute. Another.

>KALI

Doc breathed a sigh of relief. His fingers flew over the keyboard.

>MISSION COMPROMISED. ABORT. REPEAT. ABORT.

>VERIFY ABORT CODE

Doc typed it in.

>ABORTING. GOOD LUCK. CONTACT SFOB FOR FURTHER ORDERS.

And that was it. Doc was on his own. "Shut it down," he said to Hamid.

"The General wished me to switch programs," Hamid said.

Doc raised his rifle. "If you access the vault door override, I'll kill you."

"I'm sure you will. The General wished to talk with you face-to-face, or as much as seeing each other via computer will facilitate."

The screen cleared, and a new image appeared. The video wasn't the greatest quality, but Doc had to remind himself that it was 1998. Cell phones were still just phones, not smartphones, and computer technology had a way to go.

General Raju was seated behind a large desk, the edges of which weren't even in the image. He was glaring at the camera. "I can see you, Doctor Ghatar. I see you are stained with the blood of one our brave soldiers. That is an act of war for which you will pay the price."

There was a loud clang from the vault door, and Doc looked that way.

"What you are hearing," Raju said, "is my engineers breaching the door. They assure me they can do it. It will take some time, but you are going nowhere. If you open the door now, I promise you a swift execution. If you do not, I promise you extended misery and pain before the mercy of death."

"Has the international incident with India been resolved?" Doc asked. "Was it Indian commandos who attacked the Prime Minister's motorcade?"

"That is of no consequence in this discussion between the two of us," Raju said.

Another loud clang, then a vibration rumbled through the floor and continued.

Hamid nodded in understanding. "They're drilling into the locking mechanism."

"How long?" Doc asked him.

He shrugged. "I have no idea. I am not a mechanical engineer."

Doc wondered if his time would be up before they found out. Checking his watch, he saw that it was one-thirty in the morning here, which meant he'd only been in the bubble for about six hours.

All he needed now was time.

The download informed him there were four pins holding the door shut. It didn't have the information on current drilling techniques and how long it would take to disable all four of them. Edith had missed those details in her preparation.

He'd forgotten Raju was still on the line.

"We will find out how long it will take," the General said.

"Yes, we shall," Doc said. He turned the computer monitor off. He gestured with the muzzle of the rifle. "Go over there," he said, indicating a chair at another console.

Hamid walked over then sat down. Taking a length of rope from his pack, Doc tied him securely to the seat. "This will be over in a bit, and you'll be fine."

"I do not think you will be," Hamid said. "General Raju has a very unsavory disposition. If I were you, I would fear what he will determine to be your fate."

"Fate?" Doc smiled. "Curious you would use that word. This is what is supposed to be."

"Who are you?" Hamid asked. "Truly, you are a very strange man."

Doc went over to the console and sat down. "We must wait now."

"Wait for what?"

"For the time to pass. For the storm to pass. Whatever we wish to call it. For cooler heads to prevail."

The phone rang.

And rang.

"Are you going to answer?" Hamid asked.

"No."

They sat, the floor vibrating from the drilling, the phone ringing. Time passing. After several minutes, the phone stopped ringing. The vibrating didn't stop.

Doc forced himself to stop checking his watch. It didn't make the time pass any faster. The phone rang again, continued for a minute, then stopped. For the next several hours, the drilling was continuous, the phone intermittent.

Doubt began to chip away at Doc's resolve.

Would he be pulled back before the vault door was breached? What should he do if it were breached? He had the rifle and several magazines of ammunition. How long could he hold off an assault force? What if the crisis wasn't over by the time he was pulled back or the vault door breached? What if the Pakistanis still went through with their intent of a first strike against India?

He resolved that last issue with some logic. If he were pulled back and the door hadn't been breached, then the Shadow's bubble would implode, and things would go back to normal history. He hoped.

But that brought its own questions, and since he had nothing other than time and worries, Doc allowed himself to ponder them.

Nada would have told him not to, because as more hours passed, Doc's confidence was evaporating. There was a very dark side to having too many vagaries of the variables.

"Is there a change in that vibration?" Doc finally asked Hamid as he checked his watch.

"I do not know," Hamid said. "But I must relieve myself. I would prefer not to wet my pants, if you do not mind."

Doc realized he had to do the same. He untied Hamid. They walked to an empty spot on the outer wall then urinated.

Done, Hamid went back to his chair. "I promise I will not try to attack you if you do not tie me up. My old limbs need to move."

Doc knew what Nada would say about that promise. He picked up the rope when the phone rang once more.

"Do you want me to answer it?" Hamid asked.

Doc also knew the correct reply, but his uncertainty trumped his common sense. "Go ahead."

Hamid walked to the phone, his legs stiff, leaning heavily on his cane.

"This is Hamid." He cocked his head, listening. "Yes, sir." A few seconds. "Yes, sir. I will do that." Then he hung up. He spoke to Doc. "The General insists you talk to him via the video on the computer. He says he will kill someone you know if you do not respond."

"Kill who?" Doc asked.

"He did not grace me with that information." Hamid indicated the computer. "Shall I?"

Doc nodded, knowing he'd made a big mistake allowing Hamid to answer and allowing the demon of doubt to win.

The screen came alive. Raju was standing in front of his desk. To his right, on his knees: Sergeant Lockhart. His uniform was muddy and torn. Blood dripped from his mouth. His hands were tied behind his back. His head drooped.

This is my fault. Doc gritted his teeth.

"We went up the mountain past where you killed out soldier," Raju said. "We found this."

He grabbed Lockhart's hair and lifted his face to the camera. His eyes were unfocused, and Doc knew Lockhart still was partly out of it from the shot he'd given him. "Look at the man who abandoned you," Raju said to Lockhart, pointing with the gun at the monitor.

Lockhart blinked several times, but didn't say anything.

"Open the vault door, or I will kill him." Raju drew his sidearm then pressed the muzzle of his gun to the back of Lockhart's head. With the other hand, he held up the note Doc had left with the sergeant. "'*I am sorry. This is for the greater good. Head for the PZ ASAP'.*" Raju crumpled it and tossed it aside. "What greater good? The only good you Americans care about is your own. We have reports the Indians have mated their warheads with their platforms. They will attack us, and we have no way to deter them. Millions will die. Millions of *my* people. What greater good does that serve?"

"They won't launch," Doc said. "They're reacting, too."

"You know nothing. You have one minute to open the vault."

Another minute closer to being pulled back and the bubble collapsing, Doc thought.

Raju was staring the camera. "You are not moving." He shoved the gun into the back of Lockhart's head, jarring him. "Beg your comrade for your life."

The sound of an explosion reverberated through the containment facility. Doc looked toward the door. It was intact, but there was a bulge in one part, where the engineers trying to break in had inserted explosive and disabled one of the locking pins.

Raju heard it and smiled. "They are getting there." He looked down. "Beg."

"Screw you," Lockhart said.

"There's no point in hurting him," Doc said. "I have my orders."

"And what orders are those?" Raju asked. "Your orders were to try to open the Depot for your task force, which is now returning to base. You left your comrade here, unconscious, behind you. You are acting on your own."

"I'm doing the right thing," Doc said, as much for himself as Raju.

Hamid was watching him and the screen, back and forth, as if observing a deadly tennis match.

"Your minute is up," Raju said.

"He will do it," Hamid whispered harshly.

"You have not moved," Raju said, "so you have determined his fate."

"Wait!" Doc yelled.

"You still have not moved," Raju said. "What am I waiting for?"

"I tell you that it will achieve nothing to—"

Raju pulled the trigger. The sound of the shot echoed out of the speakers. A burst of blood spurted from Lockhart's mouth, and he toppled forward. The camera panned down to show the dark hole in the rear of his head and the circle of blood slowly spreading on the wooden floor.

Doc turned the monitor off and stepped back, taking deep breaths.

"I warned you," Hamid said. "General Raju is ruthless."

"I get that," Doc said.

"I do not understand what you are doing," Hamid said. "You are accomplishing only a temporary solution. Once they breach the remaining three pins and open the vault door, they will remove the warheads. Unless, of course, India launches first and destroys us."

"But what if, by then, India doesn't launch?" Doc asked. "Wouldn't that be proof they don't plan to?"

"Today?" Hamid shrugged. "Yes. But what about tomorrow? And the day after? And the people will not forgive the assassination of the Prime Minister."

They will if it never happens, Doc thought. "I just need a little time."

"To do what?" Hamid asked. He spread his hands wide and implored, "Please, open the vault door. My country is at stake."

"You think launching these weapons against India will save your country?" Doc asked. "You're a physicist. You know what will happen if Pakistan and India have a nuclear exchange."

"The goal is deterrence," Hamid reasoned. "If India finds out we do not have access to our nuclear weapons, then they *will* launch a preemptive strike."

"They won't," Doc said.

Hamid snorted. "Do you want to know how I am certain they will?" He didn't wait for an answer. "Because *we* would. If India did not have nuclear deterrence, we would have destroyed them long ago."

Doc quoted, "*If India builds the bomb, we will eat grass and leaves for a thousand years, even go hungry, but we will get one of our own. The Christians have the bomb, the Jews have the bomb, and now the Hindus have the bomb. Why not the Muslim, too, have the bomb'?*"

Hamid nodded. "The People's Leader, President Zulfikar Bhutto. You know your history. So, you should understand where things stand between my country and your parents' country."

"Bhutto was executed," Doc said. "And his daughter, who is in exile, will return one day. And she will be assassinated."

"How do you know this?"

"Don't you see how insane all of this is?" Doc asked. "You need to believe me. Nothing will happen."

"You are gambling millions of lives on that," Hamid said.

"Tell me something, Hamid," Doc said, trying to get the image of the pool of blood around Lockhart's head out of his mind. "Why would India send a commando team to assassinate your Prime Minister and do nothing else? Not follow through with at least a conventional attack? In fact, such an assassination should be the prelude to a nuclear first strike. Yet that hasn't happened, has it?"

Hamid stared at him.

"Does any of this make sense?" Doc pressed.

The phone rang. Both Hamid and Doc looked at it as if it were a poisonous snake.

Doc reluctantly answered it.

"Turn the computer back on," Raju ordered. "There is someone who wants to speak to you."

"Who? You killed the only person I know here."

"That isn't quite true, is it, Doctor Ghatar?" The phone clicked dead.

Doc felt a chill sweep over him. He turned the computer on.

Raju was behind his desk. He leaned forward, seeing Doc in his monitor next to the camera. "You have been a fool! You will open the vault door. Now!"

Doc said nothing.

Raju got up then walked around his desk, the camera tracking him. He stopped in front of his desk, where he'd executed Lockhart. There was a dark stain on the floor, but the body was gone.

"Your delay allowed us to learn some things." He drew his pistol then pointed the muzzle to the right. The camera panned that way. Two soldiers held a frightened young woman. "Do you recognize her?"

Doc had no clue who she was. "No."

The camera went back to the general. "You do not know your own family, Ghatar? You are a physicist. You *are* Doctor Ghatar, who taught at the Tata Institute of Fundamental Research. You emigrated to the United States two years ago. You have turned your back on your country of birth and joined the Western warmongers. You have altered your appearance somewhat, but not enough."

Doc felt a band of panic constrict his chest. He'd always favored his father's features. And his father *had* been a professor at TIFR a little over two years ago.

"It is surprising you do not recognize your cousin, Doctor Ghatar," Raju said. "Has it been too long since you saw her? Let me reintroduce you, then. Doctor Ghatar, this is your cousin, Zoreed Ghatar."

The division of India and Pakistan in 1947 had split many families. Not everyone had packed up and gone one way or the other. Doc knew his father had relatives in Pakistan.

"We are tracking down more of your family," Raju continued. "One of my captains has radioed that he has secured your cousin's two children. They will be here shortly. Will you open the vault?"

"No."

General Raju went up to the young woman, and placed the pistol to her forehead. "You are causing me to stain my office once more. Will you open the vault?"

Doc didn't say anything.

"I will take that as a no." The sound of the shot was surprisingly loud coming out of the computer's speakers. The image of the head snapping back, the blossom of blood, skull, and brains blowing out the back was something Doc knew he'd never forget.

Delphi, Greece, 6 June 478 B.C.

"I'm sure there are those who will mourn Pythagoras of Samos," Pandora said, "but to accuse me of killing him hurts my feelings."

"You lie," Cyra said, echoing Scout.

Pandora sighed, pulling the daggers back and taking two steps to the rear. "Face me, my little darlings."

Scout and Cyra turned.

Pandora sheathed the blades. She held up both hands, empty, palm out. "Use your Sight. Both of you. You have enough to see Truth if I allow you into my head. At least to see my Truth of the past few hours."

Scout stared into Pandora's eyes for several seconds. Finally, she said, "You could be fooling us. Presenting us with..." She faltered.

"But my mother *saw* you," Cyra said.

"Did you look into *her* with the Sight?" Pandora asked.

"She's my mother," Cyra said. "She's the Oracle."

"Reminds me," Pandora said, turning to Scout. "Figured out the mother thing yet?"

Scout took Pandora's tactic. "Can't you *see* who it is?" she asked. "The assassin?"

"No," Pandora admitted.

"So much for your great Sight," Scout said.

"Do you remember Xerxes Dagger?" Pandora said.

"Yes," Pandora said.

"You could not see him at first. This one is worse. Whoever it is has shielded himself from me. He is a predator of the highest order. Nasty creature."

"Then how do you know it's a he?" Scout asked.

"I can sense a male spirit," Pandora said. "And these assassins. Their lack is their mark."

"Lack of what?" Scout asked.

"Humanity."

"You don't seem to like men so much," Scout said. "So why do you care so much about Alexander's forefathers?"

"Some men are important," Pandora said.

"You didn't seem impressed with Alexander the Great's legacy last time I was here," Scout said. "Why are you so concerned that he's born?" She knew Cyra was behind the conversation, confused, with no clue who they were talking about, but Scout "knew" Pandora had not killed Pythagoras, and that she had told the truth: he was not *the* Pythagoras. The Charioteer of Delphi would never be sculpted, but Scout couldn't see how that would barely be more than a ripple, although she imagined Edith Frobish would be terribly upset.

Much more was at play here.

"I have my reasons," Pandora said. "Seems you would care also."

Scout had checked on it when she returned, and learned that despite the fact the empire Alexander founded had quickly dissolved after his death, his effect on the world was profound: he destroyed the Persian Empire, ensuring that Western civilization would develop; founded Alexandria and the Ptolemy dynasty in Egypt, which would last until some other guy named Caesar put the kibosh on that; Alexander spread Greek culture across a wide swath of the world he passed through, bringing about the flowering of the Hellenistic Age. In essence, he set the stage for the Roman Empire that would follow. He also appeared to be quite a ruthless dick, in Scout's opinion, slaughtering many who stood in his way, and a lot who were trying to get out of his way.

All of that made Scout wonder what, exactly, were Pandora's motives in protecting Alexander's forefathers. Why had the Oracle lied? Why was Scout really here?

Another race was lining up. Scout turned to Pandora. "I don't know who you are. Where you're from. When you're from. You need to tell me more about you before I can even think of trusting you."

"Tell me something," Pandora said. "How long has it been for you since we last met? I know it was not two years. Your mind has not matured two years, worth."

"I really wish it were longer since our last meeting," Scout said. "In fact, I'd be happy to never see you again. I think you're a little cray-cray."

Pandora frowned. "I'm not aware of the term."

Scout twirled her finger around her ear. "Crazy."

"We're sisters," Pandora said. "Did you consult with your teacher in your time to learn more about what we are?"

"That's none of your business."

"That's a no." Pandora shook her head. "A poor steward, sending you through time so ill-prepared. Especially if you let them, whoever you work for, know you ran into me. I don't think they have your best interests at heart." She nodded toward Cyra. "Your mother doesn't have yours at heart, either, priestess."

"You lie," Cyra said.

"I could have killed both of you," Pandora said. "You'll have to accept that as enough of a sign of good faith for now. The priority is to find this killer."

Cyra was still behind. "Why would my mother say it was you, if it wasn't you?"

"I don't think she likes me," Pandora said.

"She's not alone in that," Scout said.

"Come with me," Pandora said, indicating a thick grove of olive trees. "It's best if we are in private for this."

"For what?" Scout asked.

"Come," Pandora said, the timbre of her voice vibrating with power.

Scout and Cyra followed, their will suborned for the moment to Pandora. They slid between the trees, deeper into the grove, until they were alone in a small clearing.

Pandora held out her hands, one toward Scout, and the other to Cyra. "If we work together, combine our power, we can find him."

Scout stared at the offered hand. "Do we have to dance in a circle and sing *Kumbaya*?"

Pandora's voice shifted up into power once more. "Take my hands."

Scout and Cyra did so before they could consciously make a decision about it, their fingers interlacing with Pandora's. They also took each other's hands, making a complete circle.

"Close your eyes." Pandora's fingers tightened on theirs. Now her voice was in their heads: *He is the essence of nothingness. Not anger. Not revenge. Not despair. A hole in humanity. He is what is not human.*

It made little sense, but Scout understood. She could feel Cyra's presence, stronger than before when Scout had taken over her body. And Pandora's presence was a pulsing tower of light, of power, pulling Cyra and Scout into her own stream, into her Sight, and then outward, a circle flowing, reaching out and—

Danger close!

Scout gasped as pain slashed into her brain. She almost passed out, falling to her knees. Cyra's hand was jerked out of her own, along with Pandora's.

Scout opened her eyes, seeing Cyra tumbling over next to her, unconscious.

"Forget her," Pandora ordered, drawing a dagger and tossing it to Scout as she scrambled to her feet.

Just in time, as a man dressed in a short blue tunic entered the clearing. "You summoned me."

He was short, wiry, with a narrow face and dark, piercing eyes. There were two daggers in sheaths hanging off a leather belt, but his hands were empty.

"Why did you kill Pythagoras?" Pandora asked.

Scout was getting the balance of the blade. She took a half step, away from Pandora and in front of Cyra.

He looked from Pandora to Scout, then back at the older woman. "He was the honey that sweetened the pot to bring me to the three of you." He looked down at Cyra. "Too weak. Like her mother."

"Who are you?" Scout asked.

He drew his blades. "My name is Legion, for we are many."

"Going to be one less," Scout said.

United States Military Academy, West Point, New York, 6 June 1843 A.D.

"'Time, time, time, is on my side, yes it is'," Ivar sang to himself in a low voice, and then changed the lyrics to his reality, "but no, it isn't."

"What was that?" Grant looked over from the easel.

"Oh, just a song I remember from when I was younger," Ivar said.

"I have no musical talent," Grant said.

"But you are an artist," Ivar said. His eyes were black, his nose swollen, and he looked like hell. He could feel every beat of his heart in his face, pulsing, and it was in rhythm with the Rolling Stones song.

"I do this to relax," Grant said. "With the test coming later today, I wanted to take my mind from it."

He was doing a landscape of the Hudson River and the far bank. The two were in a garden at the foot of a set of stone steps that descended from the edge of the Plain. It was a quiet place, a cliff wall on one side, and a steep drop down to the Hudson on the other. Kosciuszko's Garden, the download informed Ivar, had been built by the man who'd designed the fortifications at West Point during the Revolutionary War.

"I don't know what got into McClelland," Grant said. "We graduate in a few weeks. It's not normal for graduating cadets to even bother with the incoming class." He grinned. "You're the class of '44's problem, although you'll find some yearlings, the class just ahead of you, '46, to be the most vicious at hazing. It seems as soon as some plebes get out from under the boot by becoming yearlings, they want to try the boot on and stomp on the ones afterward, as if they have no memory of what they felt when they went through it."

"How do you feel about the hazing?" Ivar asked.

"It's stupid and pointless," Grant said. "One can't treat a soldier the way we treat plebes, so it's developing and inculcating the wrong leadership style. The Army is indeed harsh, but my fear is that if we go to war on a large scale, our Army will be made mostly of volunteers, and one certainly cannot treat *them* like plebes."

"Are you concerned about Mexico?" Ivar asked, knowing he was skirting close to thin ice, given what he knew was coming, but it wasn't every day one got to sit next to Ulysses S. Grant and have a chat.

"It seems inevitable," Grant said, "and it will be purely an imperial move to grab land. Mexico is no threat to the United States." He'd paused in his painting, and a frown crossed his face. "I fear worse than Mexico, though."

"Slavery."

Grant nodded. "It is an inevitable problem. Let us hope the politicians sort it out, but they seem to have a predilection for making things more complicated rather than sorting them out."

"Mister Grant!" A voice called out from the top of the steps. An older man made his way down. He was in his forties, dressed in civilian clothes, and had an unruly mop of prematurely silver hair. Ivar began checking the download, but Grant supplied the answer.

"Professor Weir. May I present a newly arrived cadet, Mister Ivar."

Weir shook Ivar's hand. "You appear to have been on the wrong end of some hard object."

"An accident, sir," Ivar said.

"Professor Weir is the Professor of Drawing," Grant clarified. Drawing was an integral part of the course of studies at West Point. Not to make artists, but because in this pre-camera age, the ability to draw was critical in engineering, topography, exploration, and a host of other skills graduates would be called upon to accomplish.

"And Mister Grant is my best student," Weir said.

"At the moment, perhaps," Grant said. "But in a few weeks, you'll have a new best."

Weir held up three fingers. "You are in the top three since I began teaching here. That is what I wanted to speak to you about, with graduation so near. I was talking with Mister Havens the other day, and he said that your temperament was just the right type to be a teacher. That got me to thinking."

Grant put the pencil down. "I have hoped to be called back to the Academy some years hence to teach in the Mathematics Department."

That hope was in the download, and it had never come to fruition, with Grant ending up fighting in the Mexican War and then being cashiered out of the Army in 1854 when stationed on the West Coast—reportedly for intemperance, although his official record held no blight against his character. He would then go through seven very tough years trying to make a go of it as a civilian and constantly failing. Despite his poverty, though, he would free his wife's, i.e. his, only slave, instead of selling the man for a considerable amount of money.

But *this* opportunity was nowhere in the download, which caused Ivar some consternation.

"There is a very good chance I will have an opening in my department shortly," Weir said. "Would you allow me to put your name in for consideration if this becomes a fact?"

"This is a surprise, sir," Grant said.

Ivar wondered why Havens would have put such a bug in Weir's ear. It seemed out of— and then he spotted McClelland, leaning over and peering down the stone stairs into the Garden. Realizing he'd been spotted, McClelland disappeared.

"It's something to consider," Weir said. "I have enjoyed my time teaching here, Mister Grant. And it might be better for you to be here, than at some lonely frontier post."

"I've received my first posting," Grant said. "While I will not be in the dragoons, where my heart desires, I will be in the Infantry and assigned to Jefferson Barracks, along with my good friend Frederick Dent. Another dear friend, Lieutenant Longstreet, is already there."

That clicked for Ivar. Grant would end up marrying Dent's sister, Julia. Historians were uncertain what her influence on his life was, but one thing for certain: when he wasn't around her, he tended to drink and fail. When she was in his orbit he flourished, in the military at least, not so much in civilian life.

None of that mattered for Ivar except in one fundamental: Grant never taught art at the Academy.

Weir nodded. "I understand. Keep my offer in mind, though. I look forward to observing you display your talent with horses later today."

Weir took his leave.

Grant didn't pick up the pencil to continue the drawing. He paced back and forth at the edge of the garden overlooking the river. "I thought I knew what the immediate future held. This is unexpected."

"You had no problem with the unexpected this morning," Ivar said. "You handled jumping that creek quite easily."

"That's different," Grant said. "That was a task that needed to be done. This is a choice, a personal one with no clear-cut objective. I do want to teach, but I don't think in art."

"You said mathematics," Ivar said.

Grant nodded.

"Won't accepting Professor Weir's proposal negate the possibility of ever being a professor in the mathematics department?"

Grant nodded once more. "That is true."

"Then stick to your original course," Ivar said, knowing there would be no mathematics department in Grant's future. "By the way, did you return the pistol to Mister Hill?"

"No." Grant gestured toward the small satchel of painting supplies next to the easel. "I've not crossed paths with him yet today."

"I'll take care of it, then," Ivar said. "Besides, you have a more important matter to attend to this afternoon, don't you?"

"Yes." Grant removed the pistol and handed it to Ivar. He checked a pocket watch. "And I must attend to the matter of York now."

"Good luck," Ivar said as Grant packed up his easel and supplies. "There is something I, too, must attend to now." He tucked the pistol inside his tunic.

Chauvet Cave, Southern France, 6 June 32,415 Years B.P. (Before Present)

Moms fervently wished she were back in the Possibility Palace, in a hospital bed like the one Eagle had occupied. The rock pressing into her side and the deep, throbbing pain in her shoulder and arm indicated otherwise.

She opened her eyes to darkness, then blinked and focused. There was a dull glow in one direction: the cave.

Why aren't I back? she wondered. The mission was over. The cave, and its inhabitants, were safe. The art was preserved.

Moms sat up, groaning as the pain in her shoulder multiplied. Eagle had been right when he said the shoulder was the most complicated joint in the body. She checked, and the fur had stopped the bleeding. She got to her feet and walked to a point where she could see the cave.

There was a body lying just outside the entrance, curled into a ball.

What had she missed?

Moms scrambled forward, climbing, crawling, then running toward the cave. It was a young boy, and Moms dropped to her knees next to him. Before she could check for a pulse, she heard his snores, and relief flooded her. His mouth was wide open, gasping for oxygen, the snoring so loud, it was vibrating his body.

They'd kicked him out because of the noise? Sleep apnea? That seemed rather much, given the possible dangers out here. Moms stood, then walked to the edge and peered into the narrow opening. The red glow of the dying fire filled the space. The others were on the floor in several clumps around the fire, close together for warmth.

No security. Nada wouldn't have approved.

None of them stirred as Moms stealthily entered the cave. She paused, her eyes tearing, her throat irritated. Their faces were flushed and red, and they looked so peaceful.

She knew why they weren't stirring and why the fire was dying.

She got to her knees, her breathing shallow, but the smoke was much less than it had been because the same lack of oxygen that had killed all of them had also tamped the fire down to red embers. She blinked tears out of her eyes.

Moms crawled back outside the cave. She grabbed the boy, waking him.

He was sluggish, then startled to be woken by a stranger. He grunted something, but Moms just shook her head. She looked at the little boy, whose apnea had caused him to be the first to awaken, to stumble outside, desperate for oxygen. The canary in the coal mine. The others had passed out before they had a warning, before they had a chance.

What had she missed?

It was an old fire pit, one that had been used many times. The only way— Moms looked up the rock wall.

No one ever looks up.

The download confirmed the Chauvet Cave had been found from above in 1994, via a very narrow fissure that led downward into it. This front entrance had been blocked long ago by a landslide, which was to occur probably about six thousand years from now, and the reason everything inside had been so well preserved for so long.

The download confirmed that radiocarbon dating indicated two main periods of activity in the cave—now, and around five thousand years from now, when more drawings were made. Indeed, footprints belonging to a child with a dog walking next to him had been preserved from that latter era, one of the earliest signs of the domestication of dogs.

Checking that the boy was all right and signaling for him to stay put, she went to the wall. Her anger at herself defeated the pain in her shoulder as she climbed. Fresh blood seeped out of the wound. The top of the ridgeline was a difficult seventy feet. She reached the top and saw the reason.

The gutted warrior had crawled up here and completed his mission as best he could. He'd blocked the opening in the rock that served as the vent for cave's fire pit with brush and branches, and rocks to anchor it all down. The dust that had once been him was on top of the makeshift arrangement. He'd lived long enough for his body to seal the vent completely. Moms pulled the brush out of the way and was hit in the face with smoke as the cave began to vent.

"Brilliant, Brilliant," Moms muttered, then her brain turned inward. "Stupid. Stupid." She'd assumed he was mortally wounded and posed no danger. Nada's take on assuming was the same as everyone else's—no special insight needed there.

Kill the artist and kill the art?

Moms hustled to the edge and climbed down as best she could, using her one, somewhat good arm.

She reached the bottom.

The boy wasn't there. She looked about, close to panic, then saw him inside, kneeling next to the girl, her head in his lap. He was moaning something primal, pain-filled, and even if the download had been able to translate, Moms wouldn't have needed it. She took a look around. The fire was crackling, fed by fresh oxygen drawn into the mouth of the cave and now vented properly.

The boy crawled to a woman and shook her. He made a mewling noise when he realized she wouldn't wake. He started slapping the woman's hand, trying to rouse her.

One of the tribe wasn't with the dead around the fire. A man farther back in, with a hand stretched out. Moms went to him. He had several sticks next to him, the tips black or red. One was in his hand. He, too, looked like he was asleep, his cheeks rosy behind the beard, his eyes closed. Except his chest wasn't moving.

The artist.

On the cave wall in front of him were the horses, the only paintings done so far. The horses were so beautifully rendered that in the flickering firelight, they appeared to be running. Moms was enraptured by the images, forgetting time and place.

Where were the rest of the paintings discovered in her time? The bear? The Venus? The rhino? The bison, so well rendered they would end up with bear claw marks scratched through them during a time when the bears ruled the cave? Where were the other herds of animals? The red dots? The hand prints?

They were yet to come. If they were to come.

She startled when she realized the boy was next to her. He knelt, putting his hands into the man's furs, gripping. He grunted something.

"Father?" Moms said.

The boy glanced at her, then buried his face in the furs covering the man's chest.

His world was gone. Moms sat back, looking at the horses.

This was the beginning.

She had to make sure it wasn't the end.

The Present

Our Present
Area 51

"A LIVE GRENADE?" Eagle asked Orlando.

The Colonel turned the Jeep off the hardtop onto a dirt road. A piece of plywood had a warning spray-painted on it in unsteady letters: *No Trespass: We Will Shoot Your Ass.* A skull and crossbones were painted next to it.

"It wouldn't have been a real test if it weren't a real grenade," Orlando said.

"I should—"

"Oh, relax. It had altimeter arming built in. Wouldn't have gone off above eight thousand feet. If none of those yahoos had done anything, it would have just rolled around, and we could have kicked it out or put the pin back in. But she did something. Damned impressive."

"But why have it explode on the way down?"

"She didn't, and doesn't, know there was an altimeter arming device," Orlando said. "She's always going to believe it was live from the get-go."

"What if one of the others had done that?" Eagle asked. "I was able to hook into her straitjacket with the lowering line. But if one of the other—"

"They didn't," Orlando said. He glanced over at Eagle. "I been doing this for a long time. I didn't actually expect anyone to jump *out* with it. Jump on it. Try to throw it out. Run away. No one has ever grabbed it and jumped with it. What's as interesting as Lara jumping, is you going after her."

Eagle didn't like the change in direction. "So she's suicidal."

"You said she tossed the grenade away after she left the plane," Orlando pointed out.

"Yeah, but she didn't have a chute."

"If she were suicidal, she'd have held on to the grenade," Orlando said.

Eagle shook his head. "But, again, she didn't have a chute."

"Maybe she knew you'd come after her?"

"How could she know that?" Eagle asked.

Orlando shrugged. "Good question."

Eagle sighed, tired of going in circles with Orlando. "Any problems with the autopilot landing?"

"Nah," Orlando said. "Machines can do stuff like that, but they can't think. They don't got the instincts a real pilot has."

"Boris?"

"Pissed in his pants," Orlando said. "Seriously, if that's the best the Russkies got, I don't know why we worry about them. He's on a plane home. In the old days, they'd greet him with a bullet to the back of the head for getting sent back. Now, they'll probably kiss him."

"Princess?" Eagle asked.

"Had to shoot her," Orlando said. "Not fatal, but she's gonna need a knee replacement. She tried to cut me. Women. Can't trust 'em."

"Ms. Jones was a woman."

"She was Ms. Jones."

"Moms is a woman."

"She's Moms."

"Scout?" Eagle tried.

"I like her," Orlando grudgingly admitted. "Something about the kid."

Eagle knew he'd never dent Orlando's misogyny. "Why'd you call her Lara?"

Orlando shrugged. "First thing that came to mind when I saw her."

"Doctor Zhivago?"

"Who?"

"She's not Russian," Eagle said. "Sounds American. How'd she end up with the Russians?"

"How'd she end up in a straitjacket?" Orlando asked as a way of answering.

"Where are they taking her?"

"Your boss, Dane, wants to talk to her."

Eagle had a good idea what that "discussion" entailed.

Orlando looked at him. "I don't suppose you want to tell me what unit you guys are in now. Who Dane is."

"Sorry," Eagle said. They were approaching what appeared to be a derelict gas station.

"Don't suppose you want to tell me what happened to Nada. You gotta remember, I knew who he was. Before."

"Best not get into that, Colonel," Eagle advised.

The brakes screeched as Orlando stopped them a hundred yards shy of the building. Two guards popped up from spider holes, weapons trained on the Jeep. A third man, coming out of his hole behind the Jeep, walked up and put a handheld in front of Orlando's eyes. It beeped, and a green light flickered.

"Proceed, Colonel."

"Ever wonder if, one day, they're just going to let you pass, since they know you?" Eagle said, as Orlando threw the Jeep into gear.

"They do, I'll have their ass." Orlando pulled to the front of the crumbling station. "I'll wait."

Eagle got out, then went to the rusting soda machine and pushed the button for a grape soda. The soda machine slid to the side, and a stairway beckoned. Eagle went down the stairs, the entrance sliding shut behind him.

He entered a room that only someone on a government contract could design: depressing, gray steel-reinforced concrete walls, curving to a popcorn ceiling. Eagle knew there was twenty feet of steel-reinforced concrete above it.

The Den.

The evolution of the place's name was part of the history of the team. It had been tabbed a "bunker" on the official specs, but that had sounded too last-days-of-Hitler. Someone during the Cold War days had suggested the Zoo, via *The Spy Who Came in from the Cold*. But when the Cold War faded, that had changed to Lions' Den, then simply Den.

The generations of Nightstalkers who'd passed through had given it personality. Various knives, axes, guns, etc. were on the wall, mementoes of missions past. A vertical log, half chipped away from thrown knives, spears and axes, stood in one corner. Eagle smiled as he remembered everyone ducking whenever Doc took his turn throwing an axe.

A large table was in the center. Etched into it were the names of all the Nightstalkers who had made the ultimate sacrifice. The table had originally been in Area 51, in the room where the very first Nightstalkers, under a different name, were assembled to battle Rifts. It had been moved out here when the team moved, many years ago, away from all the scrutiny focused on Area 51 by alien conspiracy people.

Eagle ran his fingers over the names, all code names conferred onto each team member as they joined.

There were a lot of them.

He looked about, and his desire to strip the place in order to make the team room in the Possibility Palace wilted. The new team, whoever they were, whatever missions they were being tasked with, were the Nightstalkers.

Traditions always had to start somewhere.

Plus a name was missing. It was the first for the Time Patrol: Nada.

The Time Patrol needed their own traditions.

The Missions Phase V

Normandy France, 6 June 1944 A.D.

"DAWN ISN'T FAR OFF," Brigit said as she led the way along a cow path.

They halted as a tremendous storm of heavy firing erupted to the west and north, dwarfing the artillery that had been pounding away.

"It must be five-forty-five," Mac said. "The fleet bombardment. The battleships *Nevada* and *Texas*. The *Nevada* was sunk at Pearl Harbor. And the *Arkansas*." He smiled as he thought of Arkansas, and Kirk chopping wood and taking care of his siblings. How he was alive because Nada was dead, and that was how fate worked sometimes. Moms had said something about fate and scales, and Mac imagined that life and death were balanced somehow in the larger frame of things.

Mac allowed the download free rein, because it kept him from thinking too much on other things. "The British battleships *Ramillies* and *Warspite*. Twelve cruisers. Thirty-seven destroyers. They're firing up the beach, and will shift inland since the first troops land on Utah and Omaha Beaches at zero-six-thirty."

"And we must destroy this bridge as part of all that," Brigit said. She was walking along the path faster than what Mac considered safe, given the darkness, but it was obvious she knew it well.

"Yes."

"Look." Brigit halted, and Mac came up next to her. The rail line curved on a raised bed toward the trestle bridge. "You can destroy that?"

Mac took the load of explosives off his back and put it down. "Yes. It's my expertise."

"A strange thing to become an expert in."

"I spent most of my time in"—He considered how to phrase it—"in my last war, defusing bombs."

"That is a good thing. So, you were saving lives."

Strange, he'd simply thought of it as defusing the IEDs, not saving lives, but he had saved a lot of lives. Mac began sorting out the demo, inserting fuses, and running det cord. He worked by feel. He didn't really need to see what he was doing. He had the diagram of the bridge in the download, and knew exactly where the critical points were and what each would require.

"You will destroy the bridge, and then it will have to be rebuilt," Brigit said. "War is so futile."

"This was, is, a good war," Mac said. *It might have been the last one*, he thought.

"Indeed?" Brigit looked at him, her eyes glinting in the pre-dawn. "How so?"

"The Germans have done terrible things."

"Oh, yes. The camps. The camps everyone pretends don't exist."

Mac regretted saying that because now he knew what had happened to her husband and baby. "You can go back now," he said. "You'll be safe, and it will soon be over here. The Allies will pass by, and you can make your farm beautiful again. And you can have another Maurice, and he will wear flowers, and perhaps you will think of me now and again and maybe smile."

"Yes. I will think of you and smile. Now, do what you have to do."

Mac crawled out from the treeline, up onto the tracks. He jogged forward, his arms full of explosives, all wired together, and thought, *Tripping now would be really bad.* But even worse was seeing the German step up onto the rail line ahead of him, a Sturmgewehr 44 selective-fire rifle in his hands.

Mac stopped, and couldn't help but think Roland would love to get his hands on that weapon, the grandfather of all modern automatic rifles. *"Oberführer."*

"I was wagering with myself," the German said, "who would come. Would it be Procles, with you as a prisoner, or just you?"

"Did you win your bet with yourself?" Mac asked, hoping that Brigit was heading back to the farm.

"It was fifty-fifty."

"Why?" Mac asked.

"Why, what?" the *oberführer* was a tall, thin man. He wore a long gray coat, just like the other SS Officer. He didn't have a cap on, and his blond hair was too long for a soldier.

"Why are you attacking us?"

"That question is too large for the two of us," he said. "Like you, I am a soldier doing a mission."

"Why did you kill the boy?"

"One life?" The *oberführer* was confused. "You care about one life in the midst of all this? And more so, in the middle of the even larger picture of why the two of us are here?"

Mac realized the shore bombardment had ceased. It was that moment just before the sun came up. There were tens of thousands of soldiers, American, Canadians, British, and Free French, heading toward the Normandy coastline in landing craft, a sad percentage of whom would be dead before nightfall.

Mac could hear vehicles approaching in the distance, the clatter of tracks from armored vehicles, the rumble of diesel engines from trucks.

"We are surrounded," the *oberführer* said. "It will take them a while to get organized, but they will be here shortly. When they catch you, they will execute you as a spy. Even I cannot stop that. This is not the way I wanted this to happen. I wanted to speak with you."

Mac really hoped, prayed to the God he didn't believe in, that Brigit had left.

"But there is a way," the *oberführer* said. A Gate appeared beside him, a dark, inviting portal away from all this. "Come with me. There is much we can learn from each other."

"You shot a boy in the back of the head," Mac said. "There's nothing I can learn from you. I wondered at times about our missions. Our war. But now, I know it is right, too. It's a just war."

The *oberführer* sneered. "You're a fool."

Mac winced, not from the pains of his bad knee or the broken fingers or the scrapes from being pulled out of the well, but because he could see Brigit's slight form creeping up onto the rail line behind the man pretending to be a German officer, but representing something so much worse. He saw the glint of first light on the knife in her hand as the top edge of the sun broke the horizon behind her.

The *oberführer* realized too late as the blade slid across his throat. Blood spurted forth in a geyser from his severed carotids. He staggered for the Gate, trying to escape, but Brigit shoved him in the other direction and he fell off the embankment, tumbling to the dirt. The Gate snapped out of existence.

Mac walked up to Brigit. "You didn't leave."

She nodded at the bridge. "Hurry. There is not much time."

"Go back to your farm."

The *oberführer*'s body crumbled into dust.

Mac ran to the bridge, ignoring his torn knee. He moved swiftly, placing the charges, then running the det cord.

When he was done, he took the roll of det cord and walked backward along the side of the embankment to his pack. Brigit sat next to it, but he'd expected no different.

He wired the cord into the detonator.

The vehicles were closing in. Brakes squealed. Commands were shouted in German.

"You should go now," he said to Brigit.

"No."

"You have to go."

"No."

"I thought you were going to think of me and smile."

Brigit smiled. "I am thinking of you."

Sjaelland Island, Denmark, 6 June 452 A.D.

Heorot emptied as darkness approached, except for the thanes of Hrothgar, Beowulf, and ignored in their dark corner, Jager and Roland.

Jager had refused to talk further of his world, his life, Grendels, or anything. He withdrew into a mode Roland was familiar with: pre-combat.

Roland watched as the thanes took their armor off and put swords and spears aside. After all, Heorot was now safe.

He was startled when Jager spoke after such a long silence. "This poem of that—" He indicated Beowulf. "Why is it important?"

"I'm told it is," Roland said. "It is part of the start of"—the download confused him with possible answers, so he went back to the Met, to what they had seen—"art."

"'Art.'" Jager said the word. "I was told stories of it by the old ones. They used a word with it: beautiful." He sighed. "I'd like to know what 'beautiful' is before my Hunt is over. What art is." He shrugged. "But it does not matter. She comes. I sense her approach."

They were both ready. Roland had ceded the Naga to Jager, given his greater experience fighting Grendels. He had the spear. If Mac had been there, he'd have commented that it was the ultimate sacrifice Roland could make: to give up his weapon.

"Does she have a name in the poem?"

Roland checked. "No. She is termed an Aglaeca, which means a ferocious fighter."

"'Aglaeca.'" Jager nodded. "That works."

The fire began to die down. More fell asleep. Roland wondered how much longer he had here. If he were pulled back before—

"If the poem is important," Jager said, his eyes scanning the hall, "then we must follow the words as best we can and kill her in her lair. I do not like the field of Hunt in here. We let the Mother take whomever she takes. Follow her back to the lair. Kill her."

Roland nodded. He felt the pressure of time, unsure what hour he had arrived the previous night. It had been late, given how quickly dawn came after the battle. He had some hours, but—

The front doors were thrown open, and Aglaeca was there, larger than Grendel, stooping to enter Heorot.

There were just two guards alert and awake, and they were dead within seconds. It went against Roland's nature to hold back from a fight, but this wasn't a fight. It was a slaughter as Aglaeca plowed her way toward the throne, slaying any thane who woke at her approach.

"She's going after Beowulf," Roland said. "We can't—"

Jager was already moving. He shouted something in a language that Dane, and the download, didn't recognize.

Twenty feet short of Beowulf, Aglaeca paused. Her entire body had to turn in order to see to the side, as she also had no neck. Larger, fifteen feet tall, covered in scales, her only noticeable difference from Grendel was a ridge of black scales on the top of her head, a foot high, and continuing down to her back.

Jager yelled again as Roland ran up next up to him, spear at the ready.

Aglaeca snatched the severed arm from the post to which it was hammered. She rumbled for the door, carrying the body like a doll in one hand, the arm in the other. The monster disappeared into the darkness as the inside of Heorot began to finally awaken, at least, those who hadn't been killed.

"Why did it run?" Roland asked. "It could have killed Beowulf."

"It knew the language I spoke to it," Jager said. "It knows I'm a Jager."

"But why not fight?"

"Her survival is her priority," Jager said. "Even more than revenge. That was another way they were able to defeat us. They can sublimate their emotion to their purpose. Often, we humans can't do that."

Roland nodded.

"Time for me to finish it," Jager said.

"I'll help," Roland said. He looked over. Beowulf was awake, but still drunk. He was trying to make sense of what had happened, but other than Roland and Jager, no one had witnessed the complete assault. It would be a while before any sort of coherent group could be put together to go in pursuit.

"Beowulf is alive," Jager said. "When I finish it, he can take credit. That is your task. This is mine."

"I'm coming with you," Roland said. "You can use the Naga."

Jager shrugged and sprinted for the door. Roland ran after him. They loped through the darkness, Jager slightly in the lead, bent forward at the waist, his eyes toward the ground. There was a full moon, and Aglaeca's tracks were easy to follow. Roland could also swear he heard Jager sniffing every now and then, as if tracking a scent.

The terrain became treeless, a moor that extended to the horizon. Jager suddenly halted, holding up a fist. Roland stopped, providing security.

"In there," Jager said, indicating a dark pool. The surface was black, with even darker swirls in it, as if a painter had dipped a brush into deepest shadows then spread it. "They build hollowed-out lairs in places that are only accessible via water. In the beginning, the kraken would guard the water. That should have been something we considered more carefully. What it meant. But we killed all the kraken. And we'd killed almost all the Grendels. What we didn't know was there were a few lairs we didn't get. That's where the mothers were. Everything else was all a great diversion, and it worked quite well. When the spawn burst forth from the dark waters, they overwhelmed us."

Roland didn't like getting in water. He'd had a brutal time passing the various swim tests his military schooling had required him to take. He'd always felt if he wanted to swim, he'd have joined the Navy, not the Army. He was a rock, muscle-bound and solidly built; there wasn't much buoyancy built into his body.

Jager walked around the edge of the pond, kneeling occasionally. He stopped at one point. "It's down here."

"How do we do this?" Roland asked.

Jager smiled sadly. "This is my hunt. We have a tradition in the Jagers. *Had* a tradition. Every hunt is remembered by a trophy. Thus, every Jager is remembered by his trophies. My lodge, my home, is long gone, along with my trophies. And this will be my last. Promise me to take my trophy with you."

Roland thought of the walls of the Den back at the Ranch, where the Nightstalkers had hung their forms of trophies from various missions. "I will."

"Good."

Roland looked at the water with some apprehension. "Should we tie off so—" And then he was stunned as Jager slammed the haft of the Naga staff into the back of his head.

Roland fell to his knees, dazed. He heard a splash and knew that Jager had gone in. He tried to stand, but his head was spinning, and he fell backward, hitting the ground hard. Roland had been caught on the edge of an IED blast early in his career while on a tour in Iraq, and this was a replay, his mind trying to process, to get his body to move, but unable.

Roland heard distant voices approaching. Men. Afraid. Questioning.

He carefully sat up, wincing at the pain in the back of his head. He looked at the dark surface of the pool. There was no sign of Jager. Turning his head, he could see a party of warriors tentatively approaching in the full moon, their weapons at the ready, torches held by young thanes to light the way. Beowulf was in the lead.

Ripples began to disturb the surface of the pool. Roland stood up, spear at the ready, hoping to see Jager appear, ready if it was Aglaeca.

"What are you doing?" Beowulf demanded as he arrived with the other warriors.

"Jager is in there," Roland said.

The water was frothing as if the entire pool were boiling, air bubbles bursting, but no sign of either man or beast.

"Then he is a dead man," Beowulf said. "We will wait until the monster emerges and slay it." He didn't sound overconfident.

Roland was watching the water. "There is blood." At least, he thought so, but the water was so dark and foul, it was difficult to discern. "Jager will prevail."

The download was intruding: according to the epic poem, Beowulf dove into the water after making a brave speech about who should get the treasures he'd just received from King Hrothgar if he didn't return. But the warrior didn't look like he was getting wet any time soon.

"I'm going after him," Roland said.

"You're mad," Beowulf said.

Roland graced him with a smile. "I am."

He took a deep breath and—

Aglaeca's hand broke the surface. Beowulf and the other warriors took several steps back, but Roland raised the spear over his head, ready to strike. Aglaeca's head appeared, mouth wide open, fearsome fangs exposed, but the eyes were vacant, dead. The body floated, then rolled over, facedown, the Naga buried deep into the base of the skull.

Jager burst to the surface, gasping for air, his face streaked with dirty water and blood. He was next to the monster, thoroughly spent. Roland grasped Jager's hand, pulling him ashore.

"You're wounded," Roland said. "I'll—"

"No need," Jager said.

Beowulf and the warriors were coming forward, emboldened by the death of the beast.

"Get it out of the pool," Roland ordered as he was pulling aside Jager's tunic. Puncture wounds were spaced across the right side of his chest. Aglaeca's claws had struck home at least once. Air bubbled out of two of the wounds.

"You got a sucking chest wound," Roland said to Jager. "I can—"

"No." Jager's voice was low, but firm. His head was up for the moment, looking down at his own body. "There is poison in their wounds. When they are that many and that deep, there is no recovery."

Beowulf and several warriors had managed to loop a rope around the Aglaeca's body. They pulled it out of the water onto shore.

Jager's head slumped back. "It is my time."

Roland gently moved Jager's body so that he could hold his head off the ground. One of the warriors pulled the Naga free from the body. He looked at Beowulf, then at Roland and Jager, and carried it to them, an offering of respect.

Roland took the Naga and placed it across his lap. Then he looked down at Jager. "If it is to be your time, then let me send you off with an epic tale, my friend, of a mighty hunter."

Roland had Jager's head gently cradled in one hand, as he began to speak in a soft but powerful voice:

"*'They praised his acts of prowess*
worthily witnessed: and well it is
that men their master-friend mightily laud,
heartily love, when hence he goes
from life in the body forlorn away.
Thus made their mourning the men of the Jagers,
for their hero's passing his hearth-companions:

quoth that of all the kings of earth,
of men he was mildest and most beloved,
to his kin the kindest, keenest –'"
"That is beautiful," Jager said. "The way the words play. It is—" He died.
And then, Roland was gone.

Kala Chitta Range, Pakistan, 6 June 1998 A.D.

Two more explosions had rocked the vault. Doc checked his watch. He'd been here seventeen hours.

Doc had turned off the computer after Zoreed was killed. The phone hadn't rung, which he hoped meant General Raju had run out of leverage and was waiting for his engineers to finish their job. Which they were pretty close to achieving ,with just the one pin remaining.

He was staring through the observation window at the rows of warheads. Billions of dollars worth of research and development and graft, all to be able to destroy an enemy while also being destroyed.

The phone rang. Hamid grabbed it before Doc could stop him.

"Yes, sir." Hamid hung up. "The General insists we contact him via the computer. He says there is something both of us need to see."

He didn't wait for permission. He turned the computer on. Doc headed over, but Hamid gasped in anguish before he could get there, staggering back as if shot.

Doc looked at the screen. Two bodies lay on the floor, pools of dark blood haloing their heads on the polished wood floor: a woman and a teenage boy.

"Ah!" Hamid cried out. "That is my wife! My oldest son! Why, General?"

"Because you are in there with him," Raju said. The camera panned back. Raju held a pistol in his hand, which he waved. "If you are not an ally of his, then you most certainly did not give your life defending Pakistan's greatest treasure. I do not think you understand how serious this is, Ghatar."

Hamid staggered back, then slumped into the chair. He put his face in his hands and moaned in grief.

"He had nothing to do with this," Doc said.

"You did not open the door when asked," Raju said. "Their blood is on your hands."

"You are evil," Hamid said.

Doc assumed he meant Raju, but when he looked over, Hamid was glaring at *him* from the chair.

Hamid's grief quickly shifted into anger. "You are evil to just watch that and do nothing. You have cost me my family."

"And if these weapons had been released and used?" Doc asked. "How long do you think your family would live? How many millions would die?"

"You are evil," Hamid said.

"I am doing the hard, right thing," Doc argued. "He"—Doc pointed at the image on the screen—"killed your family. He is holding the gun."

Hamid looked from Doc to the screen, then back at him. "You are all crazy. All of you soldiers."

General Raju's voice intruded. "Doctor Ghatar. I told you one of my officers was tracking down Zoreed's children." He gestured to the right, and the camera turned that way. A boy and girl stood between two soldiers. The floor beneath their feet was stained with their mother's blood. Doc wondered if they knew she was dead.

"Twins," Raju said. "How sweet." He fired, and the boy's head snapped back, and he tumbled to the floor. The girl screamed and tried to run, but the closest soldier grabbed her.

Hamid stood up. "Do not shoot her, General."

Raju laughed. "And why not?"

Hamid slowly walked forward, leaning on his cane. "There has been enough death."

"Not nearly enough," Raju said. He focused on Doc. "I no longer care if you open the vault door, Ghatar. My engineers say it is a matter of minutes. I gave orders for you to be taken alive. You will experience a long time dying." He gestured, and the soldier shoved the girl away.

Raju fired, hitting her in the shoulder, knocking her against the bookcase. He fired again, a headshot, and her body tumbled next to her brother.

"I told you not to shoot her," Hamid said.

The general looked at the camera. "You do not speak to me. You are nothing. You will die before the American."

"That is what I knew," Hamid said. He slammed his fist down on the keyboard, and the computer went dark.

"What are you doing?" Doc asked, utterly confused, stunned by the blatant murders.

"We are dead men," Hamid said. "We can simply be dead and forgotten, or we can be dead and remembered as men who stood for something."

"And what is that?"

"Peace."

Hamid limped away.

Doc followed. "What are you going to do? We're trapped."

Hamid stood at the door leading into the Core. He typed on the keyboard next to the shielded door that led inside. With a brief whoosh of atmospheres equalizing between the observation room and Core, the door swung open.

Doc followed Hamid inside. The Pakistani physicist typed on the inner keyboard, and the Core door swung shut.

"This will gain us time," Doc said with approval. "It's not as secure as the vault door, but it will—" He paused as Hamid opened a cabinet and pulled out a cordless drill and a hammer. He tossed his cane aside. With one tool in each hand, he headed for the closest warhead, limping badly.

Doc intercepted him, putting an arm out. "No."

"We're dead men," Hamid said, pushing past. "You were the one lecturing me about nuclear weapons. Let's end this here. Now." He smiled grimly. "This death will be swifter than the one Raju has in mind for you. I am the one sacrificing the quick mercy of the bullet. I am doing this for my wife. For my son. For all Pakistanis. For all Indians. For humans."

He put the tip of the drill to an access panel on the side of the warhead and turned it on.

Doc remained still. How much time did he have left? According to his watch, he'd been here over twenty hours.

But had he accomplished his mission? Did the bubble depend on that? The fraking vagaries of the variables.

"You can help," Hamid said. He had the access panel off. He pointed toward the locker. "There's another drill and hammer in there." He raised the hammer over the warhead's core.

"Hold on," Doc said. "We've got some time. Let's access them all first."

"We don't need to access all of them," Hamid said. "Several will do the job. Everything in here, including us, will become so irradiated, nothing in here will be touched for generations."

Belatedly, Doc checked the download for data on *why* the Kala Chitta Range Depot had been closed.

Classified. Even those who'd been paid off had said nothing.

A secret, even in time.

But Pakistan had nukes in Doc's time. He had no doubt of that. They wouldn't be destroying the capability to make more, the knowledge or technology. What would be accomplished here?

Hamid was staring at him, hammer raised.

The answer was here. Now. If they didn't do this, and Raju got access to these weapons, he *would* use them. It would take time, months, if not years, before Pakistan rebuilt its arsenal. Doc thought of the twins. "Just wait on that a few minutes."

He went to the locker and retrieved a drill and hammer.

An explosion rocked the Core.

"They are in the Observation room," Hamid said. "I do not know how long the door will hold. It is built to keep radiation in, not intruders from entering."

Doc looked over at one of the observation ports. A cluster of faces was peering in, soldiers. Mouths were opening, yelling, but it was utterly silent in here until the sound of a drill penetrated the quiet.

"Tickling the dragon's tail," Doc said as he walked over to a warhead.

Hamid laughed for the first time. "Ah, yes. The first lesson every nuclear physicist must learn. Never play with the dragon. It has been a long time since University. Who said that? Was it Fermi?"

"Richard Feynman was the one who said messing with any core was tickling the tail of a sleeping dragon." Doc removed one of the screws on the access panel.

"The Demon Core," Hamid said. He'd put the hammer down and was opening the next weapon, giving Doc a reprieve. "How many did the Demon Core kill before they used it in a weapons test?"

They never used it in a weapons test, Doc thought. It had been used to open the very first Rift at Area 51, and had been drawn through to the other side. But it had killed a lot of people over the years via Rifts.

"I wonder," Doc yelled over the noise of their drills, "if Slotin subconsciously tickled the tail out of guilt. After all, he assembled the core for Trinity, the first nuclear weapon." He was referring to Louis Slotin, who'd played with the Demon Core, made the slightest mistake with a screwdriver, and died twenty-five days later from the radiation that had blasted him.

Not a good way to die.

As Doc moved to another warhead, he paused. The pitch of the drilling from outside changed.

"There can be no more delay," Hamid said.

Before Doc could say anything, Hamid smashed his hammer down on the core inside the warhead in front of him. Then he waved the hammer at the men observing through the thick glass.

All the faces disappeared.

The drilling stopped.

Doc could swear he felt a wave of warmth wash over him.

Hamid smashed another core.

Doc raised the hammer above the core in front of him and—

Delphi, Greece, 6 June 478 B.C.

Scout shifted into the ready position, the double-edged dagger in a reverse grip as she'd been trained. Out of the corner of her eye, she saw Pandora also going on guard.

Legion didn't do any of those spinning knife things so popular in movies in Scout's time as he pulled his weapons out. He had a blade in each hand, held about waist-high, and his eyes shifted back and forth between Pandora and Scout, as if deciding which entrée to dine on first.

"I had thought one of you would have dispatched the other by now," he said as he shifted his feet slightly.

Scout felt a chill slide though her body. He was deadlier than Xerxes Dagger; it wasn't just Pandora's warning. She could feel it. He had only one purpose: killing.

"You tried," Pandora said. "But you people have never understood the power of our sisterhood."

"It's not *that* powerful," he said. And in the midst of speaking, he lashed out, so fast Scout barely had a chance to attempt a defense.

The tip of one of his blades sliced along the forearm of her knife hand, peeling skin back.

Scout hissed in pain and started to take a step back, felt Cyra's body behind her heel, and held her ground. The cut wasn't deep or disabling, but it hurt like hell and, worse, was bleeding freely.

Pandora had not moved during the attack, seeing no opening.

Legion lifted the blooded blade to his lips, and his tongue darted out, much like a snake's, tasting. "Very nice."

"What did you offer the Oracle to set me up? To set us up?" Pandora asked. She took a half step away from Scout, trying to widen the distance, forcing him to commit one way or the other, and in doing so, expose himself, if only for an instant.

"What everyone wants. At least, what every human stuck in this existence wants."

"Life," Pandora said.

"Time. More time." Legion cocked his head. "I thought the girl would be faster. She's not very well-trained."

"I'm getting real tired of hearing that," Scout said.

His blade struck Pandora's before Scout was even aware he'd attacked and she'd defended. Sparks flew as metal hit metal. Pandora danced away as his other blade sliced through her billowing tunic.

Scout belatedly attacked, but he was already facing her, blocked her thrust, then flicked the tip of his blade at her face. She felt a sting above her left eye as she jerked back, trying to avoid the counterattack.

In her rush, she forgot about Cyra's unconscious body and fell backward. Scout scrambled, terrified he would press the advantage and finish her.

But he'd gone back to his ready position and was looking at Pandora. A thin, horizontal line of red appeared in her white tunic.

Breathing hard, Scout got to her feet, stepped over Cyra, then held her ground. She felt something wet on her forehead, and then a drop of blood dripped into her left eye. She wiped at it with her free hand.

"Eighty-seven cuts," Legion said. "That's the most I've inflicted before the end. It takes a while to bleed out. There is an art to it. Anyone can butcher. It takes an artist to end a life without a single fatal blow."

Scout blinked and shook another drop of blood away from her eye. She looked at Pandora. *Do you have a plan?*

Pandora gave a slight smile. *Very good. Awareness of others. You should run. Leave him with me.*

"So not fair," Legion said, as if he knew they were communicating. "But a fight is never fair. It won't help you."

"We killed Xerxes Dagger together," Scout said. "We're going to kill you. And how come you guys have names like Dagger and Legion? Why not Fred? Or Joe? Or Billie-Bob?" *I can't leave Cyra.*

Scout blinked blood out of her eye. The cut in her arm was throbbing. A faint voice whispered in her mind.

Legion fixed her with his dead gaze. "Xerxes Dagger? I wondered why he didn't come back." He twirled the blades.

Showing off, Scout thought, and knew she'd scored something on him.

"He was my brother." Legion came at her, and Scout jumped back over Cyra, bringing her dagger up, parrying his first blade as he stepped over the body. But the second one— she could see it, almost slow motion, but faster than she could move to block it—the tip touched her shoulder, a blaze of pain, arcing toward her neck to finish her, but then it was jerked back in surprise.

Scout slashed, slicing his forearm to the bone as he belatedly tried to blocked her, his focus diverted by the ceremonial dagger Cyra had slammed through his foot, pinning it to the ground.

He barely had time to register that pain as Pandora's hand slithered around, gripping his forehead, pulling his head back as her other hand drew her dagger across his neck.

Scout was drenched as his heart pumped his life out. His eyes were blinking, confused, not understanding what had happened.

His blood is cold .

Scout slammed her dagger into his heart, twisting, shredding it.

"You can't—" Legion managed to say before he died. His body fell backward, but Cyra's dagger kept the foot pinned, the lower leg straight, so he fell awkwardly.

But it didn't matter, because in just seconds, the body crumbled inward to dust.

Scout knelt and cradled Cyra's head. "Are you all right?"

Cyra nodded. "Help me up."

They stood, facing Pandora.

"Impressive," Pandora said. "I wasn't quite sure we could defeat him."

"Who is he?" Scout asked. "What is he? Him and Xerxes Dagger. Are there more like them?"

"Oh, yes," Pandora said. "There are more."

"Are they Shadow?" Scout asked.

"A good question," Pandora said. She looked at Cyra. "Your mother betrayed us. Betrayed the sisterhood. She wanted Scout to come after me. For us to fight, even while she knew the beast we just killed was prowling about. He would have killed those I have to protect." She shifted to Scout. "He would have damaged your timeline badly. He's already touched it by killing Pythagoras of Samos."

"So he's Shadow," Scout said, tired of asking questions.

"He's evil," Pandora said, without answering. "Pure evil. And—" She paused. Her voice dropped to a whisper. "She comes." Her eyes were blank, her mind somewhere else.

"Who comes?" Cyra asked.

Pandora came back to them, to the here and now. "Time is fleeting." She pointed at Cyra. "You must deal with your mother. You must become the Oracle." Then she looked at Scout. "We *are* sisters. Some day, you will understand that."

Scout stared at Pandora. "Tell me something. Is hope still trapped in your *pithos*?"

Scout blinked as everything went black for a moment, then light was back, but Pandora wasn't in front of her. A hand rested on the back of her neck, the fingers like icicles, extending up to cradle the back of her skull.

I could kill you, Pandora's said inside Scout's head. *Draw the life out of you, leaving just the shell of your body, which would crumble into dust, just like his, since it is not of this time. There would be nothing of you left. How long do you think you will remain in the memories of those who sent you here so foolishly? So unprepared?*

Scout thought of Moms and Roland and Eagle and Mac and Doc and Ivar and most especially of Nada, a memory himself.

Interesting, Pandora said. *Your ties to them are strong. Did you ask them who your true mother is? Do they even know? Do you know who you are? Do you really know who anybody is?*

The blackness flickered once more, and when reality was back, Pandora was gone.

"What happened?" Cyra was looking about for Pandora. She took a sharp breath as she saw someone else. Scout also saw her.

A woman dressed in a black robe, her hair and most of her face hidden by a hood, was standing at the edge of the clearing. She had a book in one arm. It looked heavy by the way she held it in the crook of her arm.

"Your mother has passed on," she said to Cyra.

"What? What?" Cyra repeated, understanding, but not accepting.

"She was tired and hurting," the woman said. "She's not in pain anymore."

Scout saw that the woman's eyes were pure white. "Who are you?"

"It's time for you to go," the woman said to Scout.

Darkness fell.

United States Military Academy, West Point, New York, 6 June 1843 A.D.

Ivar used the download's map to search the Academy, dodging upperclassmen every time he got close to one after being stopped and hazed several times.

There wasn't time for such tomfoolery, Ivar thought, then smiled to himself at the turn of the antiquated phrase.

Unable to track McClelland down in his room in the barracks or the mess hall, he finally decided that if the cadet was an agent of the Shadow, then he would be where his target was: Grant. Ivar trailed behind as a large contingent of cadets began to drift over to the stables, since it was well known in the Corps that Grant was making an attempt at the Academy jumping record. The wagering was intense, the Corps split over whether Grant could pull it off. There were some who predicted disaster, given the nature of the Hell-Beast.

Of course, none of them, other than Jackson, had been there this morning when Grant jumped the stream. And not even Jackson knew what Ivar did: Grant *would* succeed.

Ivar didn't enter the riding hall. He pushed through some bushes on the side, found a convenient tree, and climbed until he had a view through one of the high windows. The interior was an oval, tanbark-covered floor, surrounded by stadium seating. The stands were over half full, and a steady line of men in gray were entering, taking the rest of the seats. Ivar scanned the crowd for McClelland.

He spotted Benny Havens seated amongst a contingent of civilians, a rather stout woman next to him. Ivar assumed that was his wife, Letitia. If Havens was Ivar's Time Patrol contact, he might have spoken to Weir about wrangling Grant an assignment at the Academy under the misassumption that the mission was simply to keep Grant safe. Much like Doc's and Moms's contacts had thought that was their mission during Ides, given they had no clue what the future held.

Grant walked in from another door onto the arena floor, leading York. A buzz ran through the crowd. Grant was in his dress uniform, a saber dangling at his side. He seemed frail, especially compared to the massive horse.

Two enlisted men were setting up a couple of props and a bar under the supervision of the Master of Horse, which Ivar thought was a pretty cool title, one Scout might like.

But the jump was secondary; McClelland's whereabouts was the priority.

Grant mounted York and trotted the horse to a spot in front of a reviewing stand. He drew his saber and brought the hilt to his chin, blade up, saluting Major Delafield. The Superintendent stood, returned the salute, then reclaimed his seat. Grant slid the saber into the scabbard.

He walked York to the bar then leaned over, saying something to the Master of the Horse. The sergeant nodded and gave an order to the two men. They raised the bar. The excitement in the hall rose with the bar.

Where the hell is McClelland? Ivar wondered, since it seemed every cadet in the Corps was now in the riding hall. *What would Nada do?* he thought. And the answer was obvious: *Think like the enemy.*

But this enemy wasn't making sense. McClelland had been there when Jackson challenged Grant, and spurred it on, but he'd attacked Ivar, not Grant.

What would Moms do?

Look for the unexpected. McClelland wasn't in the riding hall. Then he had to be outside. Why? Doing what? Getting ready to do what? Ivar looked left and right. No sign of McClelland. He climbed down and began to circumnavigate the large hall. The river side was built on top of the cliff, leaving no room to walk. Ivar hustled the other way, around the front of the hall to the far side.

The noise inside suddenly ceased, and he knew Grant was getting ready to make his attempt.

And there was McClelland, lying on his stomach, peering in through an opening at ground level, a musket to his shoulder. He was mostly hidden by some bushes, but Ivar caught the glint of sunlight on the barrel. McClelland had pulled back a plank from the outer wall. Ivar realized he had a field of fire underneath the stands onto the riding floor.

Ivar drew the dueling pistol and ran forward. He stopped just behind McClelland and got to his knees. He could see inside, and Grant was on York, facing the bar. He was leaning forward, his mouth next to the beast's ear, his lips moving.

Ivar pulled back the hammer on the flintlock, the noise unmistakable.

"Put the musket down," Ivar said, proud that he'd used musket instead of rifle.

McClelland looked over his shoulder while he did as ordered. "I was just going to spook the horse."

"You seemed to be aiming," Ivar said. He took a quick glance inside. Grant gave York the gentlest of nudges. The horse began to trot, then broke into a gallop. Grant was leaning forward, one with the horse, as they approached the bar. York leapt, flowing over the bar with inches to spare, then landed on the far side.

The crowd exploded into cheers.

Mission accomplished? Ivar wondered.

"Get up," he ordered McClelland. "Leave the weapon."

Ivar escorted him toward the cliff, away from the crowd exiting the riding hall.

"When I spread the word among the upperclass that you pulled a pistol on me, you won't last a week here," McClelland threatened.

"When I spread the word you were going to shoot Grant," Ivar said, "I think you won't be around much longer."

"Told you," McClelland said. "I was just going to spook the horse. Make him miss the jump. I have a lot wagered against Grant."

They were in a small opening, between the trees and the hall and the cliff. Ivar blocked the only way out.

"We wait until everyone is back in the barracks," Ivar said.

"And then...?" McClelland asked.

Good question, Ivar thought. If McClelland were Shadow, he should get pulled back when the bubble collapsed, just as Ivar was, and everything would be back to normal. But what if he were from this time, the real McClelland, and had been suborned somehow by the Shadow?

The damn vagaries of the variables.

What would Roland do? And Ivar knew he was hitting the bottom of the barrel when he got to that point, but the answer was obvious: *Shove McClelland over the edge of the cliff.*

"Who are you?" Ivar asked. "Are you from the Shadow?"

"What the devil are you talking about?"

"Why were you trying to kill Grant?"

"Told you, I was just going to scare the horse. Keep him from making the jump. Why would I kill him? I'm not a murderer. You're crazy. You were crazy this morning."

That made sense. If Grant failed in front of the entire Corps, how would that affect him? Would that be the seed of a weed of doubt that would cripple him the rest of his life? Make him question himself under stressful situations, such as when Robert E. Lee was turning his flank?

McClelland's eyes shifted, and Ivar knew he'd made a mistake. That was confirmed as he felt the round muzzle of a weapon pressed into the flesh at the base of his skull.

"I'd be putting the pistol down, lad," a familiar voice said.

Stupid, stupid, stupid, Ivar thought as he bent over and put the pistol on the ground, the gun to the back of his head maintaining contact all the way.

"Go and join him," Benny Havens said .

Ivar walked over to McClelland on the edge of the cliff.

The cadet took a step forward, saying, "Glad you finally—"

"Stay there for a moment," Havens said.

"But—" McClelland was at a loss. "You said if I did what you asked, all would be square between us. The debt forgiven."

"The debt is forgiven," Havens said, but his eyes were on Ivar. "Should I let him go? He's just a simpleton, trying to repay a gambling debt. He knows nothing. But he did give you a beating."

"Excuse me," McClelland said, trying to muster some indignation. "You said—"

"Shut up, lad," Havens said.

Ivar was beginning to understand. "You ordered him to attack me, correct?"

"Correct."

"Did you order him to kill me?"

"No. Just to put you out of commission so this here event could be taken care of. Didn't work, as we see." Havens didn't seem upset about his plan falling apart.

Ivar glanced at McClelland. "Looked like you were getting ready to kill me with that axe."

McClelland shook his head. "Just trying to crack your skull. Make you go to the Surgeon."

Ivar realized McClelland was too stupid to lie. "This is between the two of us," Ivar said to Havens.

"Get out of here," Havens said to McClelland. The cadet hastily departed toward his inglorious future as a drunk and failure.

"A degenerate gambler," Havens said. "The worst kind of man. There's no cure for him." He lowered the pistol.

Ivar stared at Benny Havens. "Why are you working for the Shadow?"

"Is that what you call it?" Havens asked. "My wife calls them demons, sent by Satan. They've come only a few times since the first." He went to a log then sat, a tired, old man. "Every time in the middle of the night, to tell me of their bidding."

"These demons wanted you to get Grant kicked out?"

"At the very least," Havens said. "Dead would have suited them fine. That's too far for me, though. I'd never do that."

"What do they look like?" Ivar asked, although he already had a good idea.

"Beings floating in the air, with blood red eyes that bulge from a smooth, white face. And long, red hair. There are always a pair. They have no lips, but the wife and I can hear them. I know that sounds crazy," Havens said, "but it's the God's honest truth. I've seen them with me own two eyes several times."

Valkyries. Emissaries of the Shadow. "Why do you do their bidding if you know they're evil?"

"Our daughter."

The download indicated the Havens had been childless, part of the mystique of their long "service" to the Corps, as a number of cadets, mainly those who favored liquor, viewed them as a sort of surrogate parents. Edgar Allan Poe had called Benny the '*only congenial soul in the entire God-forsaken place*' while William Tecumseh Sherman had labeled him '*a rascal not worth the remembrance.*' An interesting dichotomy in points of view.

"What about your daughter?" Ivar asked.

Havens stared off into the unseeing distance. "They took her the first time they came. She was just a teeny baby. They came and took her, and told us they were going to hold her. That we were to tell no one about them. That we were to say our girl had died of the baby sickness, or else we'd never see her again. Letitia just 'bout went insane. Took all I had to keep her quiet. I just about went crazy, too. I never was no God-fearing man, and now demons had come into our house and taken our baby. How's a man to deal with that?"

There were tears rolling down Havens's cheeks, and the pistol was forgotten in his hand.

He looked at Ivar. "What did we do to deserve this punishment? How did we cross God? Letitia, she's always been a God-fearing woman. She doesn't even cuss. So it must be on me. My fault."

"It's not your fault," Ivar said. There was no way he could explain the Shadow to Havens, not that the rules of Time Patrol would allow him to. "Did you provoke Pickett to challenge Grant?"

Havens glumly nodded. "His girl was up the week past. She did talk to Sam. But I got Pickett aside last night, told him I overheard words. Words I invented to stir his blood. I put the worm in his brain, and once it fed on enough rum, it turned."

"What else did they ask you to do? Besides Grant?"

Havens shook his head. "It makes no sense. First thing they asked was three months after they took our daughter. They came back. Wanted me to get the cadets to have a party in the barracks for Christmas. Back then, I didn't see the harm, but I didn't see the reason, either. Why would Satan care about a party?"

"The Eggnog Riot," Ivar said.

"Aye."

A Christmas Day party in the barracks in 1826, when so many cadets got so drunk, they ended up rioting. With just that, the Shadow, via Havens, had almost wiped out the careers of an impressive list of West Point alumni before they graduated: Jeff Davis the most notable, along with a future Governor of Mississippi, a future Supreme Court Justice, a future Secretary of State of the Republic of Texas, and a Confederate Army General.

"But it didn't work as they wanted," Ivar said.

"I don't know what they wanted, other than me giving them the kegs. A bunch of the poor lads got kicked out."

"But the important ones didn't," Ivar said.

"How's that?" Havens asked.

"Nothing," Ivar said, but his brain was racing. How could one be sure that among those thirteen cadets who'd been expelled, there wasn't someone who might have affected history on a large scale if they'd graduated?

The vagaries of the variables.

Ivar shook his head, trying to dislodge the doubts. "But I don't understand why it didn't work."

"What are you talking about?"

"It would seem the Shadow would want Jeff Davis expelled, at the very least. That would be a ripple. You did what they asked. What stopped it from—"

"We didn't let it."

They were startled at the woman's voice. She was between two trees, a slender figure dressed in a black robe, a black hood hiding her hair and putting her eyes in a dark shadow. All that was visible was the lower part of her face, smooth, unlined, and of indeterminate age. She held a book in the crook of one arm.

Ivar and Havens popped to their feet.

"Who are you?" Ivar asked. "Who is 'we'?"

She ignored him. She glided forward, her robe barely moving. She reached out with her free hand then placed it, palm open, on Benny Havens' chest. "You have a good heart." She gestured toward the log. "You need to rest."

"I am so tired," Havens agreed. He sat on the ground with his back against the log.

She put her hand on his head. "Rest."

Havens closed his eyes, his head lolled over, and he was asleep.

"Who are you?" Ivar asked, eyeing her hand suspiciously.

Then he saw her eyes and took a step back, almost off the cliff. They were white. Completely white, yet he sensed she was seeing him more clearly than anyone ever had.

"My names are legion." She smiled. "I've always wanted to say that. People are just too serious about everything, aren't they? A little levity is important, don't you think?"

"Maybe give me one of the legion of names?" Ivar asked, not feeling the levity at all.

"It's time for you to go," she said.

"You're not Shadow," Ivar said. "Are you a Goddess? Like Pandora? Pyrrha?"

She laughed. "You are amusing. Goddesses? Even they must conform to my two sisters and me in certain things. We don't have power. We are what we are." She tapped the book. "I just read from the book, and it is what it is."

"What book?"

She held up the book she was carrying. "The Book of Fate."

Ivar was lost. "What about his daughter?"

She shook her head. "She's not in the book. I took that memory from him just now. I've already taken it from his wife's. They will never miss what they never had."

"I don't understand."

"Of course not," she said. "And Ivar?"

"Yes?"

"You are you. And your heart is just fine."

Chauvet Cave, Southern France, 6 June 32,415 Years B.P. (Before Present)

Daylight tinged the opening of the cave.

Moms shook herself awake, surprised she'd slept. Loss of blood, yes, but her brain wasn't working right. Had they stretched her too far, sending her so far back in time? She didn't know why she thought of it that way, stretched, but the word applied. She wasn't all here.

She giggled. If she wasn't, where was the rest of her?

"Hard to think," Moms said out loud. She knew it was bad, talking to herself, but the words seemed to anchor her in the here and now, and she'd take what she had to in order to do that.

There was movement, and she looked over. The boy was back with the girl, most likely his sister, her head on his lap. He was stroking her hair, cooing something to her. Very bird-like. Very caring.

Moms got up, her body stiff, her shoulder throbbing. It took a lot of effort to walk to the artist. Moms made a noise to attract the boy's attention and pointed at the sticks. He stared at her blankly.

Moms picked up a stick. She went to him, found a piece of bare rock, then scraped on it. The charcoal needed to be fresh. All she made was a slight smudge.

There was a skill to it.

It could be done. The boy could tell others how to do it. What he had seen his father do. But why would they listen? How would they understand the concept?

Moms stood. The boy remained with his sister. She had to make sure he made the next steps: the art and the artist.

He had to bring people here. To see. But how could he bring other people to this place of death? How could he show them what was so important that they needed to leave their own cave?

She still had the rest of the day to achieve something, anything. But not much of the day was left, judging by the sun.

Moms looked down the valley. From her trip so many years ago, many millennia in the future, she knew there were a lot of caves in the valley.

Which meant there were other humans.

Moms sat next to the boy and watched the valley. She was rewarded within five minutes. A thin tendril of smoke drifted up about a kilometer away.

"Come," Moms said.

The boy looked at her, confused, but not scared.

These were not people to whom fear came easily.

Moms took him by the hand. Her heart fluttered when she saw that he was clutching one of the drawing sticks in his other hand.

"Good," Moms said. She reached out and ruffled his hair. She gathered the other sticks.

She led him to the trail next to the Ardèche River, toward the smoke. A narrow trail turned off from the main one, climbing up toward a cave.

Moms halted. She knelt and pointed at the stick in his hand, then pantomimed drawing. He frowned.

Moms ran her finger in the dust and snow, drawing the outline of a heart. She pointed at the sticks. Then up at the cave.

"Go."

He headed up the side of the valley.

Moms moved away, then took an overwatch position where she could see the front of the cave. The boy arrived at the flat space in front of the cave and was immediately surrounded by people. There was a commotion for a while at the arrival of a stranger.

One of the women drew the boy aside. She gave him some food.

Moms waited.

So much resting on just a boy.

The boy went inside the cave. Moms sighed. She'd tried. The cave would be found. Inhabited again by both humans and cave bears. Maybe someone would make the connection between the images on the wall and a man's hand, and then the next connection of how to make those images.

Maybe.

Or had that one man, the boy's father, been such an aberration, his mind so far out of the bell curve, that—

The boy came out of the cave with the stick in his hand. The tip was dark with charcoal. He walked to a section of flat rock next to the entrance. He began to draw with the charcoal-tipped stick. A rough approximation of a horse's head began to appear under the boy's hand.

Several men and women gathered behind him, watching. Curious.

One of the men cried out. He pointed at the image the boy was drawing, then pantomimed something, and Moms realized he was trying to indicate a horse galloping. The others caught on, excited.

A woman gently took the boy's arm, the one that held the stick, then waved it about, crying out.

Magic.

It was magic.

And now, it was theirs. It was in the boy's genes, and it was in the imagination of all who'd seen. They would go to the cave eventually. The boy would lead them here. They would know what the horses were. Would make more drawings.

Moms crept away, back up the valley. She climbed wearily back up to the Chauvet cave.

The bodies still appeared to be asleep. She took the woman the boy had gone to and dragged her next to the father. Then she picked up the girl. Moms gently carried her over and sat down, back against the wall, under the horse drawing. Moms stroked the girl's hair, slowly untangling the dirty knots. She thought how all life had a reason, even when the reason wasn't you.

Once the hair was untangled, Moms rocked the girl, murmuring something, some lullaby long-buried under years of despair and pain. Moms began to cry, because someone had to cry for the dead.

She remembered his name. The man who'd taken her here, so many years ago, so many millennia in the future.

And she continued to cry.

The Return

ROLAND WAS SLIDING through the tunnel of time, forward.

To one side was another timeline, where Grendels were climbing out of dark pools, thousands of them, a plague of death against which the Danes could not stand. Then the rest of the Viking world succumbed, and the beasts spread into England, Germany, and around the world, until that timeline coalesced into a black orb of nothingness.

Just death.

Roland noted that timeline in his peripheral vision outside the tunnel he was traversing back to the Possibility Palace, but his focus was on the small piece of scale from Aglaeca he held in his hand.

A trophy with which to remember a hunter.

* * *

Doc was tumbling in the tunnel of time, moving forward. He was spinning, disoriented, only catching glimpses of other possible timelines. Many ended in the bright flash and utter darkness of nuclear war.

But the journey was so brief, there was little time to take it in.

All he knew was that he felt warm, as if the radiation he and Hamid had loosed in the Core of the Containment chamber had coated his body.

How many rads?

How many rads had he received from the dragon's tail?

* * *

Scout was sliding through the tunnel of time, forward.

She looked about, searching for other possibility timelines sprouting off, but there was nothing. As she'd suspected, Pythagoras of Samos and his sculptures were not—

A thin, gold line shot off above her. She tried to see what it was, what that timeline entailed, but it was so narrow and opaque. Was it even a timeline? What did it mean?

Scout watched as it faded into the dimness of possibilities.

Something was different.

Who was her mother?

* * *

Ivar was in the tunnel of time, but not returning. Not yet. He was stuck, and for a moment, he panicked, but then he saw that while he wasn't moving, the scene around him was. West Point was slowly evolving. A barracks torn down, and a new one being built.

Cadets in gray scurried back and forth, faster and faster. Parades whirled across the Plain. Ivar was moving up, away, gaining a bird's-eye view as the seasons whipped by, but then he suddenly slowed.

A cemetery in Highland Falls, just south of the Academy, on the high ground above where Havens's tavern had been. Cadets in a square, surrounding a grave. Distantly, echoing in the tunnel of time, the sound of deep voices sang:

Come tune your voices, comrades, and stand up in a row.
For singing sentimentally we're for to go.
In the Army there's sobriety, promotion's very slow,
So we'll sing our reminiscences of Benny Havens, Oh!
When this life's troubled sea is o'er and our last battles through,
If God permits us mortals there in his blest domain to view,
Then we shall see in glory crowned, in proud celestial row,
The friends we've known and loved so well at Benny Havens, Oh!
Oh! Benny Havens, oh! Oh! Benny Havens, oh!
We'll sing our reminiscences of Benny Havens, Oh!

Ivar saw *her*, dressed in black, holding her book, outside the circle of cadets around Benny Havens's grave. She looked up, as if she could see him, flicked a hand, and then Ivar was accelerating through time, back to his own.

There were images on other sides. Other possibilities. The Stars and Bars flying over the half-finished Washington Monument, with Robert E. Lee standing in front, being sworn in as the new President of the Confederate States of America, while a U.S. flag flew over a new capital in Philadelphia.

Another Civil War, years later, over the same issues. Deadlier, bloodier, no reconciliation.

There were other timelines: no Jefferson Davis, a different president of the Confederacy, one who managed to draw England into the war; that one flared into red so thick, Ivar couldn't see through.

But Ivar knew.

Fate.

It is as it should be.

★ ★ ★

Moms was sliding through the tunnel of time, forward. To her own time.

Her eyes were closed, her face crusted with dried tears.

It was a long journey, and she feared what awaited. She knew, without knowing how she knew, that there was as much sadness ahead of her as that which she had left behind.

Normandy France, 6 June 1944 A.D.

The shouts from the German soldiers were getting closer.

"Do you know my only wish for all these long years?" Brigit asked. "I wished to die with someone I loved. For a long time, it was enough to have Maurice, since I never thought I could love another person again after my baby and my husband."

"What were their names?" Mac asked.

She whispered them in his ear. "And what is your real name?"

Mac told her. He thought of how hard it had been for her to live the way she'd been forced to, and he knew she'd been finished for a very long time, but it had only been habit that her kept her living. Her essence of being human.

She wrapped her arms around him. "Thank you for burying Maurice."

The first bullet from the approaching soldiers clipped a branch above them, showering them with spring blossoms.

"Ah, yes," Mac said. "For Maurice."

He felt her body shudder as a machine pistol chattered. She went limp.

He could be pulled back now, Mac thought, as Doc had been, just before the firing squad, but he knew he wouldn't be. The Fates were ruling today.

This was his.

He pushed the detonator, and the det cord burned at four miles per second, reaching the explosives, and the bridge was gone.

Mac screamed at the top of his lungs in the sudden silence after that: "Maurice!"

He held Brigit in his arms, and a peace settled over him that he'd not known for so long, and he wondered if he'd ever known it at all, and then, as he'd always hoped, everything was darkness, and all was peace.

The Possibility Palace

"IT IS PROTOCOL FOR US to acknowledge the death of a team member because no one else will," Moms said. "We must pay our respects and give honors."

They were in their team room: Moms, Scout, Ivar, Doc, Roland, and Eagle.

Moms's shoulder was bandaged and her arm in a sling. Eagle had progressed past his sling, but he still had a wrap around his shoulder. Scout's forearm was bandaged, the long wound bound; stitches decorated her forehead above her left eye. Ivar sported a large bandage over his nose. Doc was pale, shaking, and pumped full of medications to battle the dose of radiation he'd received. The prognosis was he'd recover, but they all knew that long-term, the radiation would come back to haunt his body.

With a grimace, Moms pulled her arm out of the sling. She took Eagle's hand on one side, and Scout's on the other. The rest of the team completed the circle around the table.

"He was named Mac by the team," Moms said, "but in death, he regains his name and his past. Sergeant First Class Eric Bowen, U.S. Army Special Forces, MOS Eighteen-Charlie,

Engineer, from the great state of Texas, has made the ultimate sacrifice for his country, for his world, and for mankind. We speak his rank and his name as it was."

They all spoke together: "Sergeant First Class Eric Bowen."

Scout spoke up. "As long as a name is remembered, we live on."

Every member of the team nodded.

Moms continued. "We, the Time Patrol, have seen many things and been to many places, and many times. We don't know the limits of science, and we don't know the limits of the soul. If there is some life after this, or some existence on a plane we can't conceive of, then know our teammate is there, in a good place. Because that is what he deserves for performing his duty without any acknowledgement, and for making the ultimate sacrifice. If there is nothingness in death, then he is in his final peace and will not be troubled any more by the nightmares of this world, or the demons that haunted Mac."

Moms took a deep, shuddering breath and tried to gain the composure to continue.

Eagle spoke into the void. "There will be no medals. No service at Arlington. There is no body to bury. He is in the past. We know he succeeded in his mission. History confirms it."

"All we can do," Scout said, "is keep him in our hearts."

The team remained silent, then the circle broke. Eagle held up a chisel and hammer.

"We are no longer the Nightstalkers. We've been the Time Patrol for a while. We have to start our own traditions. We have to own our own place. This room. That starts here. Now." He nodded to the wall where the Badge of Merit he'd taken on his mission on the Ides was mounted on a plaque, the only decoration in the room. "The best way to do that is to remember those who went before. Since we've become Time Patrol, we've lost two teammates."

He put the tip of the chisel on the wooden table, then tapped the hammer, and a sliver of wood was removed. He adjusted, then tapped again. And then a third time, making a letter:

N

Then he offered the tools to Scout. She made the next:

A

Moms was next:

D

Then Roland:

A

Doc began the next name right below Nada's:

M

Ivar continued:

A

And Eagle finished it:

C

Moms went to the door and opened it. Edith Frobish was standing outside, waiting patiently. She had a large cooler. Moms helped her carry it in. They opened the lid.

"Pearl beer," Moms said, passing cans out. Once everyone had one, Moms opened hers, then held it up.

"To Mac."

"To Mac," everyone responded.
"To the Time Patrol," Eagle said.
"To the Time Patrol."
"To Nada," Scout said.
"To Nada."

The Possibility Palace: Down the Hall

Dane sat across from Lara, regarding her without comment. Frasier was on his side of the table, leafing through a thin file, translated from Russian.

"What little is in here, is heavily redacted," Frasier complained. "But from what I can read, she did some very, very bad things."

"Bad things," Lara whispered. "Yes. Bad things." She was speaking to herself as if she were alone in the room.

"We've all done bad things," Dane said.

Frasier shoved the folder over to him. "Not like this."

Dane didn't have to read it. "I know."

Frasier pointed out the obvious. "And she's not Russian. How did she end up over there?"

"Here, there," Lara said. "Now, then. What does it matter?"

"I'm sure it's an interesting story," Dane said.

"The Fifth Floor," Lara said.

"What's that?" Frasier asked.

Dane shook his head. "Not now. We'll get to that." His focus was on the girl. "You're going to make a choice."

Lara nodded . "Whether to join the Time Patrol."

Dane nodded. "How do you know that?"

She'd been brought here unconscious, through the Gate from underneath the Met. The only part of the Possibility Palace she'd seen so far was this room.

"It is all everyone here thinks about," Lara said.

"You know what people are thinking?" Frasier asked.

"At times." She smiled. "Why do you think they sent me in the straitjacket?"

"What am I thinking right now?" Dane asked.

"I don't do parlor tricks," Lara said. She shrugged. "I don't know. It doesn't work like that. But if enough people think or feel something, it is easy to"—She paused, searching for the word—"see."

"The Sight," Dane said. He tapped a finger on the tabletop. "In the course of history, there are billions and billions of lives. The reality is, few of those individual lives make an impact. That's not to say that in their personal lives, for their family, their friends, and even their enemies, all those people aren't important. But if any of those people ceased to exist, blinked out of existence, the course of history would not change."

Lara stared at him, expressionless .

"Even those we think are historically significant," Dane continued, "whether by the weight of their entire life, or by a single, momentous action, such as Oswald assassinating Kennedy, might not even be important, since someone else might do the same."

"We're replaceable," Lara said.

"Pretty much everyone," Dane said.

"Who am I replacing?" she asked. "There's a group of sad people here. They miss someone."

"That's not important right now," Dane said.

"Would they miss me some day?" Lara murmured. "It would be nice to be missed. I doubt they miss me on the Fifth Floor. But maybe they do, but not for good reasons."

As Frasier opened his mouth to say something, Dane gave a subtle signal with his hand, silencing him. "What is needed to be a member of the Time Patrol, Lara, is that you are a person who will never, ever, use our capability and go back and change something for personal reasons. Every person has something in their past, some point where we wish we had chosen differently. Many points, probably. But you can't ever use time travel for personal reasons."

He held up three fingers. "You now have to make a decision to take one of three paths. First, you may choose not to choose. To walk away. Second, you may go back to that key moment and change what happened. Third—"

"You will not allow that second choice if it changes history," Lara said.

"True," Dane said. "But as I said, most of us aren't that important. If you choose to go back, and it doesn't affect the timeline—and it most likely won't—you *will* be allowed to go back but that will be it and you will never be Time Patrol. And if you begin to interfere in the point you go back to by knowing the future, you will receive a visit from one of our operatives at that time, and be Sanctioned."

"Killed."

"Yes."

"I imagine that will also be the result if I choose not to choose."

"No," Dane said. "You'll be sent home."

"'Home'?" Lara laughed. "What home? The Fifth Floor? Before that? Which home? Which person?" Lara shook her head. "You will not allow me to leave this place, knowing what I know."

"You won't know what you know," Frasier said. "We'll wipe your memory from the time you arrived at Area 51 until just before you get back."

"Ah," Lara said. "But how do you know this key moment?"

"We know," Dane said. "We have our own people with the Sight."

"And my final option...?" Lara asked.

"Accept who you are now," Dane said. "Where you are now. All that has happened to shape you into who you are. And choose to be part of the Time Patrol."

"When do I have to make this choice?" she asked.

"Now," Dane replied.

"I can really go back and change it?"

"Yes." Dane said. "We both know the moment."

"Do you?"

A flicker of uncertainty crossed Dane's face.

"And if I change it," Lara said, "that won't change the timeline?"

"No."

She stared at Dane, unblinking. Tears glistened in her eyes. She looked down for a long moment, blinking hard. When she looked up, the tears were gone.

"I will stay here and be Time Patrol."

The Metropolitan Museum of Art

Edith Frobish stood on the balcony overlooking the main hall of the Metropolitan Museum of Art, her hands on the railing, her fingers rubbing the metal nervously.

She'd checked. There was no record of the Charioteer of Delphi in Greece or in the art world. It had never existed.

As far as the art in the Met?

It was all there. Nothing fading, nothing gone.

But there were differences. She'd walked the museum before it opened this morning. Every spot that was supposed to have art in it did: paintings on the wall, sculptures on their stands. But some were different. Subtly different.

But different.

The End
For Now

The next installment in the Time Patrol Series
<u>Independence Day</u>
Excerpt follows bio and book listings.

Our History Afterward

Sjaelland Island, Denmark, 6 June 452 A.D.

Beowulf is cited as one of the most important works of Old English Literature and might be the oldest poem. It begins a long line of literature that continues today.

Kala Chitta Range, Pakistan, 6 June 1998 A.D.
Pakistan and India still are on a razor's edge with regards to nuclear weapons. A nuclear exchange between the two countries could happen quickly.

Control of Pakistan's nuclear arsenal continues to be of grave concern to the rest of the world. Fear of radicals seizing it has the majors powers drawing up contingency plans to avoid such an event.

Delphi, Greece, 6 June 478 B.C.
There were two well-known Pythagoras from ancient Greece. One was Pythagoras of Rhegion who is the more famous as a philosopher and mathematician. The other Pythagoras of Samos who was a sculptor.

Art as a recorder of history is a touchstone of the Time Patrol.

United States Military Academy, West Point, New York, 6 June 1843 A.D.
U.S. Grant did set a horse jumping record that stood for many years at West Point. He wanted to go into the Cavalry but was instead branched into Infantry. For more on this event and his early history through the Mexican War, West Point to Mexico is free.

Chauvet Cave, Southern France, 6 June 32,415 Years B.P. (Before Present)
More ancient cave drawings are being discovered. No one quite knows when mankind made the leap to conceptualize thoughts with external images. The Chauvet Cave is known to hold some of the best preserved. It was discovered in 1994. It received World Heritage status in 2014.

Normandy France, 6 June 1944 A.D.
Before the landings, on 5 June, Eisenhower wrote a statement which would remain in his uniform pocket for long after D-Day: *"Our landings in the Cherbourg-Havre area have failed to gain a satisfactory foothold and I have withdrawn the troops. My decision to attack at this time and place was based upon the best information available. The troops, the air and the navy did all that bravery and devotion to duly could do. If any blame or fault is attached to the attempt it is mine alone."*

It is interesting to note that Eisenhower ended the statement by mislabeling it as written on 5 July.

If the landings had failed here are some possibilities:

The aerial bombardment of Germany is stepped up, eventually with nuclear weapons.

Eisenhower would have had to offer his resignation and it would have been accepted.

Roosevelt would not have won another term as President.

Russia wins the war on its own in 1946 and all of mainland Europe is under the hammer and sickle.

The fact, though, is that Eisenhower never had to make that statement.

About the Author

Thanks for the read!
If you enjoyed the book, please leave a review. Cool Gus likes them as much as he likes squirrels!
Any questions or comments, feel free to email me at bob@bobmayer.com
Subscribe to my newsletter for the latest news, free eBooks, audio, etc.

Look! Squirrel!
Bob is a NY Times Bestselling author, graduate of West Point, former Green Beret and the feeder of two Yellow Labs, most famously Cool Gus. He's had over 70 books published including the #1 series Area 51, Atlantis, Time Patrol and The Green Berets. Born in the Bronx, having traveled the world (usually not tourist spots), he now lives peacefully with his wife, and labs. He's training his two grandsons to be leaders of the Resistance Against The Machines.

For information on all my books, please get a free copy of my **Reader's Guide**. You can download it in mobi (Amazon) ePub (iBooks, Nook, Kobo) or PDF, from my home page at www.bobmayer.com

For free eBooks, short stories and audio short stories, please go to
http://bobmayer.com/freebies/
Free books include:
Eyes of the Hammer (Green Beret series book #1)
West Point to Mexico (Duty, Honor, Country series book #1)
Ides of March (Time Patrol)
Prepare Now-Survive Now
There are also free shorts stories and free audiobook stories.

Never miss a new release by following my Amazon Author Page.

I have over 220 free, downloadable Powerpoint presentations via Slideshare on a wide range of topics from history, to survival, to writing, to book trailers.
https://www.slideshare.net/coolgus

If you're interested in audiobooks, you can download one for free and test it out here:
Audible

Connect with me and Cool Gus on social media.
Blog: http://bobmayer.com/blog/
Twitter: https://twitter.com/Bob_Mayer

CONNECTIONS BETWEEN SERIES VIA PLOT AND CHARACTERS:

Technically the first *Time Patrol* book is the fourth *Nightstalker* book. You can start the Time Patrol series with Time Patrol, but if you want to know about what they did before, as Nightstalkers, then those three books show that.

The Fifth Floor is part of Time Patrol, but different in that it's the backstory of one of the characters: Lara.

The universe of *Atlantis* is the same as that in *Time Patrol* with the Shadow trying to change a timeline. They are just different timelines. Thus we have characters from Atlantis such as Dane and Foreman showing up in the Time Patrol.

The *Cellar* becomes involved in the *Nightstalkers* and *Time Patrol*, with Hannah and Neeley playing roles.

NIGHSTALKERS SERIES:
1. NIGHTSTALKERS
2. BOOK OF TRUTHS
3. THE RIFT

The fourth book in the Nightstalker book is the team becoming the Time Patrol, thus it's labeled book 4 in that series but it's actually book 1 in the Time Patrol series.

TIME PATROL SERIES:
1. TIME PATROL
2. BLACK TUESDAY
3. IDES OF MARCH *(free)*
4. D-DAY
5. INDEPENDENCE DAY
6. THE FIFTH FLOOR
7. NINE-ELEVEN
8. VALENTINES DAY
9. HALLOWS EVE

AREA 51 SERIES:
1. AREA 51
2. AREA 51 THE REPLY
3. AREA 51 THE MISSION
4. AREA 51 THE SPHINX
5. AREA 51 THE GRAIL
6. AREA 51 EXCALIBUR
7. AREA 51 THE TRUTH
(Legend and Nosferatu are prequels to the main series)
8. AREA 51 LEGEND
9. AREA 51 NOSFERATU
10. AREA 51 REDEMPTION (coming Winter 2018)

ATLANTIS SERIES:
1. ATLANTIS
2. ATLANTIS BERMUDA TRIANGLE
3. ATLANTIS DEVILS SEA
4. ATLANTIS GATE
5. ASSAULT ON ATLANTIS
6. BATTLE FOR ATLANTIS

THE GREEN BERETS SERIES:
1. EYES OF THE HAMMER *(free)*
2. DRAGON SIM-13
3. SYNBAT
4. CUT OUT
5. ETERNITY BASE
6. Z: FINAL COUNTDOWN
(at this point we introduce Horace Chase as the main character and he eventually teams up with Dave Riley, the main character from the previous books)
7. CHASING THE GHOST
8. CHASING THE LOST
9. CHASING THE SON
10. OLD SOLDIERS (coming spring 2018)

THE DUTY, HONOR, COUNTRY SERIES

THE SHADOW WARRIORS SERIES

THE PRESIDENTIAL SERIES

THE CELLAR SERIES

THE BURNERS SERIES

THE PSYCHIC WARRIOR SERIES

COLLABORATIONS WITH JENNIFER CRUSIE

All my novels and series are listed in order, with links here:
www.bobmayer.com/fiction/

My nonfiction, including my two companion books for preparation and survival is listed
at
www.bobmayer.com/nonfiction/

Thank you!

Independence Day

TIME PATROL

"Those who deny freedom to others deserve it not for themselves." Abraham Lincoln

Where The Time Patrol Ended Up This Particular Day: 4 July

The unanimous Declaration of the thirteen United States of America

WHEN IN THE COURSE OF HUMAN EVENTS, it becomes necessary for one people to dissolve the political bands which have connected them with another, and to assume among the powers of the earth, the separate and equal station to which the Laws of Nature and of Nature's God entitle them, a decent respect to the opinions of mankind requires that they should declare the causes which impel them to the separation.

Entebbe, Uganda, 4 July 1976 A.D.

"HAVE YOU KILLED MEN, EAGLE?" Avi asked.

"Yes."

"Many men?"

"All that I've needed to."

"That is good," Avi said. "My men are the toughest and best-trained commandos in the world. They have all killed. If you become an impediment to the mission in any way, or put any of my men in danger, I will kill you without hesitation."

It is 1976 A.D. The world's population is 4.139 billion humans; The first flight of the Concorde; The Sex Pistols; Microsoft is registered with the Office of the Secretary of State of New Mexico; Frampton Comes Alive; Jimmy Carter is elected President; Some group named U2 is formed; Son of Sam kills his first victim; The Big Thompson Flood in Colorado kills 143 people; Bob Marley is wounded in an assassination attempt; the United States of America celebrates its bicentennial.

"If I am killed or wounded," Avi continued, "and not capable, my men have my permission to do the same. Israel comes first, the Time Patrol second."

Some things change; some don't.

Philadelphia, Pennsylvania, 4 July 1776 A.D.

THE ARROW WHIZZED BY, so close Doc swore he felt the feathers on the end of the shaft tickled his cheek. He dove forward, hoping he didn't land in the literal crap, but he was already in it in the larger sense so . . .

He hit dirt, then rolled, automatically reaching for a pistol, which he didn't have.

He stayed low and looked left, then right, not sure from which end of the alley the arrow had been launched. He spotted a figure silhouetted by the slanted moonlight at one end, with a short bow in hand, and another arrow being notched. The figure was cloaked and hooded, walking forward, less than twenty meters from Doc and closing the distance.

He realized the figure was a woman by the contours and the way she walked. That was irrelevant because Doc knew he was a dead man. She might have missed at the longer distance, but at this range . . .

"Wait!" Doc begged.

It is 1776 A.D. The world's population is a little over 900 million, of which only 3.6 million are part of the fledgling United States; Norfolk, VA is burned by the British; Thomas Paine publishes Common Sense; *American Marines make an assault on Nassau, Bahamas; Adam Smith publishes* The Wealth of Nations; *the Presidio of San Francisco is founded; the Illuminati is formally founded in Bavaria (conspiracy theories have never been the same); angry New Yorkers cover a statue of King George III with graffiti and then topple it (New York has pretty much always been the same); the first submarine attack, by the* USS Turtle, *fails; Captain Cook sets off on his third journey of discovery (he's not coming back).*

But the woman kept coming, her face hidden by the overhang of the hood and the darkness.

Some things change; some don't.

Monticello, VA, 4 July 1826 A.D.

"DID YOU READ MY LETTER?" Thomas Jefferson asked the young man, his voice frail and faint.

The man nodded. "Yes, sir."

Moms was on her toes, trying to hear the words through the open transom.

"Will you do as I ask?"

The man glanced at Sally Hemings, then back at Jefferson. "Sir, I—" He paused. "I don't understand what you are asking of me. I understand the words, but not the intent."

"You don't need to understand the intent," Jefferson said. "You are just to do as instructed."

It is 1826 A.D. The world's population went past one billion around the turn of the century and is now roughly 1.02 billion; about 10 million live in the United States; New York City is packed with almost 150,000 inhabitants; Beethoven finishes the String Quartet in C Sharp Minor, Opus 131; the first commercial rail line, the Granite Railway, opens in the U.S.; the Eggnog Riot breaks out at West Point (Benny Havens explains this in D-Day); *Varina Howell Davis, who would become First Lady of the Confederacy, is born.*

Jefferson's gaze shifted to Sally Hemings. "Get it."

Some things change; some don't.

Hemings reached behind his pillow and pulled out a leather pouch. She handed it to Jefferson. With shaking hands, he untied the strings, revealing an iron rod a quarter-inch in diameter and eight inches long. There were brass knobs on both ends. The rod went through a number of thin wooden disks, two inches in diameter and a sixth of an inch thick. They slid along the rod as Jefferson cradled it in his hands.

"There are twenty-six disks," Jefferson said. "I have thirteen here. John Adams has the rest. Take this to him. He is the one who must complete the Cipher."

The young man took the incomplete Cipher. "What does the Cipher do?"

"It leads to a document. One we all signed along with the Declaration."

"What does the document do?"

"Everything, Mister Poe. It will change everything."

Gettysburg, PA, 4 July 1863 A.D.

"MAMA. PLEASE COME GET ME, MAMA!"

Roland lay between two cold corpses and tried not to listen to the plaintive cry from someone close by. A man who'd put on a uniform, whether it be gray or blue, so proudly, eager to go forth and be a hero. Pretty much the way all wars began for the young who would be the cannon fodder, with the fantasy sold to them by the old men who started the wars.

This was the reality. It always devolved to a broken man lying on the ground, crying out for that most instinctual need.

"Mother!"

Roland could hear other voices now. There was a tree to his left, shot up, its branches splintered by artillery and grape shot, but still something of a tree. Unlike the men, it might recover from this battle. In time. A cluster of about twenty men lay underneath its bony branches. Blue and gray mixed together. Just as dogs who know they're going to die crawl under a bush, men on battlefields tended to group together under trees.

Dying Trees. Edith's download informed Roland the practice was so prevalent there was a term for it. They were scattered across every Civil War battlefield. Afterward, when one side retreated, or a temporary truce was signed, and the burial parties were sent out to clean up the mess so it could start all over again, they inevitably found the bodies of those who hadn't been killed outright, clustered together.

It is 1863 A.D. The world's population is roughly 1.2 to 1.3 billion humans; the population of the United States is 31,443,321 according to the 1860 census, but two years of war have taken a toll on that and the death toll will eventually reach 700,000; the first section of the London Underground, from Paddington to Farringdon Street opens; the French intervene in Mexico, bombarding Vera Cruz; Jules Verne's first adventure novel, Five Weeks in a Balloon *is published; The 54th Massachusetts, the first African-American regiment, leaves Boston for the front; West Virginia becomes the 35th State; Between 2,000 and 3,000 people celebrating the Feast of the Immaculate Conception in a Church in Santiago, Chile, die when it catches on fire; Gerard Heineken buys a brewery; Abraham Lincoln signs the Emancipation proclamation.*

Were they afraid God might see them? Roland wondered about the wounded. Were they hiding?

Some things change; some don't.

The more practical victims were found clumped around ponds or streams, where they crawled, desperate for water.

"Help me, Lord. Help me, Lord. Help me, Lord."

Roland had to tune that chant out. The only way God, as Roland envisioned a Higher Power, could help these men was to kill them faster.

Vicksburg, Mississippi. 4 July 1863

"GOOD. 'CAUSE IF YOU WAS A SPY, I'd have to gut you right here with my knife."

"You have a knife?" Ivar asked.

The young boy, Joey, revealed a silver pocketknife in one hand. It had been there all along and Ivar hadn't seen it.

"It's a good one," Joey said. "Engraved and everything."

"Your father's?" Ivar asked.

Joey's head drooped. "No, sir. My daddy, he got his'self killed at Shiloh. At least we thinks so. He went off with the great General Sidney Albert Johnston and the Army of the Mississippi and never did come back. In '62, that was. Spring. Bunch of dads went off and never come back. Word is damn Yankees wouldn't allow the decency of claiming the dead. Just tossed our mensfolks' bodies into a trench." Joey held out the knife, with his fingers on either side of the blade, the handle toward Ivar. "Here. Take a look-see."

Ivar took it, then angled the blade so he could read the engraving in the moonlight.

He felt a rush as he read the name: *John C. Pemberton.* The Confederate Commander of Vicksburg.

It is 1863 A.D. Thomas (Stonewall) Jackson dies (mistakenly shot by his own troops); Harper's Weekly *publishes Thomas Nast's drawing of Santa Claus; the Idaho Territory is organized by the U.S. Congress; the National Conscription Act, the first draft in the United States is passed; the Football Association is formed in London (stealing the term from the U.S. but they really meant soccer); linoleum is patented and kitchens will never be the same; Henry Ford is born (when he's older he'll make some cars).*

"You know Pemberton?" Ivar asked.

"He's in our cave a lot," Joey said, his tone indicating he didn't like that one bit.

Ivar knew he was in the right place and the right time. He just had no clue what the problem was since the surrender of Vicksburg had already been negotiated between Pemberton and Ulysses S. Grant. What monkey wrench could the Shadow throw into that?

Some things change; some don't.

"The General," Joey said, taking back the knife. "He aint acting right in the head."

Mantinea, Greece, 4 July 362 B.C.

"HAVE YOU HAD VISIONS of other timelines when traveling back to your own time?" Pyrrha asked Scout.

"Sort of."

"We believe those are real timelines," Pyrrha said. "Not possibilities. They happened." Pyrrha, in mythology, is the daughter of Pandora and the only woman to survive the Great Flood along with her husband, thus being the mother of all mankind. That's in mythology. Right now, in Scout's reality, she was a pain, asking questions that Scout couldn't answer.

"Hold on," Scout said. It was growing warmer as the sun rose. The sounds of soldiers aligning themselves in tightly packed phalanxes, orders being shouted, trumpets blaring, horses racing back and force, echoed in the plain below them. "I thought those threads were what happened if we failed. Possibilities."

It is 362 B.C. The world's population is a bit more than 100 million humans. Over half of them live in India and China. King Agesilaus II of Sparta leads one thousand warriors to Egypt to assist in battling a Persian invasion; when Agesilaus is asked how far Sparta's rule reached, he extended his spear and replied 'As far as this can reach'; China begins to become unified.

Pandora, in mythology even more of a troublemaker than her daughter, spoke up. "The Shadow is trying two things. One is taking shots in the dark, trying to disrupt your timeline in order to terminate it. But it's also taking some aimed shots. Going to places where history, the history of the timelines that reached the same point, show there were splits into parallel worlds. It's trying to shatter your timeline at one of those key junctures."

Just great, Scout thought.

"Today is one of those junctures," Pandora said.

Some things change; some don't.

Order your copy now!
Amazon

Copyright

Cool Gus Publishing

http://coolgus.com

This is a work of fiction. Names, characters, places, and incidents either are the product of the author's imagination or are used fictitiously, and any resemblance to actual persons living or dead, business establishments, events, or locales is entirely coincidental.

D-Day (Time Patrol) by Bob Mayer
COPYRIGHT © 2016 by Bob Mayer

All rights reserved. No part of this book may be used or reproduced in any manner without written permission from the author (Bob Mayer, Who Dares Wins) except in the case of brief quotations embodied in critical articles or reviews.

ISBN: 9781621252832

Printed in Great Britain
by Amazon

37602565R00095